"Sharon Mondragón's stories are as charming as they are touching. I loved getting to know the knitters—and crocheters!—of Fair Meadows Retirement Community, and I loved watching their friendships grow and blossom. *The Tangled Tale of the Woolgathering Castoffs* may seem lighthearted on the surface, but it plumbs the depths of loss, grief, fear, and change . . . all with hope and a winsome reminder that there is nothing we can't bring to the Lord in prayer. If you love inspirational fiction that makes you smile and tugs at your heart, I highly recommend this book."

KATIE POWNER, author of *The Wind Blows in Sleeping Grass*

"When I read Sharon Mondragón for the first time, I knew that I had found something special, a story that I wouldn't be able to forget and characters who worked their way into my heart. How delightful for me to find that her second novel was just as good—no, even better than the first! At the start, *The Tangled Tale of the Woolgathering Castoffs* might be mistaken for a quiet novel. But halfway through, readers will find a story that captures their minds and, much more importantly, their hearts. You don't want to miss this story, especially if you enjoyed *Where the Blue Sky Begins* by Katie Powner or *The Extraordinary Deaths of Mrs. Kip* by Sara Brunsvold."

SUSIE FINKBEINER, author of *The All-American* and
The Nature of Small Birds

"Sharon Mondragón offers up another wonderful, whimsical, thought-provoking, and spiritually inspiring story, capturing my attention as a reader and stealing my heart in the process. I loved being reunited with the cast from *The Unlikely Yarn of the Dragon Lady*, and meeting the new cast of characters who joined them was icing on the cake. The author writes with such reverence—in a way that describes a true relationship with God, Jesus, and the Holy Spirit—that the scenes from the prayer chapel at Hope of Glory feel especially anointed."

CHERI SWALWELL, founder of the JESUS in the EVERYDAY
monthly membership and author of *Adventure's Invitation*

"Who would have guessed that a prayer shawl ministry in the lobby of a retirement home would change the lives not only of shawl recipients but of the shawl creators as well? In this heartwarming sequel to *The Unlikely Yarn of the Dragon Lady*, Sharon Mondragón deftly weaves residents in the retirement community and visitors with loved ones in the memory care unit into a circle of friends, all whose lives are richer by the end. This heartwarming story is an inspiration for those skilled in needlework and those of us who are not."

PATRICIA SPRINKLE, author of *Hold Up the Sky*

"I didn't know that I'd so love and savor this story about the knitting adventures of septuagenarians and octogenarians! As the Woolgatherers create prayer shawls for the caregivers of loved ones with memory loss, they don't realize that they too are on a journey of discovery with God. They receive and give God's loving embrace as they respond to nudges of grace one stitch at a time. Read, savor, and make a list of people you could bless with this enriching story!"

AMY BOUCHER PYE, author of *7 Ways to Pray* and *Transforming Love*

THE
TANGLED TALE
OF THE
WOOLGATHERING
CASTOFFS

Books by Sharon J. Mondragón

The Unlikely Yarn of the Dragon Lady
The Tangled Tale of the Woolgathering Castoffs

THE
TANGLED TALE
OF THE
WOOLGATHERING
CASTOFFS

A Novel

SHARON J. MONDRAGÓN

KREGEL
PUBLICATIONS

Library of Congress Cataloging-in-Publication Data
Names: Mondragón, Sharon J., 1957- author.
Title: The tangled tale of the woolgathering castoffs : a novel / Sharon J. Mondragón.
Description: Grand Rapids, MI : Kregel Publications, 2024. | Series: Purls and prayers ; book 2
Identifiers: LCCN 2023034505 (print) | LCCN 2023034506 (ebook) | ISBN 9780825448201 (paperback) | ISBN 9780825471193 (epub) | ISBN 9780825471186 (kindle edition)
Subjects: LCGFT: Christian fiction. | Novels.
Classification: LCC PS3613.O52435 T36 2024 (print) | LCC PS3613.O52435 (ebook) | DDC 813/.6--dc23/eng/20230818
LC record available at https://lccn.loc.gov/2023034505
LC ebook record available at https://lccn.loc.gov/2023034506

ISBN 978-0-8254-4820-1, print
ISBN 978-0-8254-7119-3, epub
ISBN 978-0-8254-7118-6, Kindle

Printed in the United States of America
24 25 26 27 28 29 30 31 32 33 / 5 4 3 2 1

So now faith, hope, and love abide,
these three; but the greatest of these is love.

1 Corinthians 13:13

CHAPTER 1

THE TROUBLE BEGAN ON THAT day of love and loneliness, Valentine's Day.

Edna O'Brian surveyed the lobby of Fair Meadows Retirement Community, definitely decorated for love. Fat pink Cupid cutouts drew their arrows at red hearts on the windows. Crayoned cards from the third-grade class at the nearby elementary school formed a giant heart on one wall. Huge vases of roses and carnations crowded the front desk, hiding the perky receptionist from view. As soon as one arrangement was whisked away to be delivered to a loved and lucky resident, another arrived with a swoosh of lobby doors to take its place.

Edna turned her back on the mass of flowers and pulled her brown cardigan more tightly around her. None of those bouquets were for her. Stanley had always brought her a box of Whitman's chocolates on Valentine's Day, the kind with the key on the inside of the lid, telling you what was in each of the chocolates. She'd always saved the coconut ones for him . . .

From her seat with the Fair Meadows prayer shawl group, Edna gazed across the lobby at the dining room, also decorated in honor of the day. The tables were decked with red tablecloths and fancy silver bowls, each of which probably cost more than her entire first set of CorningWare. The bowls were filled with white-and-red-striped carnations. *Everything about this place is fancy*, Edna thought with a shake of her head.

Especially her. Jenny Alderman clapped her hands to get the attention of her fellow prayer shawl makers, her many rings sparkling in the sunlight. She teetered slightly in her high-heeled pumps and patted her dyed auburn hair. Entirely too red for a woman in her seventies, in Edna's opinion.

"Ladies, ladies . . . and gentleman." Jenny flashed her dimples at Alistair Peabody, the lone man in the group. Once she had the attention of the prayer shawl makers (*and probably everyone in the lobby*, Edna thought), Jenny said, "And now for the moment you've all been waiting for. We had some great ideas for a name for our prayer shawl group. There were so many good ones, it was hard to decide."

Edna suppressed a snort. She bet Susan Thomas, the member who'd suggested they have a contest to choose the name, was sorry she'd ever mentioned it. Whoever came up with the best name would win a gift certificate for three skeins of yarn at a fancy yarn shop. Competition had been so fierce Susan had finally asked someone outside the group to choose the winner. Moments before, the Fair Meadows activities director had delivered her decision in a sealed envelope, then high-tailed it out of there.

"Suggestions included 'Caring Hearts,' 'The Golden Needles Club,' 'Hugs for Helpers'—"

"That's mine," Edna said. She'd been lobbying hard for her idea.

"We know, we know," Susan said under her breath. Edna turned to give Susan a sharp look. Out of the corner of her eye, Edna glimpsed a chubby man, a bit like one of the Cupids on the window, making his way to the elevator. She turned to listen to Jenny again.

"Don't forget 'Knotty Knitters,'" Mr. Peabody, seated next to Jenny, said. "Knotty—sounds like 'naughty'—get it?" He winked broadly.

"We get it, we get it," Susan said. Edna rolled her eyes at the bad pun right along with her.

Jenny, however, beamed at him with a flutter of eyelashes. "Of course, we didn't forget that one, Alistair. So clever. The final two names for our group of knitters—"

"And crocheters." Edna waved her pink size Q hook in the air.

"And crocheters." Jenny nodded. "As I was saying, the final two suggestions were 'The Woolgatherers' and 'The Forget-Me-Knots,' spelled with a K."

With a glance at Edna, Rose Harker chimed in. "There were so many clever names I don't know how our activities director managed to choose." Edna had the sinking feeling Rose was preemptively trying to smooth things over with her.

Jenny flourished the envelope and slit it open with a bright red fingernail. She fished a sheet of paper out and read aloud. "You are gathering to make shawls to comfort and encourage the caregivers of your neighbors in Memory Care. The minds of these neighbors often wander or 'woolgather,' therefore I have chosen 'The Woolgatherers' as the name most appropriate for your group."

"That's mine." Laura Whitman beamed with pleasure, her eyes crinkling at the corners, where laugh lines had settled long ago. *Of course*, Edna thought glumly. She used to be an English teacher. Of course she'd won.

Laura accepted the gift certificate from The Tangled Thread Yarn Boutique amid applause (half-hearted on Edna's part).

"It's a great play on words," Jenny said.

"My idea is just as good, if not better," Edna muttered.

"Oh, don't be a sore loser," Jenny said. When Edna bristled, she hastened to add, "'Hugs for Helpers' is good, but 'The Woolgatherers' is even better."

Across the lobby, unaware he'd been mentally compared to a pudgy Cupid decoration, Sam Talbot took in the bustling activity around him as he waited for the elevator.

"Are you getting on?" A woman, followed by a pair of teenage girls, stepped around Sam to get into the elevator and stuck out her arm to hold the door open.

Sam started and turned away from the scene across the lobby, where a striking woman with auburn hair was making some sort of announcement.

"Oh, right." Sam stepped into the elevator.

"What floor?" she asked.

"Seven." Sam looked away.

"Us, too." One of the girls pressed the button for the seventh floor. "We're going to see Grandma Becca."

"Are those for your wife?" the woman, apparently the girls' mother, asked.

Sam glanced at the clear plastic box in his hand. Inside, half a dozen chocolate-covered strawberries were nestled in a bed of iridescent shredded cellophane. The whole affair was secured by a wide red ribbon, tied in a bow on top of the box. Dorothy loved fancy packages.

"For Valentine's Day," Sam said.

The elevator slid to a stop at the seventh floor.

"Happy Valentine's Day," the girls chorused as they stepped out and turned left toward the patient rooms.

"You, too." Sam took a firm grip on the box of strawberries and strode to the nurses' station.

"She's in the dayroom." Eileen, the weekend charge nurse, smiled as he approached. The nurses all wanted to be called by their first names in Memory Care, something about being a family. Sam couldn't get used to it. Eileen grinned at the box of strawberries. "She's going to love those."

"Indeed she will." Sam smiled back. "It's a tradition. I always get her chocolate-covered strawberries for Valentine's Day."

Sam crossed the reception area toward the blare of the dayroom television, waving the box in goodbye. He stopped in the doorway, scanning the room until he found her. There she was, his Dorothy. He admired the silver hair that fell to her shoulders, as thick and wavy as it had been the first time he'd glimpsed it across the quad on his way to Calculus III. Her hair hadn't been silver then, but a rich brown. The autumn sunlight had brought out flashes of auburn as she walked.

Sam pulled his mind back to the present. Dorothy sat at a table with an aide, intent on working a jigsaw puzzle. Her eyebrows drew together as she tried to fit a piece into the picture. The aide attempted to guide her hand toward the edge where the piece belonged, but Dorothy resisted. She continued to jam the edge piece against one in the center, applying more force with every shove. Sam's heart sank as he watched. Lately it seemed . . . *no, she's fine,* he told himself. She is *not* getting worse. The aide glanced up and beckoned him over. He held the gift in front of him, where the lavish bow would catch her eye, and stepped over to the table.

"Look who's here, Dot," the aide said, her voice bright and cheerful.

Sam clenched his teeth. The staff insisted on calling her by that absurd nickname, as though she were a grease spot or the period at the end of a sentence. She was *Dorothy,* his Dorothy.

Dorothy *did* notice the bow first and a smile curved her lips. Then she raised her lovely hazel eyes to his.

"Happy Valentine's Day, sweetheart," he said, smiling, too.

To Sam's dismay, however, his wife's smile disappeared. Her eyes widened in alarm. Dorothy trembled as she dropped the puzzle piece. She leaned over and tried to hide behind the aide.

"The Fat Man! Oh, no, it's the Fat Man!"

"Now, Dot." The aide disentangled herself and gave Dorothy a reassuring pat. "It's your husband, Sam. There's nothing to be afraid of. Look, he's brought you a present."

Dorothy stood, took a panicked step back, and almost tripped over the chair behind her. Sam instinctively reached out to steady her. She gasped and looked around the room wildly.

"Help me! Please, somebody help me! The Fat Man is trying to get me!"

Across the room a man rose unsteadily to his feet to come to Dorothy's rescue. A nearby aide, however, spoke softly to him, telling him the lady was all right.

Sam gaped at his wife in shock. What was going on? He looked behind him where another aide stood. He was six feet tall, at least, muscled, but not fat. He glanced at his own stomach, wondering. Dorothy, afraid of him? No, it had to be someone else. If someone was scaring his Dorothy, he'd thrash him to within an inch of his life.

"Dorothy, it's me. It's your Sam." He tried to sound reassuring, but he heard the desperation in his voice. He set the box of strawberries on the table. He pulled a card from his coat pocket and tucked it under the ribbon. "For you, Dorothy. Like always. Happy Valentine's Day, sweetheart."

"No, no." Dorothy put her hands out in front of her as if to ward off Sam and his gifts. "I'm Dot. I'm Dot."

"Of course you are," soothed the aide as she stood and put her arm around Dorothy. Dorothy buried her face in the aide's shoulder. Her voice was muffled, but Sam still heard what she said.

"Make him go away. Please, please make him go away." She began to sob and tremble like a child waking from a bad dream.

"I'm sorry. You'd better go," the aide said softly over Dorothy's head. "Take the box, too. It will just upset her if you leave it."

Sam's shoulders slumped as he retrieved the strawberries and shuffled out of the dayroom, confused, disappointed—and angry.

"What's going on?" Sam demanded at the nurses' station. "Two days ago, she was a little confused, but after a few minutes she knew exactly who I was. And she wasn't afraid, either. What's the matter with her? She said something about . . . about . . . a fat man." He absently put his hand on his belly. "Is somebody around here scaring her? Some of those aides are pretty hefty dudes."

"I'm so sorry, Mr. Talbot," Eileen said. "I'm not aware of anyone trying to intimidate her, but I'll check into it."

"There had better not be." The hand on his stomach tightened into a fist.

Eileen's voice took on a placating tone. "Dementia is an unpredictable disease. I know it's frustrating. Maybe she'll know you next time." She gave a wan smile. "If you leave the box with me, I'll make sure she gets it. And the card, too."

"Won't it confuse her even more, chocolate-covered strawberries appearing out of the blue? Or worse yet, scare her, make her feel the 'Fat Man'"—Sam sketched air quotes with his fingers—"won't leave her alone?" His face felt hot as he realized Dorothy had meant him. She thought *he* was the Fat Man. What kind of man went around scaring his wife?

"She probably won't remember if I give them to her later. She won't wonder about where they came from. They'll appear like magic, like presents from Santa."

"Santa *is* a fat guy," Sam said, with a rueful half smile.

"And plenty of little kids think he's great until their parents take them to the mall to sit on his lap. Then they start screaming their heads off and want nothing to do with him," Eileen said.

"Yeah," Sam said. "Our youngest was like that. I never expected to be Santa—on Valentine's Day." His hand shook as he passed the box of treats to Eileen.

"You mustn't take it personally, Mr. Talbot."

Sam looked away so he wouldn't be able to see the pity in Eileen's eyes.

"Hard not to. I really didn't mean to scare her."

"I know you didn't. Listen." Eileen cocked her head toward the dayroom. "She's calmer already."

"Out of sight, out of mind, then?"

"Apparently," Eileen said.

There seemed to be nothing more to say, yet Sam lingered. "Does she need anything? A new puzzle? More of that shower gel she likes?"

"She has everything she needs at the moment."

"I'll be going, then." Sam sighed and turned toward the elevators. "Make sure she gets those strawberries," he called over his shoulder.

"Will do." Eileen's voice was cheerful, but Sam glimpsed a line of worry between her eyebrows as the elevator doors slid shut. Sam's stomach clenched as he wondered if his own worst fear had finally come to pass, the fear that the days of his Dorothy knowing her Sam had come to an end.

CHAPTER 2

IN THE LOBBY, ROSE HARKER followed the rest of the newly dubbed Woolgatherers to the Fair Meadows van as it idled under the porte cochere. Gus, the van driver, slid open the van door with a flourish.

"All aboard The Tangled Thread Express," he greeted the group. The young man looked sharp in pressed black pants, crisp white shirt, black tie, and black leather bomber jacket. He handed each woman into the van as though she were his own grandmother—even Edna, who insisted she could get herself into the van, cane and all, without any help. And she did, with only the lightest touch on her elbow as she struggled and swayed like a wind-blown leaf. Rose smiled as Gus deftly made it seem as though Mr. Peabody was the one helping *him* get Mr. Peabody's walker into the van instead of the other way around. She noted the grateful squeeze Alistair Peabody gave Gus's shoulder as he climbed in after his walker.

Last to board, Jenny settled herself at the front, next to Gus. Gus donned his black leather driving gloves and checked his passengers in the rearview mirror.

"Buckle up tight, everyone," he called out as he revved the engine. "Here we go."

Next to Rose, Susan closed her eyes and gripped her armrest. She'd put on her seat belt right away. "Not too fast, not too fast," she pleaded under her breath.

Rose turned to Susan. "How are you doing with that new stitch?"

"I could use some help," Susan admitted. She let go of the armrest to pull her work in progress out of the knitting bag in her lap.

Once Susan was focused on her work, needles clicking as she struggled with the purl stitch, Gus shifted into drive. As he eased his foot off the brake, a heavyset man stepped off the curb in front of the van, apparently lost in thought. Gus jammed on the brakes and gave his horn a short, friendly tap.

The man stopped and blinked at the van. Jenny waved at him. He simply stood and stared for a moment. Finally, he slowly raised his arm and waved back. Then he continued across the driveway. On the other side of the porte cochere, he turned to watch the van pull out.

Rose tapped Jenny on the shoulder. "Who was that?"

"I don't know." Jenny shrugged. "I saw him by the lobby elevators when I was announcing the winner of the contest. He had a box with a ribbon on it, so he must have come to visit someone."

"You sure don't miss much," Rose said.

"No, I don't." Jenny gave a delighted laugh. "He looked like he needed a smile."

"He did seem a bit sad," Rose said. "Kind of dazed, too. I wonder if he's okay to drive." She turned in her seat to scan the parking lot, where she saw the man standing by a silver sedan. Rose realized she sounded like her daughter Rosalie, who had decided Rose was definitely *not* okay to drive the day Rose mowed down the mailbox while backing out of the driveway. Not long after, Rose had found herself ensconced at Fair Meadows, none too happy about it.

"He'll be fine." Jenny waved Rose's words away. "You worry too much." She turned around to chat with Gus and flutter her eyelashes at him.

"She's incorrigible," Susan whispered to Rose.

"They don't seem to mind, though," Rose said with a chuckle. "Old *or* young."

"Keep your eyes on the road, young man," Edna called from the back row. "None of us wants to meet our Maker just yet."

"Yes, ma'am." Gus glanced into the rearview mirror and saluted, then pulled to a careful stop at a red light.

"That's more like it," Edna said. "If you'd just let me sit in the front,

I could make sure we all get there in one piece. I always sat in front with my Stanley, and he never had an accident."

"Lucky Stanley," Laura said under her breath.

"I'll get you there safe and sound, Mrs. O'Brian." Gus turned carefully onto Chambers Street. Moments later, he parked at the curb in front of their destination, The Tangled Thread Yarn Boutique.

"We'll be about an hour," Rose told Gus after he had helped everyone out of the van.

"Take your time. I have studying to do." He nodded at the backpack stashed behind the driver's seat.

"We'll miss you when you graduate and start medical school."

"I'll miss all of you, too." Gus leaned close to Rose's ear. "Even the backseat drivers, believe it or not."

Chuckling, Rose continued across the sidewalk to where the group had gathered to admire the window display. Baskets overflowed with red, pink, and white yarn, and lacy crocheted hearts hung above them from various lengths of invisible thread. Edna made sure they all knew the hearts were crocheted, not knitted.

Jenny led the way into the shop, where the proprietor, a young woman wearing a red cardigan with white hearts worked into the yoke, greeted them warmly.

"Ladies, welcome to The Tangled Thread."

"And gentleman," Mr. Peabody called out.

"And gentleman," she said with a laugh. "I'm Ariadne, and I'll be happy to help you find what you need today. Make yourselves at home and browse to your heart's content."

"Ariadne," Rose said, "we need machine-washable yarn, since the people we make prayer shawls for need their shawls to be easy to care for."

"We have plenty to choose from." Ariadne conducted a tour of the shop, pointing out the yarns that would fit the prayer shawl makers' requirements.

After the tour, the Woolgatherers quickly dispersed to ooh and aah at the rich and varied colors. Hands reached out to squeeze the yarn.

"This is so soft." Susan put a hank of machine-washable merino against her cheek. "The different shades of blue remind me of the ocean."

"That would make a very peaceful shawl," Rose said.

She buried her fingers in a skein of plum-colored yarn. The color reminded her of Amy, one of her knitting students. Amy's spiky purple hair had taken some getting used to, but Rose's heart had quickly warmed to the young woman. Despite being a new mom and working full-time at the local mall, Amy still managed to meet with Rose and her church prayer shawl group, the Heavenly Hugs Prayer Shawl Ministry, at their Wednesday meetings in front of Macy's during her lunch hour. Rose was guiding her through making a tiny hat for little Heaven Leigh—sky blue to match the baby's eyes.

"Look at this, Rose," Laura said, a skein of golden yarn clasped to her heart. "This is the exact color of aspen leaves in the fall. The exact color."

"It's calling your name?"

"My husband and I always went to the mountains for a week in late August, when the aspens were just beginning to change color. Our last hurrah before school started." Laura's brown eyes were warm with memory. "This is going to be a very happy shawl." She hurried off to fill her arms with the rest of the yarn she would need.

Rose left the purple yarn behind and made her way over to the far wall where Mr. Peabody stood with his hands on either side of his walker, examining a selection of tweedy yarn.

"I'm trying to decide," he said as she came alongside him. "The brown or the gray."

"Don't you want something brighter?" Rose asked.

"Some of us feel more comfortable with meat-and-potatoes colors," Mr. Peabody said. "Men are caregivers, too."

"Good point," Rose said. "I'd go with the brown, then. Nobody wants a gray steak."

"Now you're talking." He loaded three skeins of warm brown yarn into the tote attached to the front of his walker. "Notice the thin strand of red that runs through this?"

Rose nodded.

"That's how I like my steak—medium rare."

"Yoo-hoo, Alistair," Jenny called across the shop. "Come help me pick out my yarn."

"Duty calls." With a debonair wink, Mr. Peabody turned his walker in Jenny's direction.

"What about this yarn, Rose?" Susan approached with an armful of skeins, having abandoned the ocean-colored yarn. "It's bulky weight, so it'll be really warm. I can't decide between the red, the pink, or the white. They're all on sale."

"Which color lifts your spirits?" Rose asked.

Susan lowered her voice. "I really like the first yarn I found, but . . ."

"I understand." Rose couldn't always afford the yarn that spoke to her heart, either. "The shop offers a fifteen percent senior discount on the second Saturday of the month. Would that help?"

Susan pulled her phone out of her purse. A lock of gray hair fell across her forehead as she entered numbers into the calculator. When she finished her calculations, she pushed her hair back in place and grinned at Rose.

"Aren't discounts great? Now I can get the yarn I really want. Thank you, Rose."

Moments later, Laura approached the register, arms full of the yarn that filled her heart with memories of aspen leaves in the fall.

"Would you like me to wind it for you?" Ariadne asked.

"Yes, please," Laura said. "I can hardly wait to start this shawl." Soon the yarn swift and ball winder whirred away, creating neat cakes of yarn out of the hanks Laura had chosen.

Edna arrived at the register as Ariadne finished winding the last of Laura's yarn.

"*I* don't need fancy yarn," Edna said, loud enough for everyone in the shop to hear. "Acrylic is good enough for me." She plopped four skeins on the counter.

"It is for me, too," Laura said. "But I won the contest, so today I get to splurge."

"I still think 'Hugs for Helpers' is better than 'The Woolgatherers,'" Edna said.

Laura closed her eyes for a moment, as though praying for patience. When she opened them again, she said, "The name is appropriate because when a person is woolgathering, they're lost in thought, staring off into space, somewhere else in their mind, like a person with dementia. But it also refers to us, because we gather wool to make shawls for the people who care for people with dementia."

"*You* might be gathering wool," Edna said with a sniff. "Like I said, acrylic is good enough for me. And Hugs for Helpers is a good, straightforward name. It tells exactly what we do, nothing fancy."

"Your name was good, Edna." Laura's tone was gentle but firm. "Mine was the one that got picked, though, so we should just move on."

"Good idea." Edna grasped the handles of her shopping bag. "In fact, I'm going to get started on my new shawl right now." She stalked out of the shop to the waiting Fair Meadows van. Dismayed, Rose watched Edna climb into the van.

Over by the window display, Jenny stiffened. "She's sitting in my seat," she said through gritted teeth.

"That's all right." Mr. Peabody maneuvered his walker around a bin to stand next to her. "You can sit next to me on the way to Cracker Barrel. And next to me at Cracker Barrel, if you want."

The glare she'd been directing at Edna melted from Jenny's face as she turned toward Mr. Peabody.

"You say the sweetest things, Alistair." She gave his arm a warm squeeze. "I'd be delighted to sit with you."

Thirty minutes later, the rest of the Woolgatherers emerged from the yarn shop laden with their new purchases, all of which were tucked into The Tangled Thread's signature brown paper bags. A tag stamped with the shop's logo fluttered merrily from the yarn handles of each bag.

At the sound of their happy chatter, Gus stowed his textbook in his backpack and came around to open the sliding van door. Once again, he carefully helped each Woolgatherer inside, deftly collapsing Mr.

Peabody's walker and sliding it under the middle bench seat. He shut the door against the biting February wind. Behind the wheel once more, he revved the engine.

"To Cracker Barrel, right?" he said, glancing at them in his rearview mirror.

"To Cracker Barrel!" they shouted.

"But not too fast," Susan pleaded under her breath.

CHAPTER 3

"Good morning, Woolgatherers," Rose greeted the Fair Meadows prayer shawl group on Monday morning as they took their seats in the corner of the lobby they had staked as their own. Once they were settled, needlework in hand, Rose passed a 3 x 5 card to each member of the group.

"Our shawl-maker's prayer." Jenny sounded both delighted and relieved. "I'm glad you did this, Rose. I had no earthly idea how to write a prayer."

"I'd like us to pray this together whenever we meet, but each of you can pray it when you sit to knit"—Rose glanced at Edna—"and crochet on your own. Let's pray."

The Woolgatherers bowed their heads and read the prayer on their cards aloud along with Rose.

"Father God, we ask you to remember all those who have loved ones who do not remember them. In the embrace of these shawls, may they be strengthened, encouraged, loved, and known."

When they finished the prayer, Rose raised her head to find one of her knitting students, Nan, standing just outside their circle of chairs, wiping her eyes with the end of a bright-red scarf.

"That was so moving," she said in a voice thick with welling tears. "I needed to hear that."

"Good morning, Nan." Rose smiled at the slim middle-aged woman. "Are you coming or going?"

"I'm on my way to visit Mom." Nan dabbed at her eyes again. "I'm sorry. Don't mind me."

"How *is* your mother these days?" Rose asked.

"More bad days than good lately," Nan said.

Sympathetic murmurs rose from the group of shawl makers.

With a glance at the tote on Nan's arm, Rose said, "Do you have time to knit with us afterward?"

"I do," Nan said. "But that's not the only reason I brought it. It's for my time with Mom, too. If she's having another one of those days where she doesn't know who I am, my knitting might spark a conversation. She was an accomplished knitter and tried to teach me when I was a kid. I'm afraid I disappointed her back then. I wasn't very good at it or very interested, either."

"You're coming along nicely now, though," Rose said. "She'll love seeing your work."

"I hope so." Nan waved as she headed to the elevators that would take her to the memory care unit.

Susan tsked over her work. "It must be so hard for her, never knowing if she's going to be her mother's child or a stranger each time she walks into her room."

"It certainly must keep things interesting," Mr. Peabody said.

"I admire the way she continues to search for ways to connect with her mom whether she recognizes her or not," Laura said.

Jenny, however, had apparently had enough serious talk.

"Look at this, everybody." She held up her shawl. It cascaded from her needles in waves of peacock blue, turquoise, and emerald green. "I want to hurry and finish this so I can start another one with my new yarn."

Oohs, aahs, and murmurs of "gorgeous" and "wow" ran around the circle, wrapping Jenny in admiration.

"Beautiful," Mr. Peabody said from his seat opposite her. "Just like you."

Edna frowned as Jenny blushed becomingly. "All of you may have time to sit around and gawk, but I have a shawl to make." She jabbed her crochet hook energetically into the shawl she was making.

"Yours is lovely, too," Laura said. Rose was glad Laura had apparently decided to let bygones be bygones over Edna's comments about the name contest.

Edna shrugged, focusing on her work as though it required her total concentration.

The rest of the needleworkers settled into their work as well, counting stitches, consulting patterns, asking murmured questions of Rose, the most experienced knitter of the group.

"This has to be the Woolgatherers."

Rose shifted in her seat only to start at the sight of the middle-aged woman standing at the edge of their seating area.

"What a surprise." Rose pushed to her feet to envelop the woman in a hug as warm as her smile. "Everyone, this is my friend, Fran McMillan. We knit together in the Heavenly Hugs Prayer Shawl Ministry."

"I know who you are," Jenny said. "You're the one with the boyfriend. Howie, right?"

Fran blushed all the way to her brown eyes and nodded.

"Rose told us all about it," Jenny said. "He sounds like a very nice man."

"He is." Fran's blush deepened.

"So, what brings you out this way?" Rose asked Fran before Jenny could ask any more questions about Fran's dating life.

"Oh, I was just in the neighborhood." She waved a bit vaguely. "I remembered this was one of your days to make shawls in the lobby, so I decided to come by and meet all of you. Rose has told the Heavenly Hugs all about you, too. It's wonderful you're making shawls for caregivers."

"Have a seat. Did you bring your knitting, by any chance?" Rose eyed the large tote on Fran's arm.

"I always have my knitting with me," Fran said with a laugh as she sat on the couch between Laura and Rose. "I never know when I'm going to have to sit and wait somewhere. I even knit when I'm in the drive-through line at Starbucks."

Rose's face lit up at the mention of the coffee shop. "There's a coffee shop going in across the street, on the ground floor of those loft condominiums they're building. I'll be able to get lattes and blueberry scones anytime I want."

Susan, an advocate for all things healthy, shuddered. "Scones are not good for you. And I don't think it's safe for you to try to get across the street before the light changes, what with your cane and all."

Rose bristled. "Susan Thomas, I may not be able to drive a car safely anymore, but I am still perfectly capable of crossing the street. And I'll eat as many scones as I want."

Susan raised her hands in mock surrender while Fran chuckled.

"It really isn't wise to try to get between Rose and a blueberry scone," Fran said, then settled in to her knitting.

Later, when Fran took her leave, Rose walked with her to the lobby doors.

"Fair Meadows is pretty far out of the way for you, Fran," she said. "What really brought you to this part of town?"

Fran's eyes were bright as she held a finger playfully in front of her lips. "I can't tell you yet. It's a secret . . . and a surprise!"

Sam Talbot opened his eyes on Monday morning to slivers of sunlight coming through the blinds on his living room window. He groaned. He'd fallen asleep on the couch watching Netflix again. White letters on the black screen of his television asked if he was still watching his latest binge, *Blue Bloods*. He found the remote on the floor next to a half-empty bag of microwave popcorn. He clicked "Exit" and checked his watch. It was after eight a.m., meaning it was time to get ready to go to Fair Meadows, the only thing on his agenda that day.

Sam shoved aside the afghan he'd pulled off the back of the couch the night before and sat up. With a grunt, he stood and stretched to get out the kinks that sleeping on the couch had left all over his body, scattering stray popcorn kernels on the floor. He shuffled off to the bathroom. He dropped his sweatpants and T-shirt next to the laundry basket, where a pile of dirty clothes threatened to trip him on the way to the shower. As Sam stood under the gush of hot water, he passed his hand over his chin and discovered stubble. Should he let his beard grow so he'd look even more like Santa Claus? It was tempting to forgo the hassle of shaving, but he'd never had a beard. There would be even less hope of Dorothy knowing him if he showed up with a five o'clock shadow and eventually a full beard. He decided against the idea.

Standing in his closet, Sam considered Dorothy's name for him, the "Fat Man." Sure, he'd put on a few pounds lately, but was he fat? Sam thought not, as he pawed through the hangers in his closet in search of one of the three pairs of slacks that fit him. He studied his profile in the mirror as he threaded his belt through the loops of his gray slacks. He noted the paunch, not unlike that of many men his age. Heck, when he worked as a corporate engineer, men much younger than he had sported bigger ones. Come to think of it, in a suit, those big stomachs made those men look imposing and prosperous. He decided to ignore the fact he had to notch his belt three holes over from his pre-going-to-visit-Dorothy days.

At least I'm not bald, Sam thought as he tucked in his shirt. He sighed as he remembered Dorothy's hands running through his hair. She'd loved to make it stand on end so he would look like a mad scientist. Then he'd chuckle maniacally and chase her through the house. The chase always left them breathless as she never let him catch her until they were in the bedroom. Sam swallowed hard. Best *not* to remember that. She would never know him that way again.

The sound of laughter turned Sam's head as he made his way across the Fair Meadows lobby. There was that woman with the auburn hair again. After he punched the elevator button, he turned to look at her, sitting with a group of women in a sea of bright colors—yellows and reds and blues. The doors slid open behind him, and he stepped inside while continuing to take in the cheerful scene. Absently, he pressed the button for the seventh floor and let out a sigh as the door glided closed.

"Dot's going to love those," Patsy, the weekday charge nurse, said as Sam stepped out of the elevator with the bouquet of carnations.

"Dorothy," Sam said automatically, his mind still on the lively group in the lobby.

"Right. Dorothy," Patsy said. "She's in her room."

Sam's mind returned to the present with a jolt. "Is she all right? She's always in the dayroom in the morning. She's not sick, is she?"

"No, no, she's fine. Just getting a slow start. She slept in this morning."

"Are you sure she's all right?"

"Oh, yes." Patsy gave an airy wave. "She stayed up a bit later than usual visiting with friends."

Friends? Dorothy had friends in Memory Care? Sam shook his head. She couldn't even remember her husband. How could she have friends?

The sound of laughter floated out into the hallway as Sam walked to Dorothy's room. The door was slightly ajar. He rapped his knuckles on the doorframe, even though it seemed ridiculous to knock on his own wife's door.

"Come in." Dorothy sounded so delighted that Sam took heart.

"Good morning." Sam pushed the door open and took an eager step inside. "I brought you something, sweetheart."

There was, however, no answering endearment, only a sharp intake of breath as Dorothy's eyes widened.

"Oh, no, I thought you were—but you're not. Go. Away."

"But Dorothy, I brought you carnations, your favorite."

Dorothy squeezed her eyes shut and whimpered, more agitated by the second.

"No, no, no. Go away, Fat Man. Go away."

"I'm sorry, Mr. Talbot," said the aide who had been helping Dorothy fix her hair.

Dorothy opened her eyes, revealing a sudden clarity. "That is not Mr. Talbot," she said crisply. "Mr. Talbot is my husband. I ought to know my own husband, and that is not him."

"But—"

The aide mouthed "sorry" and tilted her head toward the nurses' station.

"I know, I know," he said. "Leave them at the desk. You'll make sure she gets them later." He turned in defeat and trudged to the nurses' station, where he related the most recent absurdity of his wife's disease to Patsy.

"She stared straight at me and said Mr. Talbot is her husband, but I'm not him," he said with bewildered outrage.

"She may be remembering you at a different, earlier time in your lives together," Patsy said. "I don't imagine you look like you did when you two were first married or even the way you did ten years ago."

"You'd think she'd at least recognize the hair," he muttered. "I've always had a good head of hair."

"But maybe back then it was darker?" Patsy said.

"I guess." He looked away, as though white hair was something to be ashamed of. "I could dye it."

Patsy smiled. "You could, I suppose. But you're fine just the way you are, Mr. Talbot."

Sam wondered about that as he pushed the elevator button. He doubted very much that he was fine, not after his wife had looked straight at him and told him he wasn't who he was.

CHAPTER 4

"HOLD THE ELEVATOR, PLEASE." SAM stuck out his arm to hold the door for the slightly breathless middle-aged woman hurrying to catch the elevator. He recognized her as the woman who'd been taking her daughters to visit "Grandma Becca" on Valentine's Day.

"Thanks." She smiled at him.

Sam knew he ought to smile back, but his whole face felt too heavy to make the effort.

"You're welcome." Sam immediately regretted how gruff he sounded.

"Tough visit?" the woman asked, her voice soft and kind.

Sam nodded, not trusting himself to speak.

Silence hung between them as the elevator began to descend.

"You?" Sam finally managed to say.

"It was surprising," she said. "I really didn't see it coming."

"Me neither," Sam said.

The elevator bumped to a stop.

"I hope your next one is better," she said.

"Thank you," Sam said. "It can't get much worse," he said under his breath as he watched her walk over with a bounce in her step to the group with the brightly colored yarn. The group greeted her warmly and made room for her to sit. She leaned forward and gestured as she talked. From the way the others were beaming at her, she must be sharing good news. How could anyone come off the memory care floor happy and excited when the people you loved weren't really there anymore, or worse yet, said you weren't really there anymore? Sam's shoulders slumped as he crossed the lobby. He shivered as he stepped through the automatic doors into the bitter wind of a bleak February day.

Edna glanced up from her crochet as Nan rushed into the cozy corner where the Woolgatherers sat making their prayer shawls.

"You'll never guess what happened!"

"Scoot over, Edna," Rose said from her seat on the couch. "Nan can sit between us and then we can all hear her."

"I'm too old to scoot," Edna muttered, but moved over anyway.

"What happened?" Laura leaned forward, her face bright with interest.

"Remember I said I was going knit while I sat with Mom if she was having a bad day?"

Edna nodded along with everyone else. She knew about the bad days.

"Well, it *was* one of those days. She didn't recognize me, but she didn't seem to mind me sitting with her at a table in the dayroom. I pulled out my knitting to have something to do. After a while, I realized she was watching me—intently. Then she asked me what I was making. I told her I was knitting a shawl. She leaned over and examined my work.

"'Nice work,' she said. 'Very pretty.'

"I thanked her and told her my mother had taught me to knit when I was a teenager. Then I saw her moving her fingers in her lap as if she was knitting. I asked her if she was a knitter. She looked at her hands, knitting away.

"She said, 'I suppose I am.' And then she smiled.

"I dug around in my bag and found some needles and half a skein of yarn. Before I knew it, she'd cast on and we were knitting together. It was so wonderful to simply sit and knit with her. The staff said I could leave the yarn and needles with her. She's going to need more yarn soon, though. I'd forgotten how fast her needles could fly," Nan finished.

"What's she making?" Edna asked.

"It looks like a scarf to me," Nan said. "But it could be a sweater for an octopus for all I care. It was wonderful to do something with my mom, instead of her acting like I'm a complete stranger or not even there."

"But you're still a complete stranger, even if she's knitting with you," Edna pointed out.

"But now we have something in common," Nan said. "When we sit and knit together, we'll be connected by the knitting."

"Well, don't expect her to knit with you tomorrow." Edna felt she needed to warn this oh-so-hopeful woman. "Like with my Stanley, here one day and gone the next. That Old-Timer's Disease does whatever it wants."

"Edna." Rose's voice was gentle, but Edna heard the scolding tone all the same.

"I hope you're wrong," Nan told Edna.

"I'm not." Edna thrust her hook into her work with a bit more force than necessary to emphasize her point.

Some of the light went out of Nan's face.

"At least I had today," she said in a small voice.

"We'll pray you have more days like that. Won't we?" Rose said.

Everyone nodded except Edna.

"Won't do no good," she muttered.

Later that afternoon, Jenny knocked on the door of Rose's apartment. Something had to be done about Edna, and she was counting on Rose to do it.

"Come in, come in." Rose greeted her with a welcoming smile. "I was just about to have a cup of tea. Would you like some?"

"I'd love some." Jenny stepped inside.

They were soon settled in Rose's sitting room, cozy with knitted throws, pillows as soft and plump as Rose herself, and a basket of yarn. Rose's latest shawl project nestled in a nearby armchair where she had apparently laid it aside to answer the door. Rose poured fragrant Earl Grey from a porcelain teapot into delicate flowered cups.

"What can I do for you?" Rose offered a steaming cup to Jenny.

"I came to talk to you about Edna," Jenny said. "She's such a Debbie Downer, always looking on the gloomy side of things. She doesn't add anything positive to the group."

"Except shawls." Rose regarded Jenny over the rim of her teacup. "She's made three this month alone."

"Well, of course she has," Jenny said. "It's easy to make a shawl fast with that giant hook of hers. But she's stitching all her negativity into those shawls, too. And you saw how Nan's face fell when Edna told her knitting with her mom wouldn't last. We're supposed to be cheering up the families of dementia patients, for goodness' sake. She's not good for the group or what we're trying to accomplish with the shawls."

"Maybe"—Rose took another sip of tea—"the group is good for her. Being around positive people and doing something for others may eventually make a difference."

"Maybe," Jenny said. She wasn't ready to give up, though. "But honestly, how much are we going to have to put up with before we *eventually* make a dent in her attitude?"

Rose set her cup on her saucer with a soft clink. Her blue eyes were gentle, but her voice was firm. "The Woolgatherers is a ministry, Jenny, something we do to serve others. Edna might need our ministry as much as the caregivers for whom we make the shawls. I never knew before today her husband had Alzheimer's. It seems to have left its mark on her. I think she needs to be a Woolgatherer."

Jenny looked down, feeling like the dregs that gathered in the bottom of her teacup. She heaved a sigh and met Rose's gaze.

"All right, but I'm not sitting next to her anymore. *You* can ply her with sweetness and light."

"Gladly," Rose said. "In the meantime, though, will you pray for her?"

"I guess." Jenny shrugged, secretly doubting it would do much good at all.

Half an hour later, Rose closed the door after Jenny and let out a sigh. Truth be told, Rose also found Edna a bit of a trial. When Edna had poured cold water on Nan's hope about her mother, Rose had wanted to give her a swift kick in the ankle. But her adventures of the last few months had shown her there was usually more than met the eye when it came to prayer shawls. They seemed to have an uncanny way of opening hearts—the hearts of the makers as well as the recipients.

Back in November, her pastor had sent her church's prayer shawl group, the Heavenly Hugs Prayer Shawl Ministry, out to knit in public in a last-ditch effort to attract people to Hope of Glory Community Church. Until then, Margaret, Jane, Rose, and Fran had knitted silently in the peace and quiet of the church's prayer chapel. Margaret, the self-appointed leader of the Heavenly Hugs (and just about everything else she could manage to be in charge of), had objected strenuously, but nevertheless they had ended up knitting at the local mall during the Christmas shopping season. Knitting at the mall had done far more than bring people to Hope of Glory. The people the Heavenly Hugs had met and the situations they encountered had wrought changes in each of the knitters as well.

Rose's smile widened as she thought of Margaret, who was still inclined to take charge but not nearly as uptight and judgmental as she used to be. The silence that had once reigned between Jane and her incarcerated son had been broken with words of heartfelt forgiveness. Fran's paralyzing widowhood was fast giving way to her friendship with Howard Fuller, who she met while knitting at the mall.

And me? Rose closed her eyes as her heart overflowed with gratitude. *I'd still be moping around wishing for my old independent life instead of making a new and meaningful one here at Fair Meadows. Lord, please help Edna grow past her hard times, too.*

CHAPTER 5

AFTER ANOTHER VISIT TO AN increasingly terrified Dorothy, Sam resolved to stay away from Fair Meadows for a while. He was beginning to suspect the staff dreaded the disruption as much as he dreaded Dorothy's rejection. He stayed home on Saturday, aimlessly flipping through channels on the television, finally falling asleep to the drone of fighter planes in an old black-and-white World War II movie.

When Monday morning rolled around again, however, he found himself getting ready to visit his wife. It was what he did on Mondays, right after he trundled the trash can to the curb. As he searched the living room for his car keys, tossing chip bags and paper napkins to the side, he briefly considered adding the detritus to the trash can. But the sound of the garbage truck rumbling down the street told him he didn't have time to add anything to the can that was already at the curb.

Now, where were those keys?

"Dorothy, have you seen—"

Dorothy would have known exactly where they were. In fact, she would have been the one to put them on the hook by the door if she'd found them carelessly tossed anywhere else. Sam stopped himself midsentence. The Dorothy who remembered him, the Dorothy he remembered, would know. But that Dorothy was not here. That Dorothy was not even at Fair Meadows. That Dorothy had faded away.

He located the keys at last between the cushion and the arm of the recliner. Must've fallen out of his pocket when he'd fallen asleep. As he straightened from his search of the recliner, Sam caught sight of a well-worn book on the bookshelf in the living room. On impulse, he tucked it under his arm and headed for the florist's shop. Every Monday of his married life, he'd always bought flowers for Dorothy.

Sam stepped through the automatic doors into the Fair Meadows lobby. He turned his head at the sound of laughter. There was that bunch of knitters again.

"Oh, Alistair!" The auburn-haired woman he'd noticed last week swatted the old guy sitting next to her on the arm.

"Careful, now." The man chuckled. "You'll make me drop a stitch!"

"We're all going to drop stitches if you keep making us laugh like that," the woman sitting across from him in the knitting circle said between giggles.

"No, I'm keeping you *in* stitches," the old guy quipped.

The rest of the knitters groaned. Sam silently groaned with them, though his curiosity was piqued. A man wielding knitting needles? The closest he got to that was chopsticks and Chinese takeout.

"Puns," another knitter muttered in mock disgust. Laughter rippled across the group again.

Sam shook his head as he continued to the elevators. An old guy knitting with a bunch of old ladies? Must be desperate, he decided, what with that comb-over and all. He turned and studied the man again as he waited for the elevator to arrive. Maybe not desperate. That woman next to him . . . well, if this "Alistair" was single, he was a smart man, come to think of it.

The elevator dinged and the doors slid open. Sam backed into the elevator, his eyes still on the group chatting and laughing away.

"Seven?" a voice on the other side of the elevator said.

Sam started. A woman with a large tote bag pushed the elevator button. He'd been so focused on the group across the lobby he hadn't even noticed her stepping into the elevator. A pair of knitting needles stuck out of the top of the bag. What was it with all this knitting? She looked familiar, though.

Sam searched his memory as he nodded. Oh, right. She was the one who'd been so happy in the elevator last week about something she "hadn't seen coming."

"Me, too," she said. "I'm going to spend time with my mother. You?"

"My wife." Sam stared straight ahead. Moments later, the elevator came to a stop with a gentle thump. Sam stood aside to let the woman with the tote bag go first.

"I hope you have a good visit," she said with an encouraging smile.

Not likely. Sam refrained from voicing his doubts. He simply said, "You, too," and stepped off the elevator into the bright and sunny reception area.

"Good morning, Mr. Talbot," Patsy said, her eyebrows drawn together. "She's in the dayroom, lovely as ever." Sam nodded absently, already focused on catching a glimpse of his wife.

Sam had to admit they took good care of her here. Dorothy's hair was not only combed but also styled in soft waves that brushed the tops of her shoulders. Her outfit matched, right down to her shoes. He'd emphasized to the staff she'd always wanted to look put-together before the illness had started to take its toll. As he gazed at her loveliness, he found it hard to grasp her mind was not nearly as put-together as her outward appearance.

He stepped closer, noting with satisfaction she'd had a manicure, her nails painted in her favorite shade of rosy pink. She was seated at a table alone, leafing through a magazine. Any minute she'd turn down the corner on a page of recipes. She had always loved to try new recipes.

Dorothy, however, paged past the recipes. She paged past everything, closed the magazine, and pushed it aside. She glanced up and stiffened.

"Go away." Dorothy's voice rose with each syllable. The chair sent a screeching sound across the room as she pushed back from the table.

An aide came over and laid a gentle hand on Dorothy's shoulder.

"Now, Dot, it's your husband, Sam. He's brought you carnations."

Sam held out the bouquet and tried to smile. He was afraid it might look more like a grimace, though.

Dorothy stared at him, wide-eyed and trembling.

"That's the Fat Man. Make him go away."

Out of the corner of his eye, Sam saw another patient stand and start toward them across the room. He had a full head of gray hair and fire in his eyes.

"I'll take care of this guy, Dot," he said.

"No need, Rafe," the aide said. "Mr. Talbot is on his way out."

Oh, Mr. Talbot is on his way out, is he? Sam clenched his jaw. Dismissed like a troublemaker when all he wanted was to spend time with his wife. Who was paying for this shindig, anyway? As much as he wanted to stand his ground, though, the terror in Dorothy's eyes went straight past his pride and into his heart.

With an indignant huff, Sam stomped to the nurses' station.

"Would you make sure she gets these?" He thrust the bunch of carnations at Patsy. Realizing he was taking his frustration out on an innocent party, he softened his tone and held out the book. "I hoped she and I might read these together today, but . . ."

"I'd be happy to make sure she gets both, Mr. Talbot." Patsy glanced at the cover. "*Best Loved Poems of All Time.*"

"She loves poetry, all kinds," Sam said.

"These are her favorites?" Patsy indicated pages where the corners had been dog-eared.

Sam nodded. "I used to know some of them by heart, she read them to me so often. She loved reading to our kids, and later just to me, when they were older and didn't want to be read to anymore."

"Here's the one about the fog coming in on little cat feet," Patsy said, leafing through the pages. "And Emily Dickinson's 'I Never Saw a Moor.' She underlined it."

"She used to recite it from . . . from," Sam faltered, then swallowed hard. "From memory."

"I'm sure she'll enjoy discovering it all over again." Patsy closed the book and set it aside. "It's thoughtful of you to bring it."

Sam turned away to hide his disappointment that Dorothy would be enjoying the book without him.

"See you," he managed to say. Once the elevator arrived, he stepped inside the empty space and pressed the button for the lobby. When the doors opened again, Sam started to step out, only to be blocked by an influx of chattering women. A glance at the lighted buttons told him this was only the fifth floor. He gathered from the identical books they were holding that they were on their way to a book club, but the conversations that swirled around him were about everything but the novel. He caught snippets of cute sayings of grandchildren, accounts of the follies of grown children, and a hands-down consensus that last night's dessert had been to die for, not to mention sugar-free. Sam's mouth watered. When was the last time he'd had cherry crumble, sugar-free or otherwise?

After another stop that added a few more book club ladies to the already crowded elevator, they arrived at the lobby. The elevator doors swept open, and Sam stuck his arm out to hold them open.

"Why, thank you," one woman said as she passed.

"Such a gentleman," another said.

And then they were on their way down the hall toward the Fireside Room. Sam had seen the cozy room with its comfortable armchairs and gas fireplace when he'd toured Fair Meadows in search of a good place for Dorothy. His guide had gone on and on about all the activities Fair Meadows offered, even though Dorothy would not be able to participate in most of them. There had been broad hints he might want to relocate to Fair Meadows, too. The director had insisted on showing him one of the cottages for "active seniors," where he could live in comfort independently while Dorothy was being cared for on the seventh floor of the main building.

"Hmph." Sam snorted at the memory. They could call it a "retirement community" and talk about the "fabulous" amenities for "active senior living" all they wanted. He wasn't about to simply up stakes and move to Fair Meadows, despite luxuries like the pool and golf course. Dorothy may need to be in a place like this, but that didn't mean he did, too. He was fine right where he was. And to boot, he'd finally paid off the mortgage a few years ago.

A burst of laughter turned his attention back to the lobby. Those knitters were still at it.

Dorothy had done something with yarn, he recalled. Had it been knitting? Or the thing with a hook? He'd never paid much attention, but he'd enjoyed sitting with her in the evenings while she worked on blankets. No, not just any blankets, she kept telling him. They were afghans, although they looked like regular old blankets to him. It had been mostly afghans, but sometimes scarves, too. And hats. She'd made hats for some charity. Cancer patients? The homeless? Needy children? Something like that, or maybe all three. His Dorothy had a kind and generous heart.

Sam's steps slowed as he walked toward the lobby doors. He found himself veering toward the group that laughed and chatted as they busied their hands with . . . He drew closer to see what they were making. A white-haired woman with bright-blue eyes waved to him.

"Hello," she said.

Sam stepped over to her.

"Hi. I was wondering what you're doing, I mean, making."

"We're knitting," the woman said.

"And crocheting." A woman two chairs over waved a large pink hook at him. A few other members of the group rolled their eyes.

"Can't forget our expert crocheter, Edna," the white-haired lady said with a smile. "And I'm Rose Harker."

"I'm Jenny Alderman." The woman with the red hair gave him a warm smile, punctuated with dimples.

"Laura," a woman with a lapful of yellow yarn said.

"I'm Susan, and we're making prayer shawls." Susan was wrapped in a throw blanket, with only her hands and knitting protruding from its folds.

"Sam Talbot," Sam said. "Prayer shawls?"

"Have a seat, Sam." Rose indicated an empty place on the couch across from her chair. "We'll tell you all about it."

Sam looked away, sorry he'd asked. He wasn't sure he wanted to hear about "prayer" anything.

"Are you in a hurry?" Rose asked. "Is there somewhere you need to be?"

Sam considered taking the out Rose was offering him, but he really *didn't* have anywhere he needed to be. He sat on the couch.

"This is a prayer shawl." Rose held up her work and what looked like a river of blue yarn flowed off her lap and onto the floor. She gathered it into her lap and resumed whatever it was you did when it involved two pointy sticks. "Prayer shawls are for people who are ill, bereaved, or otherwise going through a hard time. We pray while we make them."

Sam relaxed a bit. They might say they prayed while they made those things, but he'd seen them talking and laughing with each other. Maybe they weren't religious nuts after all.

"*Our* prayer shawls, though, are for caregivers," Jenny said. "Specifically, people who care for people with memory problems. They're in really hard situations."

These folks didn't know the half of it. But he couldn't for the life of him grasp why a shawl would help anyone trying to cope with a loved one's dementia.

As if she'd read the doubt in his eyes, Rose picked up where Jenny left off.

"A prayer shawl is a tangible expression of God's love and care. When a person wraps one around his or her shoulders, it's like getting a hug from God. A shawl made with love and prayer can give comfort and courage to the person who receives it."

Sam frowned. It sounded like wishful thinking mumbo jumbo to him.

"If you say so," he said with a shrug.

"I was a skeptic, too, at first." The old guy sitting next to Jenny set aside his knitting and extended his hand. "Alistair Peabody." The strength of his grip surprised Sam. "But the people we give them to have told us the shawls really do help."

Sam shook his head. "Sorry, but I don't see how."

"Didn't anyone ever make something for you, like a scarf or an afghan?" Rose asked.

"My wife," Sam said. "She was a great one for afghans and scarves."

"So, how do you feel when you wear one of those scarves or wrap one of the afghans she made around you?"

Sam hesitated, the words catching in his throat. He pictured the blue-and-red afghan he routinely pulled over himself to watch Netflix on the couch. He wondered if he could trust himself to speak. Finally, he managed to say, "Loved."

"That's what prayer shawls are all about," Rose said. "They're a way for people to feel how much God loves and cares for them."

Sam felt a surge of annoyance. If God cared so much, why was Dorothy even in Memory Care? He needed a whole lot more than a hug from a shawl to cope with her illness. What he needed was Dorothy, his wife, his love, his companion.

"Well, that sounds very nice," Sam said, to keep himself from saying something rude. "I'd best be going now." He stood and stepped away from the group.

"Stop by anytime," Rose said. "We're the Woolgatherers, and we're here on Mondays, Thursdays, and Saturdays."

"Will do," Sam lied and then high-tailed it out to his car.

"That went well," Edna said drily as she watched Sam leave.

"What do you mean?" Jenny said. "We had a nice chat."

"Hmph," Edna snorted. "He couldn't get out of here fast enough."

"I wonder what his story is," Laura murmured.

"A widower?" Susan said. "He said his wife *was* a great one for making afghans."

"I don't think so," Jenny said. "He's wearing a wedding ring."

"You would know," Edna said.

"I still wear mine." Rose gazed at her rings with a reminiscent smile.

"If he's a widower, who's he taking flowers to?" Jenny said.

Leave it to Jenny to notice a man carrying flowers, Edna thought.

"Flowers?" Susan asked.

"Yes, flowers," Jenny said. "I've seen him bringing a bouquet on several occasions. Usually carnations, though. Not roses."

"Maybe his mother," Mr. Peabody said.

"Or his sister," Laura said.

"We'll just have to ask him." Rose shrugged.

"Good luck with that," Edna said. "We scared him off. He'll give the prayer shawl weirdos a wide berth from now on."

"I wouldn't be too sure," Rose said. "He might have been uncomfortable, but he seemed interested, too."

Edna, stomach rumbling, was about to roll up her work and head to lunch when Nan stepped out of the elevator. She hurried over to the prayer shawl group, beaming.

"She's still knitting." Nan was nearly breathless with joy. "Mom knitted with me again today."

"How wonderful," Rose said.

The other Woolgatherers nodded and smiled, except for Edna. She frowned, lips pressed together. Nan glowed with happiness, a happiness that would turn a deaf ear to the truth Edna knew only too well. That Old-Timer's *always* let you down.

"I don't know how long this will last." Nan glanced at Edna. "But I plan on enjoying knitting with her for as long as I can. She even helped me fix one of my mistakes this morning."

"Really?" Jenny asked.

"Yes, but she was different from when she tried to teach me when I was a kid. Before, she would have yanked my knitting out of my hands with an impatient huff, fixed it, and given it back to me. I'd feel about two inches tall by the time she got done, and I never learned how to fix my mistakes."

"And today?" Rose asked.

"Today, she leaned over and said, 'Excuse me, dear, but I believe you've dropped a stitch.' I started to pass her my work, but she waved it away, and then proceeded to talk me through fixing it myself." Nan sniffed and dabbed at her eyes.

Edna steeled herself against tears as Laura shook her head in wonder.

"This is amazing. It's as though dementia is helping her become a patient teacher."

"And I thought I was the only one who was going to learn patience from it," Nan said with a rueful smile.

"Wonders never cease, do they?" Susan said.

"Not when people are praying," Nan said. "Thank you, all of you. Knowing you're praying makes such a difference. I don't feel like I walk into Mom's room alone anymore. God and all your prayers are with me. I'll see you Saturday, with the girls."

"Not gonna last," Edna muttered as soon as Nan was out of earshot.

"Maybe not," Rose said. "But today she made a good memory with her mother."

"Only one of them's gonna remember it," Edna said. It paid to keep that in mind.

"I have a feeling Nan's okay with that," Rose said.

CHAPTER 6

THAT AFTERNOON, OVER AFTER-SCHOOL SNACKS, Nan told her daughters about her surprising knitting session with their grandmother.

"That is so cool." Samantha, Nan's thirteen-year-old bundle of energy, bounced in her chair. "I have a great idea. Let's all bring our knitting on Saturday and knit with Grandma Becca. I can show her my scarf." She charged off to her room and returned with her knitting. The length of red garter stitch that hung from her needles varied wildly in width. Samantha often plunged eagerly on to the next row without counting her stitches. She dropped stitches or added them with reckless abandon. She didn't have the patience to count or to take the time to fix the mistakes.

"You can't show her *that*," her older sister, Tara, said.

"Why not?"

"It's all wonky, that's why not."

Samantha glanced at her work and shrugged. "It looks okay to me. Besides, I'm having fun."

"I happen to want to do it right. If you'd just let me show you." Tara reached for Samantha's scarf.

Samantha, however, whisked it out of reach and retreated to the family room.

"I'd rather not show Grandma Becca mine," Tara told her mother.

Nan had learned to be "quick to listen and slow to speak" with Tara, the quieter and more private of her girls. She waited for Tara to find the words to explain.

Tara fiddled with the friendship bracelet on her arm.

"Grandma Becca's a really good knitter, right?" she finally said.

"Well, yes," Nan said. "She's been knitting for decades."

"I'm just a beginner. All I can do is the knit stitch. I still make mistakes. I don't want to show her until I make sure it's perfect."

"She'll love whatever you do, just like when you were little." Nan reached out and rubbed Tara's arm.

Tara's head jerked up. "That's the thing, Mom. She's not like when I was little anymore. I don't know what to expect from her from one Saturday to the next. What if all she sees are the mistakes?"

Nan lowered her voice. "Better let your sister go first, then. Any of your mistakes will pale in comparison."

Tara grinned. "That's for sure. Okay, I'll bring my knitting. But if I have any mistakes, I want to get Rose to help me fix them before I show it to Grandma Becca. Deal?"

Nan considered this. Tara had taught herself to knit from YouTube videos but asked Rose for help when she ran into problems. She stayed so long in the lobby on Saturdays getting help that Nan suspected Tara was trying to avoid visiting her grandmother. She knew she probably shouldn't be making deals with a sixteen-year-old, given the circumstances. She decided to take a chance, though, trusting Rose not to let Tara stay too long.

"Deal." They hugged on it. "She's going to love your knitting. You'll see."

Nevertheless, Nan bit her lip as she recalled Edna's warning about the unpredictability of dementia. She hoped against hope that "that Old-Timer's Disease" wouldn't disappoint either of her girls on Saturday.

"We're going to knit with Grandma Becca," Samantha called out to the Woolgatherers as the mother and daughters breezed into the lobby at Fair Meadows on Saturday morning.

"Have fun." Rose waved at her. As she watched, Tara spoke to her mother.

"Come upstairs as soon as you get it fixed," she heard Nan say.

Tara didn't look back but simply waved a hand behind her as if pushing her mother's words away.

"I need some help again." Tara sat down next to Rose. Rose laid her shawl in progress aside to examine Tara's work.

"Hmm . . ."

"Uh-oh," Tara said. "That bad?"

"No, it's not." Rose studied Tara's face to try to discern what the girl was thinking and how hard to push. "I recognize this mistake. I clearly remember teaching you how to deal with it a few weeks ago."

Tara shrugged. "I guess I forgot. Can you please show me again?"

What exactly did you forget? Rose wondered. *That you've made this mistake before? That you know how to fix it? Perhaps forgetting is what this is about—Grandma Becca forgetting you.*

Rose kept these thoughts to herself and set about talking Tara through the process of correcting her knitting. Once the problem was solved, however, Tara lingered.

"This is really pretty." Tara patted the blue shawl taking shape under Rose's skillful fingers. "Do you think I'll be able to make a shawl someday?"

"At the rate you're going, it won't be long," Rose said. "But don't you want to make a hat for yourself, or some of those fingerless gloves that are all the rage?"

"Maybe," Tara said. "But I'd really like to make shawls with the Woolgatherers."

Rose cocked her head. "You want to sit around and knit with a bunch of old ladies?"

Mr. Peabody, seated on the other side of Rose, cleared his throat.

"And an old gentleman," Rose added.

Tara shifted in her seat. "Well, yeah, sure. You're kinda cool."

"Just 'kinda cool'?" Jenny tilted her head. "I'll have you know I'm 'way cool,' to quote my own granddaughter."

"You certainly are." Mr. Peabody flashed her an appreciative grin.

"Spare me," Edna said.

"A shawl is a big project. It'll take much longer than a scarf." Rose's voice held a note of caution. "Are you sure you can keep at it?"

"I've kept at the scarf, haven't I? I'm almost done." Tara held up the length of brightly colored knitting, entirely in garter stitch.

"You'll need to learn the purl stitch," Rose said. "You'd find a whole shawl in the knit stitch pretty boring after a while."

"So, teach me," Tara said, undeterred.

"Maybe next week," Rose said.

"But I have time now," Tara started to protest, only to be brought up short by the kind but firm look in Rose's eyes.

"Now it's time for you to visit your grandmother." She held out the plate of peanut butter blossoms Laura had brought to share. "Here, take a cookie for the road."

"Okay." Tara took her time rolling up her knitting and tucking it into her backpack.

"We'll see you later, dear," Rose said as the girl heaved her backpack over one shoulder. Tara gave a small, dispirited wave, then turned and walked slowly to the elevators, munching on the cookie.

"I admire Nan," Rose said. "It can't be easy to pry them away from their teenage lives to come here every week."

"It's probably a bit scary for Tara," Jenny said. "I know it is for me. I hope I never have to move out of my cottage to Memory Care, but you never know." She gazed off into space, her knitting apparently forgotten in her lap.

"I'll never forget the day you gave Nan that blue shawl, Rose," Jenny said after a while. "She pulled it close around her and said, 'Most days my mother doesn't hug me back.' I couldn't stop thinking about how hard that must be."

"And this is why we're the Woolgatherers," Rose said. "Because God gave you the idea to make shawls for other caregivers, too."

Jenny looked startled. "God? Me? I don't know about that. It was just a nice idea."

"Prayer shawls are more than a 'nice idea.' Somehow they make things better for the people we give them to. And it *was* God who gave you the idea, Jenny, whether you realize it or not."

Jenny shifted in her chair as if uncomfortable with that notion.

Moments later, Jenny nudged Rose and said, "There's Sam. No flowers today." While Sam waited for the elevator, he turned and glanced in their direction. Jenny waved, flashing her dimples. He returned the wave a little half-heartedly, it seemed to Rose. Then the elevator doors slid open behind him. He turned, stepped inside, and disappeared as the elevator whisked him away.

"He looks like he could use some cheering up," Jenny said.

"If anybody can do that, it's you," Mr. Peabody said with a wink.

"I like to think I'm fun to be with." Jenny preened.

"And modest, too," Edna said.

Before things could escalate, Rose cleared her throat and asked for everyone's attention.

"Woolgatherers, thanks to Edna's diligent efforts, we have three completed shawls. I want to take them to church to be prayed over next Sunday. The service will be extra special because the bishop's going to be there. Would any of you like to come with me?"

"Do we have to?" Edna wanted to know.

"Not if you don't want to," Rose said.

"I'm in." Jenny waved. Susan and Laura also raised their hands.

"Anybody else?" Rose asked.

Mr. Peabody begged off, citing brunch plans with a grandson. Edna gave a decided shake of the head and no excuse at all.

"But how are we going to get there?" Susan asked, a line forming between her eyebrows. "Does your friend who gives you a ride have room for all of us?"

"Jane doesn't have room, but Gus does," Rose said. "I've already arranged for him to take us to the eleven o'clock service at Hope of Glory. He'll return at one o'clock. There's a luncheon in the parish hall after the service in honor of the bishop's visit. The Heavenly Hugs are eager to meet you."

"I haven't been to church in ages. What to wear, what to wear? Do the ladies at Hope of Glory wear hats to church?" Jenny asked, a note of hope in her voice.

"Not even Margaret Benson wears a hat to church these days." Rose chuckled. "She does dress up, though—nice suit, nice jewelry."

"I don't have many dressy outfits." The line reappeared between Susan's eyebrows.

"That's okay," Rose assured her. "Amy and Bryson wear jeans and T-shirts every week."

Susan's face cleared. "Well, I can certainly do better than that."

"The folks at Hope of Glory are going to be happy to meet you, no matter how you're dressed," Rose said. "The important thing is that the shawls are prayed over."

"Why do they have to get prayed over at church anyway?" Edna wanted to know. "We pray whenever we're working on them, at the beginning of every session. Doesn't that make them 'holy' enough?"

"Yes," Rose said. "But it doesn't hurt to have the prayers of the entire Hope of Glory community, too."

"I'd really like to meet the rest of the Heavenly Hugs and the other people there," Laura said. "Especially your Father Pete. He doesn't sound like any other minister I've ever met. Imagine sending the prayer shawl group out to knit in public to keep a church from being closed. Quite the creative thinker."

"He had a part in starting the Woolgatherers, now that I think of it," Rose said. "Knitting at the mall inspired me to knit here in the lobby. Then Jenny, Susan, and Laura joined me and the rest, as they say, is . . ."

"History," the group chorused.

Moments later, Rose noticed Sam stepping out of the elevator, shoulders slumped, hands in his pockets. Apparently, Jenny saw him, too. As he slouched toward the lobby doors, she waved and called out to him.

"Yoo-hoo, Sa-am."

Sam started and stumbled as he turned his head in her direction.

"C'mon over and visit." Jenny beckoned him to join the group.

Looking like a deer caught in oncoming headlights, Sam turned toward the group of prayer shawl makers.

Rose smiled in greeting. "How are you, Sam?"

"Okay, I guess." Sam came to a halt by Rose's chair. He plunged his hands deeper into his pockets and jingled his keys.

"Have a seat," Jenny said. "There's a place for you right here." She leaned forward and patted the chair across from her.

"Have a cookie." Laura held out the plate.

Rose saw the spark in his eyes as he spied the peanut butter blossoms. Sam leaned over and took a cookie.

"I like these. My wife used to make them at Christmas. It was my job to take the foil off the Hershey's Kisses."

"She used to?" Rose asked conversationally.

"She doesn't anymore." Sam lowered himself into the chair across from Jenny. "She can't remember to, well, take them out of the oven, or set the timer, or remember what the timer's for even if she does set it." The words came out in a rush, as if the chocolate had loosened his tongue.

"She's in Memory Care?" Rose's voice was gentle.

Sam, busy chewing and swallowing, nodded.

"How long has she been there?" Jenny asked.

"Let's see, September, October . . ." Sam counted off the months on his fingers. "Seven months. Seems longer."

"How is she?" Susan asked.

"Fine, fine," Sam said. "They take really good care of her. I can't complain."

"Still, it must be hard," Rose said.

On the far side of the circle, Edna muttered over her crochet, "Ain't that the truth."

"I do miss her. I visit several days a week, but lately she doesn't know me."

"We've noticed the lovely flowers you take to her." Jenny smiled. "She must appreciate them, even if she doesn't recognize the man who gives them to her."

Sam's chair creaked under his weight as he shifted uncomfortably.

"The staff tells me she loves them," he finally said.

"The staff?" Rose asked.

"Lately the mere sight of me upsets her, so I just leave them at the desk. They give them to her later."

"So, for her, they come from a secret admirer?" Jenny said. "How romantic."

"Not really. She doesn't wonder where they come from, according to the staff. She seems to accept that they simply appear, like magic." He slapped his hands on his thighs and stood. "I'd better be going. Thanks for the cookie."

"Stop by anytime." Rose gave him a warm smile.

"Anytime," Jenny said, with a flutter of eyelashes.

"We always have cookies on Saturdays. Here, have another." Laura offered the plate of peanut butter blossoms again.

"Don't mind if I do." Sam snagged a cookie and headed out to the parking lot.

"Poor man." Jenny resumed her knitting.

"Poor *married* man," Edna said.

"Well, of course," Jenny said, her blue eyes wide with innocence.

A little while later the elevator doors opened, and Samantha burst out like a racehorse leaving the gate. She abandoned her slower mother and sister, rushing over to the Woolgatherers, waving her red scarf.

"Look! Look! Grandma Becca showed me how to bind off. I finished my scarf."

Rose and the other Woolgatherers were soon oohing and aahing over Samantha's first completed project, passing it around the circle and complimenting whatever they could.

"Hmm," Edna said when it got to her. She passed it on without a second glance. Rose was glad the crocheter had refrained from further comment. Yes, the scarf was rife with mistakes—the width varied crazily, a few loops hung off the edges where end stitches had been dropped, and there were holes here and there. It was, however, a young girl's first attempt at the age-old craft. Young as she was, she had per-severed and finished. That alone was worth celebrating.

"Your mother is still knitting, I take it?" Rose asked Nan.

"Oh, yes. She doesn't usually know who the girls are, but she was delighted with their knitting today. I'm not sure, but she might think they're Girl Scouts working on a badge. She was a Girl Scout leader when I was growing up, and I recognized the gleam in her eyes as she worked with Samantha and Tara." She lowered her voice. "She was gentle with Samantha about her scarf and so patient teaching her to bind off."

"It's wonderful Samantha now has that memory of her grand-mother," Rose said.

"I could have taught her to bind off," Tara said. "I could teach her to at least count her stitches, if she'd let me." She subsided at a warning look from her mother.

"She'll get there," Rose said. "The important thing right now is she's enjoying it."

"Ooh, peanut butter blossoms," Samantha said.

Laura passed the plate obligingly to Samantha, urging Nan and Tara to have some, too.

"I love these," Nan admitted. "I don't make them often. It takes so long to take the foil off the Hershey's Kisses."

"You need Sam, then," Jenny said, her eyes twinkling.

"Sam?" Nan said around a bite of cookie.

"Sam Talbot," Rose said. "He stopped by to chat with us on his way out. His wife used to make these, and he always took the foil off for her."

"Stopped by to chat?" Edna scoffed. "Jenny practically hauled him over here."

"He looked like he needed some cheering up," Jenny said.

"And a cookie," Laura said.

"His wife is in Memory Care," Jenny told Nan. "It's kind of sad. He said lately she gets upset when she sees him, even though he's always bringing her flowers."

"I think I know who that is," Nan said, her face serious. "It's a bit more than upset. Sometimes Mom and I are in the dayroom when he comes. She calls him the 'Fat Man' and she's terrified of him."

"Well, he *is* a little heavyset," Laura said.

Edna snorted.

"A heart attack waiting to happen." Susan shuddered. "I hate to think what his cholesterol must be. It seems kind of mean for him to keep visiting her when she's scared of him."

Rose cleared her throat. "We don't know Sam well enough to say something like that about him, especially when he's not here to explain himself. I recommend we pray for Sam instead."

"Thank you for reminding me to pray for him," Nan said. "I've just been feeling sorry for him. I can tell he really loves her. His heart is always in his eyes, hoping this time she'll know him."

CHAPTER 7

THE SECOND SUNDAY IN MARCH dawned blustery and cold. Rose dressed warmly in slacks and a wool cardigan she had knitted years ago. After a cup of coffee and a piece of toast, she tucked one of her bright hand-knit faux fur scarves around her neck and buttoned her coat. She picked up her cane and the tote with Edna's shawls and then made her way to the lobby.

Jenny was already there, dressed to the nines. No hat, but only the better to show off her flaming red-auburn hair, Rose suspected. How she managed to walk in stiletto heels at the age of seventy-two, Rose had no idea, but she had to admit that Jenny still had the legs for them. She herself had long ago chosen comfort over fashion. She wiggled her toes inside her sensible shoes, thankful she no longer felt the need to squash them into high-heeled pumps.

Susan and Laura hurried out of the elevator just as Gus pulled the van under the porte cochere. Like Rose, they were dressed in slacks, with scarves around their necks. Susan also had a wooly hat crammed on her head.

"You should be wearing a hat," Susan told Jenny. "You'll catch your death out there."

"Rose said the ladies don't wear hats to church at Hope of Glory," Jenny said with a wink.

"You can joke about it all you want," Susan said. "Don't come crying to me if you get sick."

"I hardly think I'll get sick walking from here to the van and from the van into the church." Jenny tossed her uncovered head.

"Suit yourself." Susan huffed as she pulled on a pair of bulky mittens.

Gus soon had his passengers settled in their seats, with Jenny in the front as usual.

"Buckle up, everybody. Here we go." Gus stepped on the gas, and they were off.

Susan pushed up the sleeve of her puffy jacket and checked her watch.

"We have plenty of time," she told Gus. "No need to hurry."

"I'll abide by the speed limit the whole way, Mrs. Thomas," he said. And he did, but Rose noted how tightly Susan gripped the purse on her lap.

Once they arrived at church, Gus saw everyone up the steps and held the door for them.

"You're welcome to join us." Rose turned to Gus as she paused on the threshold, leaning on her cane.

Gus shook his head. "I'm off to the coffee shop down the street to get some studying in. But I'll be back at one o'clock sharp."

"No rush," Rose told him. "But if you do get here early, you'd be more than welcome at the luncheon. I guarantee the food will be excellent."

"I really do need to study. Maybe some other time."

"I'll hold you to that," Rose called after him as he jogged down the steps to the van. She sent up a prayer as the van pulled away from the curb. *I'll keep trying, Lord. He's going to need you and your people amid the challenges of medical school.*

With that, Rose stepped into the foyer to find the Woolgatherers already being welcomed by the usher of the day, Howard Fuller. When Howard had first started attending Hope of Glory to get to know widowed shawl maker Fran McMillan, Fran had teased him Father Pete would soon rope him into ushering. This is exactly what had happened, but Howard didn't seem to mind.

"Welcome, welcome." Howard shook hands with Jenny, Susan, and

Laura. "You must be the Woolgatherers. Fran told me about meeting you the other day. I'm Howard Fuller."

"So, *you're* Howard." Jenny raised her eyebrows. "We've heard about you, too."

Below his grizzled brush cut, the tips of Howard's ears reddened.

"All good things," Rose said with a reassuring smile.

"Here, let me take that." Howard relieved Rose of the tote bag containing the shawls. "I'll make sure they get to the front of the church to be prayed over."

Jenny scanned the foyer and asked, "Where do we hang our coats?"

"You'll probably want to keep your coats with you," Howard said. "It's none too warm in the nave. Old heating system, you know."

Rose hid a grin as Susan shot a triumphant look at Jenny.

Rose's heart swelled with pleasure as she introduced Jenny, Susan, and Laura to Father Pete and the bishop after the service. She went on to explain about their prayer shawl group at Fair Meadows.

"Another prayer shawl group?" The bishop's smile widened. "This idea is catching on. Well done, ladies."

In the parish hall, the Woolgatherers joined the members of the Heavenly Hugs Prayer Shawl Ministry, plus Howard, in line at the buffet.

"Save room for dessert," Howard told them. "The bakers of Hope of Glory have outdone themselves."

Once they were seated, Rose made the introductions.

"Everybody, this is Jenny, Susan, and Laura. And these"—Rose pointed to each woman in turn—"are the Heavenly Hugs. This is Margaret, our fearless leader."

Margaret gave a regal nod.

"And Jane, who made Nan's prayer shawl."

"Hi." Jane gave a little wave.

"You've already met Fran," Rose went on.

"Welcome to Hope of Glory," Fran said. "We're glad you're here."

"And this is Bryson," Rose said, wrapping the young man in a side hug. She smiled as Jenny, Laura, and Susan's eyes widened as they took in the bright green mohawk that stood up in spikes on Bryson's otherwise shaved head. She winked at him and said, "I'm glad they didn't make you change your hair for your new job."

"I get to work from home." He grinned. "That means I can take my laptop over to Amy's and take care of our baby while she's at work."

"Oh, you're the new father," Laura exclaimed. "Rose told us all about the Heavenly Hugs getting Amy to the hospital in time for the baby. Are they here, by any chance?" Laura craned her neck to search the parish hall for a glimpse of the baby.

"They'll be here in a minute. Our baby girl, Heaven, did what babies do." The young man wrinkled his nose. "Amy's changing her."

A few moments later, a young woman with spiky purple hair appeared in the doorway of the parish hall. A weeks-old baby snuggled into her shoulder.

"Over here, Amy!" Bryson stood and waved from across the room.

"There's no need to shout, young man." Margaret frowned. "Especially with the bishop here."

Out of the corner of her eye, Rose thought she saw the bishop glance their way, an amused smile tugging at the corners of his mouth. The sight of Margaret with her perfectly coiffed gray hair interacting with Bryson of the startling mohawk made Rose chuckle, too. But when she turned to get a better look, the bishop was listening intently to a parishioner.

Bryson settled Amy at the table and went off to fill a plate for her. She turned in her seat so everyone at the table could admire the sleeping baby.

"She's beautiful," Laura said.

"Just wait until she wakes," Jane said. "I've never seen such blue eyes on a baby."

Heaven chose that moment to wake, blinking slowly as she calmly surveyed the room. Then she yawned and went back to sleep.

"Definitely your eyes," Laura told Amy.

"But she has my hair," Bryson quipped as he returned with a full plate for Amy. In response to the raised eyebrows all around the table, he said, "My hair used to be the same color. Before I dyed it green."

Bryson reached for Heaven. "Let me take her so you can eat," he told Amy.

Once the baby was comfortably ensconced on her father's shoulder, burp cloth in place, the talk around the table turned to prayer shawls.

"Those shawls you brought are gorgeous," Fran said to the Fair Meadows ladies. "Are they crocheted?"

"They are," Rose said. "Edna is a fast and prolific crocheter."

At that moment, Father Pete strode into the parish hall.

"So glad you're here." He beamed at the visitors from Fair Meadows. "I hope you'll come again."

Susan looked cautious. "At least, whenever we have shawls to be prayed over."

"It was a lovely prayer," Jenny said, adding a dazzling smile.

At a nearby table, Rose saw one of the group of older men she had mentally dubbed "the Fishing Buddies" stand and straighten his tie. He approached their table and spoke in Howard's ear.

"All right," she heard Howard say.

With an amused chuckle, Howard introduced Clive Stanhope, a trim man in his seventies with a Clark Gable mustache. Clive shook hands all around, holding Jenny's a little longer than strictly necessary.

"So nice to see new faces around here," Clive said. Rose noted his glance lingered on Jenny's face in particular. Rose suppressed a knowing grin. "You prayer shawl ladies are bringing a lot of people to church these days. We men are going to have to step up our game."

"It's not a competition, Clive," Rose said.

"I suppose not." He shrugged. "But it beats me how you can get all these people coming to Hope of Glory just by knitting out at the mall. It's crazy."

"Maybe God will give you a crazy idea." Father Pete grinned and nudged Clive in the ribs.

Clive shuffled his feet. "I don't know about that, Father. I figured I'd just try to get more guys to come to the monthly men's breakfast." His face brightened with a new idea. "Jenny, can I get you some dessert? It goes fast around here."

"Oh, Clive, how nice," Jenny said. "I would love a piece of chocolate cake. And coffee to go with it."

Clive snapped her a sharp salute. "Cake and coffee coming up, ma'am."

"Guess I'll have to go get my own dessert," Laura said with a chuckle. "Rose, can I get you some, too?"

"A lemon bar, please," Rose said.

Susan pressed her lips together, as if to keep herself from commenting.

"I know, I know." Rose patted Susan's arm. "I usually am careful about what I eat, but sometimes you just have to live dangerously."

When Laura returned with Rose's lemon bar, Fran cleared her throat.

"I have some news," Fran said, eyes bright with excitement.

"You're not getting married, are you?" Margaret frowned. "You haven't known Howard all that long."

"No, I'm not engaged." Fran shook her head, laughing. "I'm moving."

"*Moving?*" Jane said. "Where are you going? All your kids and grandkids are here. And we'd miss you!"

Fran smiled. "It's nice to know I'd be missed. I'm not moving away, though. I'm moving across town, into one of those buildings they're converting into loft condos."

"A condo?" Margaret frowned. "But your house is so nice."

"Nice and big." Fran made a face. "Too big for just me anymore. And then there's the back yard . . ."

The Heavenly Hugs all nodded. Two summers ago, Fran had found her newly retired husband, Ed, face down in the vegetable garden. He'd had a heart attack and died instantly.

"And to be honest, I'm ready to pass the holiday celebration torch to my daughter-in-law. She did a wonderful job this year. I'm happy to help, but I don't want to host anymore. And the condo I'm buying is simply perfect, just the right size for me. It even has one of those cute stackable washer-dryer combos."

"What does Eddy have to say about it?" Margaret wanted to know.

"My son's opinion about this is immaterial," Fran said. "I'm a grown woman in full possession of my faculties. I can sell my house and move to a condo if I want."

"In other words, he doesn't approve?" Margaret said with a knowing look.

"He's getting used to the idea," Fran said. "The hardest part was making it clear I'm capable of selling the house on my own. His wife is happy about the Duncan Phyfe dining room table I'm giving her, though. It seats twelve with both leaves in."

"You go, girl." Jane high-fived her friend.

"But that's not even the best part," Fran went on. "My new place is in the building across the street from Fair Meadows."

Aha, Rose thought. "So *that's* why you were 'in the neighborhood' the other day."

"That's right." Fran grinned. "We're going to be neighbors."

Howard came up behind Fran and put his hands on her shoulders. "She's going to be my neighbor, too. I downsized last year and live in the condos on the next block."

"So, this *is* about Howard," Margaret said with a sniff. "The two of you really shouldn't rush into anything."

Fran regarded Margaret across the table. "Margaret, Ed has been gone almost two years. I'll never quite get over it, but it's time for me to go on with my life. I've seen how fleeting life can be and how it can be cut short in an instant. I intend to live whatever time is ahead of me to the fullest."

"And I'm blessed to be a part of it," Howard said. Fran gazed up at him with a happy smile.

"Just take your time and be sure, all right?"

Rose smiled to herself. Margaret always had to have the last word.

"When are you moving in?" Rose asked. "I can't wait to come visit you. All I'll have to do is walk across the street."

"I sold the house last week," Fran said. "My real estate agent told me it would sell fast since it's in a good school district. I'll be in the condo by the end of the month."

Rose felt her chest swell with gratitude as she gazed across the table at Fran. Her friend, who had journeyed through a wilderness of sudden and crushing grief, was coming out on the other side full of life and hope.

CHAPTER 8

ON MONDAY, EDNA O'BRIAN woke to a morning as gray and sad as she felt. Rain pelted the windows of her apartment, running in rivulets down the panes like a torrent of tears. She sighed and considered going back to bed. Sleep would shut out that relentless, melancholy sound. But no, it was a Woolgatherers morning, and there would be questions if she didn't go. Susan would think she was sick and come knocking at her door with that awful low-sodium chicken soup of hers and a package of unsalted saltines. Could you even call the unsalted ones saltines?

Even though she knew the breakfast in the dining room would be delicious, Edna opted for instant coffee and a Pop-Tart in her apartment. The several hours she would spend with the knitting group was about all the socializing she felt up to for the day. She pulled on a pair of elastic-waist jeans and a long-sleeved shirt. Then, because she always seemed to be in a draft down in that lobby no matter where she sat, she put on Stanley's old brown cardigan. It was getting frayed at the cuffs, but it fit like an old friend.

As Edna ran a comb through her frizzy hair, she thought of Jenny's ridiculous red hair, hair no woman her age could have without a lot of help. Jenny's hair wasn't like Penny's. Penny's bright curls had come straight from her father. A long time ago, Edna and Stanley had decided that if the long-awaited, much-longed-for baby were a girl, they'd name her Bridget. But then Stanley had taken one look at his daughter's copper-colored hair and declared she had to be "Penny." Not Penelope, but simply Penny. "My lucky Penny," he used to call her, swinging her high in the air so that her curls bounced and she squealed with delight.

Edna gazed at her reflection in the mirror. *Iron gray for me, thank you very much. Didn't have to pay a dime for it. Free of charge from Mother Nature. And from Penny and Stanley*, she added with a sigh.

When Edna finally stepped off the elevator, she saw she was the last to arrive.

"There you are, Edna," Rose called. "Come sit by me." She patted the empty space next to her on the couch.

Oh, joy, Edna thought. *I get to sit next to Sally Sunshine.* But since she'd dragged her feet getting ready this morning, it was the only seat left.

Once Edna was settled, Rose looked around the knitting circle, taking in each face.

"Now that we're all here, we can pray."

Edna dug around in her crochet bag and dredged up the card with their shawl-maker's prayer. She muttered the words along with the other members of the group.

"Father God, we ask you to remember all those who have loved ones who do not remember them. In the embrace of these shawls, may they be strengthened, encouraged, loved, and known."

At the last words of the prayer, "loved and known," Edna felt tears at the back of her eyes. She blinked them away and cleared her throat for good measure.

"I must say, I really enjoyed going to your church yesterday, Rose," Jenny said as she pulled out her work in progress, a shawl in vibrant shades of green. "You missed a great luncheon, Edna."

"Don't think you're supposed to go to church for the food," Edna said.

Jenny looked abashed. "Well, no, of course not. But the food *was* good."

"The bishop was so stern." Susan shuddered. "He's not there all the time, is he?"

"Hardly ever." Rose grinned. "He was right, though. Even though the congregation was dwindling, we didn't want to believe that the church would actually close. We weren't making an effort to reach out to people like we used to, and we didn't want to change. It took Father Pete sending the Heavenly Hugs out to knit in public to shake things up. But I didn't realize until the bishop spoke just how close we came to losing our church. Whew!"

The lobby doors swept open, letting in the sound of the rain and Nan, wiping her feet and closing her umbrella.

"Hi, Nan," Laura called. "Have a great time with your mom."

"Will do." Nan waved as she headed for the elevator, her knitting bag over her arm.

Edna shook her head as she slid her crochet hook into another stitch.

"I don't know why you have to be so negative about Nan's mom, Edna," Jenny said.

Edna stiffened and stared Jenny down. "What do you mean, negative? I didn't say anything."

"Look, there's Sam," Rose said before Jenny could answer.

Sure enough, Sam had shuffled through the doors. Raindrops glistened on the petals of the red roses in the bouquet he carried.

"I hope things go better with Dorothy today," Rose said and resumed knitting her current project, a blue shawl.

Edna sighed at the futility of such a hope and crocheted steadily on.

In the ensuing lull in conversation, Laura could be heard counting stitches under her breath. "Whew!" she said as she came to the end of the row. "It came out right." She held up her knitting, a golden-yellow shawl worked in a lacy pattern of leaves.

"It really does look like aspen leaves in the fall," Rose said.

"It's the most challenging pattern I've ever done. I'm glad I've kept at it."

"It's like a ray of sunshine on this rainy day," Susan said.

Edna glanced at Laura's knitting and resisted the urge to touch the intricate pattern. "That's a lot of work for someone you don't even know."

"I admit it's going to be hard to give this one away, but I keep thinking about how much whoever gets it will love it." Laura resumed knitting. "How special it will make that person feel at the end of a long, demanding day. I wish I'd had one just like this when I was teaching."

Edna gazed at the shawl taking shape at the end of her hook and forced herself to relax the tension on the yarn. Her fingers moved swiftly, catching the yarn with the hook and pulling through, over and over again. She crocheted without thinking, much less thinking about whoever received the shawl. She'd rather simply lose herself in the movements of the yarn sliding through her fingers and watch the pattern emerge. She focused on her work and let the various conversations flow around her.

"There's Sam," Jenny said moments later. "He sure didn't stay upstairs very long."

Edna watched Sam trudge across the lobby, looking like he'd lost his last friend, as her mother would have put it. His mouth was turned down, and his steps were slow. He still had the roses, but he didn't hold them carefully anymore. They hung by his side as he made his dispirited way toward the exit. Several rose petals fluttered forlornly to the floor.

"Yoo-hoo, Sam." Jenny waved.

Oh, great, Edna thought. *This sad sack is all I need this morning.* She glared at Jenny, but she needn't have bothered. Jenny only had eyes for Sam, or rather, for the roses.

"Sam, you bring those gorgeous roses right over here," she said.

Sam stopped and glanced at the bouquet in his hand, as though surprised he still had them.

"Oh. I meant to leave them at the nurses' station . . ." He turned toward the elevator, then stopped as if unsure of what to do. Finally, he turned around with a shrug. "It doesn't really matter anyway."

"Of course it matters," Jenny said. "Roses always matter."

Edna pressed her lips together in silent disapproval. The man looked like he had the weight of the world on his shoulders, but there was

Jenny, flirting to beat the band. Edna shook her head as Sam walked over to Jenny, drawn like a mosquito to a bug zapper.

"Come take a load off," Mr. Peabody said as Laura commandeered a chair from a nearby grouping.

"Right here." Laura gave the seat an inviting pat.

"How's Dorothy today?" Mr. Peabody asked.

"*She's* fine." Sam sank into the chair. "Now that I'm gone."

"What happened?" Rose's voice was gentle.

"I peeked in on her in the dayroom, just to check on her, not talk or anything, and planned to leave the roses at the desk. But she saw me and started screaming. I didn't mean to cause such a ruckus."

"I'm sure you didn't," Jenny said. "You were trying to make her happy."

"Flowers used to make her happy," Sam said. "*I* used to make her happy. But now I scare her. And I forgot to leave the flowers." He gazed at the roses, then thrust them at Jenny. "Here. Somebody may as well enjoy them."

"Sam, how sweet! I certainly will enjoy them. Thank you." Jenny beamed, cheeks pink and dimples flashing shyly, as if she didn't know exactly what she was doing.

Sam stood. "I'd better be going and leave you to your . . . your . . . whatever it is you're doing."

"Knitting prayer shawls," Susan said.

"And crocheting them," Edna said.

"Stop by anytime." Mr. Peabody extended his hand. The two men shook, and Sam turned to go.

"Thank you again for the roses," Jenny called as Sam left the lobby. Sam waved, and Edna caught a glimpse of a smile on his face.

Jenny buried her nose in the bouquet, inhaling the heady scent. "I do so love roses."

"Jenny Alderman, you are not keeping those flowers." Edna was surprised at how stern Miss Rosey Sunshine sounded.

"Whyever not?" Jenny said. "He gave them to me."

"They were meant for his wife," Rose said.

"And she didn't want them." Jenny tossed her head. "What was I supposed to do, tell Sam no? Refuse his generous gift?"

"Yes," Rose said. "You should have told him you would take them to Memory Care and make sure his gift got to his wife. In fact, that's what you're going to do right now."

Edna felt her mouth start to drop open and quickly shut it. She'd never seen Rose like this.

"But—"

"But nothing," Rose said. "Those are Dorothy's roses, and it's up to you to make sure she gets them."

Jenny tightened her grip on the roses, her bottom lip thrust out mutinously. Edna was reminded of what her mother always said to pouting children—"I'm gonna hang a pail on that lip."

"I'll get you some more roses," Mr. Peabody said. "In fact, it would be my pleasure."

"Oh, Alistair, would you?" Jenny turned her blue eyes, radiant with delight, on him.

"When you least expect it, my dear, a dozen red roses will arrive at your door," he said with a wink.

"All right, I'll do it." Jenny stood, squared her shoulders, and marched herself across the lobby to the elevators like a martyr on her way to face the lions.

Edna shook her head as Jenny pressed the elevator button. "It's just a bunch of flowers."

As the elevator ascended to the memory care unit, Jenny's stomach clenched with dread. It wasn't about giving up the roses. In her experience, there would always be more roses. Alistair's generous offer had just proved that. No, what really made her heart quail was going to the memory care unit. It was one thing to make shawls for caretakers, but it was another thing entirely to be among those whom they cared for.

There was nothing for it, though, she supposed as the elevator arrived at the seventh floor with a gentle thump. Not after the way Rose had spoken to her. Despite her height, enhanced as usual by her three-inch heels, Jenny had felt decidedly small when Rose pointed out the roses were really Dorothy's. She took a firm grip on the bouquet and stepped cautiously into the hallway. She was relieved there was someone official-looking at the nurses' station. A woman with warm brown eyes and a kind smile looked up from her computer.

"Yes? May I help you?"

"Yes, well, Sam Talbot meant to leave these for his wife, but he forgot." Jenny held out the bouquet, feeling like she wasn't explaining the situation well at all.

"Ah, yes. There was a bit of a fuss," the nurse said.

"And so—"

A shout followed by a clanging crash rang out from down the hall. Jenny started and shot a look of alarm at the nurse.

"No worries," the nurse said brightly. "Sometimes a member of our community has a tough day. We know what to do when that happens."

Sure enough, the shouting died away in response to the soothing voice of another person in the room.

"So, these are for Dot?" The nurse reached for the bouquet. "I'm Patsy, by the way."

"Jenny Alderman." Jenny relinquished the roses. "Dot? Isn't her name Dorothy?"

"She seems to prefer 'Dot' here. It happens that way sometimes. Are you a friend of theirs?" Patsy asked.

"More of an acquaintance of Sam's. I've never met Dorothy," Jenny said. "I live in one of the cottages here, and I'm part of a knitting group that meets in the lobby. Sam has stopped by to chat with us a few times."

"It's kind of you to do a favor for someone you don't know very well," Patsy said.

Jenny cringed inwardly. She really had meant to keep the flowers for herself. She was only doing this kindness because Rose had surprised her with a Mom Look more potent than Jenny had ever dreamed that sweet, mild-mannered woman could be capable of.

"It was nothing." Jenny waved the compliment away. *That's for sure.* Jenny found herself wishing that making sure Dorothy got her flowers had been her idea instead of Rose's.

"Would you like to meet her?" Patsy asked.

"Meet who? Dorothy?" The suggestion startled Jenny. She'd planned to simply hand over the roses and leave. This was the last place she wanted to be. She fervently hoped it would not be the last place she would be. "No, I really should be going now. It sounds like she's had enough excitement for today, anyway." Jenny backed away toward the elevator.

"Some other time, perhaps," Patsy said.

"Perhaps." Jenny tried to sound as noncommittal and unflustered as possible without being rude. Then she turned and made her way to the elevator, feeling the nurse's gaze on her as she pressed the "down" button. Another shout from the hallway sent her scurrying into the elevator when it arrived. As the doors swept shut, she breathed a sigh of relief. No, she would *not* be returning to meet Dorothy. Of that, she was sure.

CHAPTER 9

JENNY FOUND THE WOOLGATHERERS IN the middle of a heated discussion when she returned from delivering Dorothy's roses.

"Let's ask Jenny. My heart really goes out to Sam," Laura said. "And there's not really anything anyone can do about his situation. So, I think we should give him a prayer shawl."

"And I say he doesn't need a prayer shawl," Edna said. "What he needs is a swift kick in the seat of the pants."

"I don't know how you can be so mean, Edna," Susan said. "He's obviously hurting."

"He's obviously wallowing in self-pity," Edna said.

"What do *you* think, Jenny?" Susan asked.

"I'd be happy to knit Sam a prayer shawl," Jenny said. Anything to assuage the nagging sense she shouldn't have accepted the flowers and should have said yes to the nurse's suggestion to meet Dorothy.

"Or I could give him this one." Mr. Peabody offered the tweedy brown shawl he was knitting with the yarn he'd bought at The Tangled Thread.

Rose raised her hand for quiet.

"I happen to agree with Edna on this one," she said.

Laura's eyebrows shot up and Susan sputtered in protest.

"Hear me out," Rose said. "There's no doubt having a shawl would comfort Sam. It would be even better, though, for him to sit with us and make them."

"I seriously doubt he knows how to knit," Susan said.

"That doesn't mean he can't learn," Rose said. "Mr. Peabody didn't know how, and look how he's coming along."

Mr. Peabody grinned and saluted Laura with the end of one of his knitting needles. "Thanks to this patient lady here."

"I'd be happy to teach Sam," Laura said with an eager smile. "It's fun getting to teach again."

"He probably won't want to." Edna's habitual frown deepened.

Leave it to Edna, Jenny thought, *to throw cold water on the idea.*

"We won't know until we ask," Rose said. "The worst he can say is no."

"And if he does say no, we can go with the idea to give him a shawl," Laura said.

"Give who a shawl?" Nan stood at the edge of the group.

The Woolgatherers quickly filled Nan in on the events of the morning.

Nan turned to Jenny. "It was nice of you to take the flowers to Dorothy. She was at the nurses' station asking for them when I was waiting for the elevator after my visit with my mother."

"She was looking for them?" Jenny felt heat creep up her neck at the thought that she'd almost kept the looked-for roses for herself. "But she screamed when she saw Sam."

"I don't think she realizes the flowers come from Sam," Nan said. "They simply appear at the nurses' station, but they appear regularly, so she's come to expect them."

Jenny caught the glance Rose threw her way and was profoundly grateful Rose didn't say "I told you so" out loud.

"So, you're going to give Sam a prayer shawl?" Nan asked.

"We have a difference of opinion," Susan said, her voice tight.

Jenny braced herself for a diatribe from Edna, but it was Rose who answered.

"I think Sam would be better off knitting with friends than wrapping himself in a prayer shawl all alone."

"He does seem pretty forlorn. I don't think he has any family in the area. He's the only one I've ever seen visiting Dorothy, and I'm here every day. I'll bet it would do him good to hang out with all of you. I know it helps me," Nan said.

"I suppose it wouldn't hurt to ask him," Susan said. "But he'll probably say no."

"I hope he says yes," Laura said, a teacher's gleam in her eye.

Jenny hoped he would say yes, too. She just hoped Edna's sour attitude wouldn't scare him off.

On the way home from Fair Meadows, Sam stopped at his favorite deli and ordered a Philly cheesesteak on a hoagie roll. He added an order of onion rings for good measure. The comforting aroma filled the car as he drove. When he arrived home, he threw his keys on the kitchen counter, poured himself a tall glass of Dr Pepper, and settled into his recliner, his food and drink on the coffee table. Sam reached for an onion ring with a twinge of guilt. Dorothy had never been a fan of eating in front of the television, except for popcorn on Friday, their movie night. He couldn't eat at the round table in the breakfast nook, though. It was piled high with advertising circulars, pleas from charitable organizations, and magazines. Besides, it just wasn't the same without Dorothy across the table, chatting away about her day. Lord, the woman could even make laundry sound interesting.

He shrugged off the guilt at the first delicious bite of hot, crunchy onion ring. Usually at about this point, he would locate the remote and channel surf for a while before settling in for the next episode in his *Blue Bloods* binge. Today, though, he stared off into space as he chewed, remembering Jenny's pleasure in the roses. It had been a long time since Dorothy's eyes had lit up like that. Now that he thought about it, the light had been fading for months no matter how hard he tried to keep it there. And these days she closed her eyes against him in fear. It had been hard enough to worry the day might come that she didn't know him at all, but it had never occurred to him she would ever be afraid of her "Sam I Am." She'd given him the nickname when their oldest had discovered Dr. Seuss's *Green Eggs and Ham*.

He sighed and took a huge bite of his sandwich. Man, Arnie's sure made a great Philly cheesesteak. He reached for the remote.

Tara had another knitting problem, or rather, a purling problem. Since Rose didn't seem to want to teach her, Tara had gone ahead and tried to learn to purl from YouTube after she'd bound off her garter-stitch scarf (which looked considerably better than Samantha's, if she did say so herself). Purling seemed easy enough on the video, but somehow it came out all wrong when she tried to do it. The yarn she was using to practice with was a knotted-up mess, and she couldn't figure out what the problem was. She'd thrown her needles and yarn across her bedroom with a muffled shriek of frustration more than once.

Samantha seemed to be content to do nothing but the knit stitch. She was already halfway through another scarf, this one a blinding shade of electric blue. Tara, however, yearned for more. She wanted to make all kinds of things—hats and mittens, sweaters, and shawls, maybe even socks someday. But if she wasn't able to unlock the mysteries of the purl stitch, she'd be stuck with one stitch for the rest of her life, and she was already bored with the knit stitch. Tara knew there was more, so much more, but she'd have to be able to do both of the basic stitches—knit *and* purl—to knit the patterns that beckoned to her from online pattern sites.

Tara knew she would find a sympathetic ear in her mother. Her mother had also stalled at the purl stitch long ago when Grandma Becca had tried to teach her. And Tara knew her mother had given up knitting altogether until she'd met Rose around Christmastime. Now, years after she first started, her mother was not only knitting again, but she'd also finally learned to purl. Theoretically, her mother could teach her. But Tara wasn't some little kid anymore, running to her mom for help all the time.

Rose had been the one to break through her mom's mental block about purling. Tara just knew Rose would be able to do the same thing for her, making everything all clear in her patient, gentle way. But Rose obviously didn't want to teach her. She just wanted to shoo her off to Grandma Becca.

Tara pulled out her practice piece again, trying to puzzle out once more what was going wrong. She turned it this way and that, but the mess on her needles was incomprehensible. She tried tinking, taking out a stitch in hopes of unraveling the mystery of her mistake. But once she'd freed the stitch, it undid itself in such a flurry she couldn't follow what had happened. It was all so confusing. She would have to try to get Rose to teach her again on Saturday. Beg and plead if she had to.

With a sigh, Tara put away her knitting. It was only Monday. But the bright side was that she had all week to figure out how to cajole Rose into teaching her to purl.

CHAPTER 10

ON THURSDAY MORNING, THE WOOLGATHERERS met in the dining room for breakfast. The reds, whites, and pinks of Valentine's Day had given way to Kelly green in anticipation of St. Patrick's Day. The center of each table displayed a "pot o' gold," courtesy of one of the art classes at Fair Meadows. The gold-painted pots were decorated with green shamrocks and filled with chocolate coins, a rare concession on the part of the retirement community's nutritionist. Napkins in green and gold had been placed in an alternating pattern around the table.

All the green brought such a hopeful feeling that the cold and gray of winter was receding. Maybe spring truly was on its way. Rose's heart lifted even more as she gazed around the table at her knitting friends. And her crochet friend, she added mentally. Sometimes Edna didn't join them for breakfast, and this worried Rose. It wasn't that she thought Edna was skipping meals or going hungry. They all had kitchens in their apartments and cottages and could eat "at home" if they chose. But Edna separated herself from others enough already. Rose had no idea what Edna did when she wasn't with the prayer shawl group. She never saw her at any of the many activities offered by the retirement community. For all Rose knew, Edna just shuffled between Woolgatherers meetings and the dining room, holing up in her apartment in between.

It wasn't that long ago Rose had been almost as reclusive as Edna. It had been hard to let go of her old life in the neighborhood where she'd made a home for her family, raised her children, and loved her husband. She was glad, though, as she gazed at the faces around the table, that she'd responded to the nudge to knit in the lobby as a way to make friends. It had become so much more, though. Now, here she was, with not only friends but with a meaningful ministry to give comfort to those who loved and cared for people with a heartbreaking disease.

Everything had gotten better since the inception of the Woolgatherers. *Even the food at Fair Meadows*, Rose thought with a grin as she admired the steaming whole-wheat Belgian waffle on her plate, lying in a pool of sugar-free syrup and topped with fresh strawberries. She had once been sure she'd never enjoy whole-wheat anything, but these were actually pretty good.

"Aren't these waffles wonderful?" Rose said to Edna, seated next to her. Edna half-heartedly speared a strawberry with her fork.

"I'll say." Mr. Peabody poured more syrup on his waffle.

"Have a little waffle with your syrup," Jenny teased.

"Don't mind if I do." Mr. Peabody continued to pour.

Edna scowled. "This ain't real syrup. Where I come from, they're making real syrup right about now, tapping the trees and sugaring off. This stuff might as well be dishwater calling itself syrup."

"Well, you're here now," Susan said. "And sugar-free syrup is much better for you than the real stuff."

Rose frowned at Susan's criticism. "Where is it where they're tapping trees and making syrup now?" She was determined not to miss this chance to unravel the mystery that was Edna.

"Upstate New York." Edna's chest puffed out a bit. "That's where I grew up. There was a farm near my town where we always got the syrup and maple-sugar candy, too. They pressed it into a mold to shape it like a maple leaf." Edna's eyes took on the inward gaze of memory.

Rose saw the merest hint of a smile tug at the corners of Edna's mouth. "My baby brother loved maple-sugar candy. Made himself sick on it every year."

"Parents shouldn't let their children have so much candy," Susan said with a sniff.

"They didn't." Edna grinned. "We snuck it. There were six of us. Me and my four sisters and then Edward, at the end."

"The only boy," Laura said from across the table. "And the baby. Spoiled much?"

"Rotten," Edna said. "To the core," she added, laughing.

"Did he grow out of it?" Laura asked.

"Not so's you'd notice." Edna chuckled. As answering laughter rippled around the table, her face, alight with happy memory, suddenly darkened.

"Time to go." She grabbed her crochet bag and cane and hurried from the dining room.

"What was that all about?" Laura said. "One minute she's telling a fun story about her little brother and the next she stomps off."

"I hope she didn't think we were laughing at her," Susan said in a worried tone. "I was starting to enjoy hearing about her life. She doesn't talk much."

Maybe that's it, Rose mused. *Maybe she was afraid she'd opened up too much.* She wondered again why Edna was such a closed book—and how to get her to tell more of her story.

"She's right, though," Rose said with a glance at the dining room clock. "It's time to go and be Woolgatherers." She pushed back her chair, hitched her knitting bag onto her shoulder, and took a firm grip on her cane.

The rest of the prayer shawl group gathered their knitting bags and made their way to the lobby. Edna was already established in the seating area they'd claimed as their own, concentrating on her latest shawl. Once everyone was seated and settled, Rose pulled out her copy of their shawl-maker's prayer. She lingered over the words "loved and known." *Isn't that what we all want?* she thought. *But Edna sure doesn't make it easy. I don't know how to help her. Please help me help her, Lord.*

Then Rose read the prayer aloud while the others laid their hands over their work and prayed along with her.

They had been working in companionable silence for about ten minutes when Nan came through the lobby doors with a swoosh of raw March air. Susan shivered and pulled her cardigan tighter around herself.

Nan gave the group a jaunty wave as she passed by. Rose noted the color in her cheeks, probably a result of the cold wind that blustered outside. But Nan's eyes sparkled, too, and there was a definite spring in her step as she walked to the elevator. Rose sent up a prayer on behalf of Nan and her mother. Inspiration grabbed onto the tail end of her prayer.

"Our conversation at breakfast has me thinking about brothers and sisters," Rose said. "There were three of us in my family. I was in the middle between two brothers. I grew up standing between them to keep them from fighting."

"Boys." Susan shook her head.

"They're the best of friends now," Rose said.

"It was just my little sister and me growing up," Laura said.

"Was she a pest?" Susan asked. "My little brother was."

"No." Laura smiled. "She's three years younger than me and thought I was the most amazing person on the planet. She thought everything I did was wonderful and wanted to do it, too. That's when I started being a teacher. I had so much fun teaching her things—the alphabet when she was little, how to skip rope and play hopscotch when she got bigger, how to put outfits together when she was a teenager. It's not hard to rise to the occasion when someone believes you're wonderful." Laura's eyes glowed as she talked about her sister.

"How about you?" Rose turned to Mr. Peabody.

He held up a finger to indicate he was counting stitches, then let out his breath in gusty relief. "All present and accounted for." He set his knitting in his lap and looked at Rose. "To answer your question, I was an only child. It was pretty lonely at first. Once I started school, though, it was much better. So many people to be friends with."

Laura chuckled. "I'll bet you had your seat moved a lot for talking."

"I did, indeed," Mr. Peabody said with a sheepish grin. "But it didn't bother or deter me. It was simply an opportunity to make a new friend."

"I used to wish I was an only child," Jenny said. "There were four of us, all girls, and nobody could keep us straight. There was a strong family resemblance, and it didn't help that our parents thought it was clever to give us all names that start with *J*—Judy, Jenny, Joyce, and Janice. Our parents and teachers used to run through the names until they hit the right one. It made me so mad people got me confused with the others."

"I find that hard to believe," Rose said. "You really stand out."

"I had to find a way to stand out when I was a kid. In high school, I bought a hair-color kit at the drugstore with my babysitting money and bleached my hair so people could tell me apart from my dark-haired sisters. I got in so much trouble, but I didn't care. People remembered I was Jenny after that, *not* Judy, Joyce, or Janice," Jenny said with a decisive nod.

"You are definitely memorable," Mr. Peabody told her.

"Thank you, Alistair." Jenny favored him with a sparkling smile.

"You think you had it bad," Edna said with a snort. "We were all *E*s—Edna, Edith, Eunice, Ellen, Earlene, and Edward. Sometimes our mother would look straight at me or Edith and call us Edward. I wasn't *that* homely."

"I'm sure you weren't," Rose said, happy that Edna had opened up again, even if it *was* to one-up Jenny's tale of childhood injustice.

At this moment, the lobby doors opened again. Amy stood scanning the lobby, the handle of an infant car seat over one arm.

"You remember Amy, from church," Rose said to the group as she beckoned the young woman over.

The Woolgatherers, however, were much more interested in the baby stretching and yawning in the car seat. Amy lifted the baby from the seat and nestled her in the crook of her arm. Heaven blinked, eliciting oohs and aahs from the group. Amy turned to Rose. "I'm off today and want to finish Heaven's hat. Can you help me?"

Susan produced a bottle of hand sanitizer from her knitting bag and passed it around. "We'll hold the baby for you."

Heaven, however, was unhappy with this idea. She fussed in Susan's arms and wailed in Laura's. Both Jenny and Mr. Peabody passed on the dubious opportunity. When Edna tucked the baby against her shoulder and rubbed her back, however, Heaven gave a hiccupping sigh and fell asleep.

"You're a baby whisperer," Amy said in awe. "How did you do that?"

Edna shrugged. Heaven slept on.

Later, when the last end had been woven in, Amy leaned over and put the hat on Heaven. Edna turned for everyone to see. There was a soft chorus of admiration so as not to wake the baby.

"I have to get going. Thank you for holding her." Amy settled Heaven into her car seat and tucked a hand-knitted blanket around her.

"Thank you for letting me," Edna said in a husky voice. Rose couldn't be sure, but she thought she saw Edna's eyes momentarily mist with tears.

As Amy left, Sam came in, looking decidedly windblown.

"He should be wearing a hat, too," Susan said. "He'll catch his death in this weather."

The group fell silent as they watched Sam walk to elevator. His steps were slow, Rose noted, and his shoulders slumped.

"We'll talk to him when he comes back from visiting Dorothy," she said.

Sam caught a glimpse of himself reflected on the shiny back wall of the elevator and hastened to smooth his hair into place. He scared Dorothy enough as it was. No need to arrive looking like a wild man. Not that he planned on talking to her today. He would just ask after her at the desk, make sure she was okay, then peek into the dayroom to reassure himself she really was. But in case she did glimpse him, Sam wanted to appear as harmless as possible.

As he approached the nurses' station, a line formed between Patsy's eyebrows, and his stomach clenched.

"Is she all right?"

"She's fine. You know we'd call you if there were any cause for concern," Patsy said. "But after her reaction on Monday, it might be a good idea if you kept a low profile for a little while."

"I understand," Sam said. "I don't want to upset her. I won't talk to her, but can I just peek into the dayroom, just to check on her, not to speak?"

Patsy considered this for a moment. "As long as you stand well to the side of the door, I suppose it would be all right. Just don't let her see you. It took a while for her to calm down last time."

"I won't," Sam said. "Did she miss the flowers? I forgot to leave them for her."

There was the crease between Patsy's eyebrows again. "She got those lovely roses, Mr. Talbot. Your friend brought them for you."

"My . . . friend?"

"Yes. Nice lady. Lovely red hair."

"Oh, yes." Sam realized Patsy was talking about Jenny. "She is nice." He pushed himself away from the counter and stationed himself strategically by the door to the dayroom.

Dorothy sat at one of the tables with several other residents of the memory care unit. She was chatting, making her eloquent gestures, obviously regaling the others with a story. A ripple of laughter flowed over the group at something she said. He wondered which of the tales of her girlhood she was telling. She'd been fun-loving from the very start. Or maybe it was about one of their children. They'd been scamps, the both of them. He knew every story by heart, but he never tired of hearing her tell one again—which she absolutely did, again and again over the last several years, to the point their sons groaned whenever she said, "Did I ever tell you . . . ?"

"Yes, Mom, a million times. We don't need to hear it again."

But she would go right on as if they hadn't spoken, and with as much relish and glee as if whatever event she was recounting had just happened yesterday.

Sam had spoken to his sons, telling them not to be rude to their mother. She really couldn't remember she'd told those stories many times before. Couldn't they just enjoy her?

Apparently not, he thought with a sigh. They both lived out of town with their families and visited less and less. When he chided them, they pleaded the pressures of life. They had careers and wives and children of their own now. And then there had been the time when Dorothy had acted like they were people she didn't know just come to pay a call. She'd been polite, gracious even, but it was clear it was just manners. She didn't know who they were at all.

"Why, Dad?" Josh had said the last time Sam had brought it up. "What difference does it make? She doesn't know me from the mailman."

"What difference? What difference?" Sam had spluttered. "She's your mother. That makes all the difference in the world." What he'd wanted to say was, "And *I* still know you. I still need you." But he could barely form those words in his mind, let alone say them out loud.

Now Sam watched as she threw back her head and laughed at her own punch line, her hazel eyes sparkling. He wished he was at that table, listening, joining in the laughter. He'd always pictured their latter years filled with the richness and camaraderie of "remember whens." And now, he was on the outside looking in. He was hiding, trying not to be seen.

"Oh, Dot, you are so funny," the man sitting next to her said. Sam caught the glint of admiration in the man's eyes. He felt his hackles rise. He was on the verge of stepping into the dayroom to stake his claim when a gentle hand on his arm distracted him. He turned to find Patsy standing next to him.

"She really is something special, isn't she?" Patsy said.

"Yes, she is." Sam swallowed hard.

"Come back to the nurses' station," Patsy said. "I have something for you."

What Patsy had for him was a brochure about Fair Meadows Families, a support group for family members of dementia patients.

"Caregiving can get quite lonely," she said. "It can help to spend time with other people who are going through it, too."

Sam frowned. "But I'm not caregiving anymore. *You* are."

"You care about her very much," Patsy said. "You visit, you bring flowers, you keep close tabs on her welfare. You are still taking care of her."

"Not that she notices any of it."

"And that's what makes it hard," Patsy said. When Sam didn't respond, she said, "Well, you don't have to decide now. I hope you'll take some time to consider it, though. It really could help."

Sam looked into Patsy's warm brown eyes and felt his resistance give a little. He reached for the brochure and stuffed it into his pocket.

"Have a good day, Mr. Talbot."

Sam nodded and headed for the elevator. On the way to the lobby, he shoved his right hand into his pocket and curled it around the brochure. He tried to picture what it would be like to attend the support group. Did he want to sit in a circle baring his soul to a bunch of strangers? He crushed the brochure in his fist. No, thank you. Besides, he was fine. Sam dropped the balled-up brochure in the trash bin by the elevator as he stepped out into the lobby.

Over the past few weeks, it had become a habit to glance over at the group that made things out of yarn as he made his way out of Fair Meadows. They were a friendly bunch. He sensed his steps slowing as he neared them. Would someone notice and greet him, as they sometimes did?

"There you are." Jenny's voice carried across the lobby. "We've been waiting for you."

Sam glanced around in case she was talking to someone else. It would be embarrassing if she was greeting someone behind him, like that lady with the knitting bag with whom he sometimes shared the elevator to Memory Care. But no, there was no one else. She was calling to him.

"Yes, you," Jenny said, laughing. "Come on over here."

"So nice to see you," a white-haired woman—Rose, was it?—said to him. "Do you have time to visit with us?"

"Yeah, sure," Sam said. What was waiting for him at home, anyway? Not Dorothy.

"Have a seat," the lone guy said. Alistair? Was that his name? Alistair indicated the chair across from him.

"How are you?" Alistair asked.

"Fine, fine." Sam sat on the edge of the seat.

"And Dorothy?" Rose asked.

"She's fine, too," Sam nodded, wondering what to do with his hands. He was the only one without yarn or implement to occupy them. He settled for leaning forward and putting them on his knees.

"Did you get to visit with her?" Laura wanted to know.

"Well, no," Sam said. "The staff recommended I don't try to talk to her for now. It upsets her too much."

"I'm so sorry, Sam." Jenny laid her hand on his arm. For a moment Sam stared at her brightly painted fingernails. That red was a far cry from Dorothy's discreet rosy pink. When he finally looked up, he saw sympathy in every face. Except for Edna, who kept her gaze on her work. Their pity made him squirm.

"I looked in on her in the dayroom, though, and she seems happy enough," he added.

"You never know with that Old-Timer's Disease," Edna said.

Sam wondered if Edna meant that Dorothy wasn't really happy or that she wouldn't always be afraid of him.

"She was telling a funny story to some of the other residents. She was laughing and so were they. Dorothy sure can tell a good story."

"I can understand why you miss her." Rose's voice was quiet, gentle.

Sam nodded, not trusting himself to speak.

"I hope you know you're welcome to visit with us whenever you're here. Nan Sheffield usually stops by after her visit with her mom in Memory Care."

Sam realized he'd started to make a habit of talking to this group. He was touched that they didn't seem to mind. He nodded again, still not trusting himself to speak.

"Actually, Sam, we were wondering if you'd like to join our group, making prayer shawls," Rose told him.

The question startled him. One minute they were talking about

Dorothy and the next they were inviting him to make prayer shawls. What was all this about joining groups all of a sudden? And did he look like someone who knew how to *knit*?

"I'm sorry, but I don't know how to knit," Sam said. He made his voice firm and decisive, to make it clear the matter was settled.

"I didn't, either, until these ladies got ahold of me." Alistair grinned.

"And he's doing great." Jenny held out the end of Alistair's shawl in progress. "We call it his 'Meat and Potatoes' shawl."

Sam raised his eyebrows.

"The brown with flecks of red remind me of how I like my steak," Alistair said.

Sam drew back in his chair. He wasn't sure he wanted any of these ladies looking at him with such eager faces "getting ahold of him." What in the world made them think he'd want to learn to knit?

"That looks great, Alistair, but I really don't think knitting is my thing. And . . . well . . . I'm not all that religious, either." There, he'd said it. That should put them off.

"Me neither," Edna said.

"We *know* knitting isn't your thing, Edna," Susan said, a testy edge in her voice.

"I'm not religious, either." Edna lifted her chin. "But I figure I can crochet comforting shawls anyway. It's a nice thing to do for people."

"Your shawls are lovely, Edna," Rose said, before Susan could comment further. Sam caught the look Rose shot Susan, so like the ones Dorothy had used on the boys when they misbehaved in church that he was momentarily transported to those busy, lively years of their life together.

"Just come and give it a try," Jenny said. "We can teach you how to knit. You'll really like spending time with us." Her winsome smile was not lost on Sam. He knew she was trying to talk him round, but it would be churlish to turn her down flat.

Sam slapped his hands on his knees and stood. "I'll tell you what, ladies. And gentleman," he added with a nod at Alistair. "I'll think about it."

"Make sure you do." Jenny shook a finger at him with charming mock sternness.

"I think that went well, don't you?" Rose said to the circle of prayer shawl makers.

"Really?" Edna scowled at Sam's retreating back. "He couldn't get out of here fast enough."

Rose, however, chose to look on the bright side. "I think it took him by surprise. I noticed he didn't say no flat out. He said he'd think about it."

"That was just to be polite," Edna said. "It's hard to be rude to Jenny when she turns on the charm."

"It is, isn't it?" Jenny said with a wink. Mr. Peabody winked back.

"Well, we tried, anyway." Laura shrugged.

"I, for one, am not giving up yet," Rose said with a determined nod.

"We shouldn't pester the man," Edna said. "He already said no."

"He said he'd think about it," Rose reminded her. "And while he's thinking about it, we can pester God on his behalf." She took up the blue shawl to knit and pray for Sam. One by one, the others resumed their work. Rose hoped each of them was praying for him, too.

Back home, Sam shrugged out of his coat and draped it over a kitchen chair. He rooted around in the fridge and found a few of what Dorothy used to call "science experiments." Leftovers that had started to go bad. He dumped them in the trash. He wondered briefly if he should clean out the rest of the refrigerator in case there were more moldy items. But just then, his stomach growled. He grabbed the pizza box that had only been in there for three days, plopped two pieces on a paper plate, and shoved it into the microwave. He heard the pizza crackling and popping as the turntable went around. Pizza sauce speckled the inside of the microwave when he opened the door. *Rats*, he thought. Forgot to cover it again. The steam rising from the meat-lover's pizza was laden with warm and spicy scents that made his mouth water. He'd wipe out the microwave later, he decided.

He popped open a can of soda and settled himself and the plate of pizza in the recliner. He set the soda on the end table and reached for the remote. He channel surfed as he munched. There wasn't much on this time in the afternoon, so he clicked over to Netflix and selected another episode of *Blue Bloods*. Dorothy hadn't much liked cop shows, so Sam had a lot of catching up to do. He glanced over at the couch where she used to sit making things with yarn while he watched football . . . or baseball . . . or basketball. She hadn't been much into sports, either, but she'd sat with him knitting (or was it crocheting?) while he enjoyed whatever game was on.

Hmm . . . all her paraphernalia was still upstairs in what she called her craft room. He hadn't been in there since . . . how long had it been? Well before he had to take her to Fair Meadows. Sam finished off the last of his soda and clicked off the television. He threw the can and the paper plate in the trash and climbed the stairs.

Opening the door to Dorothy's craft room triggered memories of watching *The Wizard of Oz* as a child and then with his own children. It was like the moment when the movie changed from black and white to Technicolor. The room before him was full of baskets and bins of yarn in every color imaginable. There was a chair by the window. A basket rested on the low table next to it, filled with yarn and something, he couldn't tell what, in progress. Sam crossed the room to the dresser from one of the boys' childhood bedrooms and opened a drawer. It was filled with yarn, neatly arranged, as was Dorothy's way. He opened the drawer below and found zippered binders, some with needles in them and others with hooks. A nearby bookcase housed her pattern collection, dozens of books, and several fat three-ring binders with patterns in plastic sleeves.

Sam sat down heavily in the chair. He'd had no idea she had so much yarn, so many needles and hooks, so many patterns, so much stuff. He wondered if she would like to have a project to work on at Fair Meadows. She hadn't asked for craft supplies since she'd been there, and he hadn't asked if she wanted any. Did she remember how to do it? He had a feeling she wouldn't. Sitting in this room, Sam realized what a big part of her life it had been, this making things with yarn. That she had forgotten it brought home to him just how much of the Dorothy he knew was gone.

If she was done with this, if she was never coming back to it, Sam wondered what to do with all this stuff. The boys wouldn't want it, and he didn't think either of their wives would be interested, either. And he couldn't just throw it away. She'd spent years collecting the contents of this room. In a flash, it came to him. It was brilliant, a way to kill two birds with one stone. He could get the knitting group at Fair Meadows off his back by passing on what would surely be a treasure trove to them. Yes, that's what he would do. He crossed the room and selected three skeins of lavender-colored yarn, then pulled some needles and hooks out of the drawer. Carefully closing the door to the craft room behind him, he went downstairs and found a paper sack to put them in. He set the sack by the door so he wouldn't forget it on Saturday.

The problem solved, he settled into the recliner and resumed his Netflix binge.

CHAPTER 11

ROSE LOVED SATURDAYS WITH THE Woolgatherers. It was a popular day for visitors, visitors who often stopped to chat with them. Some folks simply came over to touch a shawl, as if gathering strength for the moments ahead. She always sent a silent prayer after them.

This morning, she kept her eye out for Sam. He'd had two days to consider joining their group, and she'd had two days to pray. She hoped he would say yes.

First, however, Nan, Tara, and Samantha stopped by on the way to visit Grandma Becca. Samantha proudly wore her scarf, oblivious to its many mistakes. She showed off her progress on her next scarf, which was turning out every bit as quirky as the first one. Tara declined to show off her work.

"I need to learn to purl before I can make anything else," she said, with a pointed look at Rose.

"Spend time with your grandmother first, dear," was all Rose would say.

"I can teach you to purl, Tara," her mother said.

"Whatever," Tara muttered and stalked away toward the elevator.

"I'm sorry," Nan said to Rose. "I don't know what's gotten into her lately."

"I might know what it is, but we can talk about it later," Rose told her. Tara was staring their way, arms crossed and foot tapping as she waited for her mom and sister to join her.

Nan shot Rose a quizzical look.

"C'mon, Mom," Samantha urged. "Let's go see Grandma Becca. I want to show her my scarf."

"Well, at least one of them is happy." Nan shrugged. "I suppose I should count my blessings."

"Always a good idea," Rose said. Tara's crossed arms and tapping foot sparked a memory of her daughter Rosalie deploying the same stance to get her brothers to bow to her will. She was such a force of nature that the boys usually caved, even as adults.

Rose watched Nan and her youngest daughter cross the lobby, Samantha nearly dancing with anticipation.

"What *is* going on with Tara?" Jenny asked.

But Rose declined to answer. She didn't think Tara would appreciate being discussed behind her back.

Moments later, Sam came through the lobby doors carrying a brown paper bag. He made a beeline for the Woolgatherers.

"Good morning, all." Sam stood just outside the circle of chairs. "I have something for you." He beamed as he held up the bag.

Jenny's eyes lit up. "We love presents, don't we?" She looked around at the rest of the group.

Sam pulled one of the skeins of lavender yarn out of the bag. "And I have needles and hooks, too."

"Oh, Sam, that's wonderful," Jenny said. "We weren't at all sure you'd want to join our group, but you even went out and got yarn and needles so you could learn to knit."

A round of applause erupted from the circle. Mr. Peabody stood with only a little help from his walker and pumped Sam's hand with warm enthusiasm. "Glad to have you on board."

Rose watched as a dazed expression spread across Sam's face. "Well, I, uh, I mean . . ." Finally, he seemed to gather himself together enough to try to explain again. "Dorothy isn't . . . doing whatever she did with yarn anymore. It's just sitting there in her craft room. It'd be a shame to let it go to waste."

"Indeed it would," Rose said. "It's a lovely idea for you to make prayer shawls with her yarn."

"Me?" Sam's eyes widened. "No, you don't understand. I'm bringing you yarn so *you* can make it into shawls."

"It would mean so much more if *you* made them, Sam," Jenny said. The dazed look returned. "I, uh . . ."

"Come and sit." Jenny patted the empty space next to her on the couch. "You can start right now."

"You'll teach me?" Sam asked, recovering his power of speech as he sat next to Jenny.

"No, that would be me," Laura, seated on the other side of him, said. "Unless you'd prefer Rose. Between the two of us, we've taught a number of people to knit. Now, what have you got?"

Sam handed over the paper sack.

Laura reached for the glasses she wore on a chain around her neck and settled them on her nose. She examined the lavender yarn and then pulled out the set of needles. "Oh, good. The yarn is worsted weight, a good thickness for beginners. And here are bamboo needles, size 8. Wood is so much easier than metal for beginners. We're in business, Sam!"

Laura's face was bright with cheerful excitement. Rose thought she must have looked like this often during her career as a high school English teacher. It was clear she was happy to be teaching again. Sam, however, looked like a high school boy faced with reading *Julius Caesar*. Sure, there might be a satisfyingly bloody assassination at the end, but there was an awful lot of incomprehensible gibberish before you got there.

Tara sat next to her grandmother in the dayroom of the memory care unit, her backpack at her feet. Her arms were crossed as she watched her little sister show off her hideous new scarf project.

"Not knitting?" her mother asked.

"I told you, Mom. I need Rose to teach me to purl."

Instead of taking up her own knitting after she finished admiring Samantha's "scarf," Grandma Becca leaned over and unzipped Tara's backpack.

"Um, that's mine," Tara said.

Her grandmother seemed not to have heard. She rummaged around inside.

"What are you doing? That's *my* knitting, not yours." Tara reached for her backpack.

"Tara." Her mother's voice was sharp with reproof.

"But, Mom, she's in my stuff!"

Grandma Becca, however, pushed Tara's hand away, intent on exploring the contents of the bag.

"Ah," Grandma Becca said as she pulled a misshapen swatch of cream-colored knitting from the bottom of the bag. Tara cringed inwardly. Her grandmother had managed to unearth her most recent attempt at purling. It looked worse than Samantha's scarf. She smoothed it over her knee and ran her fingers over the stitches as if she were reading Braille.

"Hmm," Grandma Becca said.

Tara squirmed as her grandmother examined the mess she'd made.

At last, her grandmother finished scrutinizing Tara's work. "Purling," she said, "is hard."

"You can say that again," Tara muttered.

"I can teach you," Grandma Becca said.

"Yeah," Samantha said. "She taught me to bind off. It was really easy."

"Purling is not easy," Tara said through gritted teeth, shooting her sister a "shut up" look, then turned her attention to her mother. "Mom, can I talk to you a minute?"

"What is it, Tara?" Her mother looked at her expectantly.

Tara widened her eyes and tilted her head toward the hall.

"Oh. Excuse us just a moment, please," her mother said to Grandma Becca and Samantha.

Out in the hall, her mother said, "What is it you can't say in front of your grandmother?" Her voice was sharp and verging on impatient, but Tara didn't care she was annoying her mom.

"Mom, I don't want her to try to teach me to purl. You said yourself she couldn't teach *you*. I won't be able to do it, and then she'll get frustrated, and then . . ." Tara closed her eyes against the scene forming in her mind.

"And then we'll go, if it comes to that," her mother said. "Just let her try. She's not the same person who tried to teach me to purl. You might be surprised."

"Or I might look totally stupid." Tara glared at her mother.

"Or you might learn to purl."

Tara knew that even, determined tone. Her mother was not about to let her out of this.

"Oh, all *right*," Tara huffed. "But if I can't do it and she loses it, it's *your* fault."

"Fair enough." Her mother looked her in the eye, unflinching. "I take full responsibility."

When Tara and her mother returned to the room, they found that Grandma Becca had tinked back all of Tara's failed purl stitches.

"Hey, Tara, Grandma Becca knows how to tink purl stitches. We should call it 'lurping.' You know, how *tink* is *knit* spelled backward, *lurp* is *purl* spelled backward."

"Not exactly," Tara snapped. "Purl backward is 'lrup.'"

"It's close enough," Samantha said with a stubborn thrust of her chin.

"Girls." There was a warning note in their mother's voice.

Tara rolled her eyes at her sister and turned to speak to her grandmother. She took a deep breath and said, "Grandma, would you please teach me to purl? I've been trying and trying, but I just can't get it."

"I'm not your grandma," Grandma Becca said, her tone kind and gentle. "But I'd be happy to teach you to purl."

Tara shot a desperate look at her mother, but her mother returned a look that clearly said, "Ignore the fact that she just denied being your grandmother."

"Thank you," Tara said, to get her mom to stop looking at her like she was a five-year-old who needed to be reminded about manners.

"There's a rhyme for this," Grandma Becca said as she gave Tara her practice piece and reached for her own knitting. "In front of the fence," she began, bringing the yarn to the front of her work.

"I know that part," Tara said, impatient.

"Good," her grandmother said, unperturbed. She slipped her right-hand needle into the stitch in front of the left-hand needle from right to left. She waited for Tara to do the same. "Catch the sheep," she went on, wrapping the yarn counterclockwise around the right-hand needle.

"Oh, like you're roping a cow," Samantha said, hanging over her grandmother's shoulder.

"A sheep," Grandma Becca said. "Back we go." She pushed the right needle back behind the left one.

Tara, tongue between her teeth, followed suit.

"Off we leap." In one practiced motion, Grandma Becca swept the stitch off the left-hand needle. "That's it," she said as Tara completed the stitch. "Now, let's do it again."

They repeated the rhyme and completed stitch after stitch all across the row. At the end of the row, Tara gazed at her work in awe.

"I don't know what I was doing wrong before, but now it's coming out right." She bent over her practice piece again, intent on mastering the stitch while she was still with her grandmother.

"Careful," Grandma Becca said when Tara was halfway across the next row. "That sheep isn't all the way off. It's leaving its tail behind."

Sure enough, Tara saw that part of the stitch hadn't been worked. It looked suspiciously like the mistake that had been making such a mess of her previous attempts at the purl stitch.

"Thank you, Grandma." Tara's heart welled with the warmth of love for her grandmother, just like when she was little and they baked cookies together.

Her grandmother set her knitting in her lap and gave Tara a sideways hug.

"I knew you could do it, Nan."

Tara froze, momentarily unable to breathe. With one word, her grandmother had ruined the moment, just like she'd ruined Saturday after Saturday ever since she had to go live at Fair Meadows. Tara let out her breath in a huff, shoved her knitting in her backpack, and stormed out of the room. Her mother caught up to her halfway to the elevator.

"Tara, wait."

"No, Mom." Tara swiped at the angry tears that threatened to spill over. "It was special, really special, like when I was little. And then she had to go and ruin it."

They'd arrived at the elevator and Tara reached out to press the down button. Nan was faster, however, and covered the button with her hand.

"How?" her mother wanted to know. "How did she ruin it?"

"She thought I was you. Do you know how hard it is to come here week after week and she doesn't know me? To remember what it was like when we did things together and she thought everything I did was wonderful?"

"You did something together today," her mother said. "And she thought it was wonderful. She said she was proud of you."

"No," Tara said, the tears finally spilling over and running down her cheeks. "She was proud of *you*."

"Oh, honey, I'm so sorry." Nan gathered Tara into her arms. Tara let herself sob into her mother's shoulder, feeling about five years old. When her tears finally came to a sniffing, hiccupping end, her mother gave her a tissue, smoothed the hair away from her face and said, "How about you go on downstairs and hang out with the Woolgatherers until your sister and I are done here?"

Tara nodded, wiping her eyes and blowing her nose. "Thanks, Mom."

Tara stood at the edge of the seating area, clutching the strap of the backpack slung over her shoulder. While the shawl makers stitched and chatted, she watched, wishing one of them was her grandmother. Well, not Mr. Peabody, of course, but one of the others. Especially Rose. But wait, there was someone new. Another man, and Mrs. Whitman was teaching him to knit. Trying, anyway. He didn't seem to be getting it. At all.

Finally, Rose glanced up and noticed her.

"Just you, Tara?"

"Mom and Samantha are still upstairs. Mom said I could come hang out with you." Tara thrust her chin out. "*And* I learned to purl today."

"Did you, now?" Rose looked pleased.

"Grandma Becca helped me," Tara managed to say before her chin began to tremble.

"Tell me about it," Rose said. Mrs. Thomas scooted over to make room.

Tara sat and pulled out her practice piece, partly because she didn't want to forget her newfound skill and partly because it was easier to talk if she had something to do with her hands. As she worked, the story poured out.

Soft murmurs of sympathy rose around her as she finished with a giant sniff.

"Cussed Old-Timer's Disease," Mrs. O'Brian muttered, loud enough for Tara to hear.

"I wish I didn't have to go at all," Tara burst out. "I'd rather remember her the way she was when I was little, before she got sick."

"You'll always have those memories." Rose's voice was gentle. "But these memories are important, too."

Tara struggled against tears again. "No, they're not. They're horrible."

"Trust me, Tara," Rose said. "In the years to come, you'll be glad you made memories with her for as long as you could." Rose's eyes took on a mistiness, as if they, too, were about to fill with tears.

"Besides," Jenny (who insisted Tara call her "Jenny" and not "Mrs. Alderman) said, "if you stopped coming, you couldn't hang out with us. We're the cool kids around here."

At the idea of elderly "cool kids" Tara laughed in spite of herself.

"Yeah, you are pretty cool. I guess I would miss you if I stopped coming on Saturdays."

"And you'd miss all the fun!" Jenny told her. "Like Sam here learning to knit!"

Sam, fiercely focused on his knitting, made a growling noise. It didn't seem like he was having fun at all.

"I know you can do it, Sam," Mrs. Whitman said.

Tara was not so sure. The man named Sam held the needles awkwardly, and when he tried to wrap the yarn around the left-hand needle, he dropped the right-hand one. It hit the floor and rolled under his chair. Tara moved swiftly to retrieve the needle. She suspected he would have a hard time getting up again if he got down on the floor himself.

"Thanks," he said when she returned the needle. With a heavy sigh, he tried again. This time he managed to hold on to the needles until he tried to maneuver the wrapped yarn to the front, the trickiest part of the knit stitch, as far as Tara was concerned. It had taken her many attempts and rewatches of videos before she'd gotten it. Sam's yarn unwound itself from around the needle as if it had a mind of its own and the right-hand needle slipped out again.

"It's no use." Sam's frustration reminded Tara of her own struggle to learn to purl. *Any minute now, he's going to throw the other needle across the lobby.* "I can't do this."

"Let's just take a break, shall we?" Mrs. Whitman said.

Sam glanced at his watch and said, "I really should be getting on upstairs."

"All right," Mrs. Whitman said with a bright smile. "We'll try again next time you come."

Sam packed up his things, and Jenny laid her hand on Sam's arm. "It's going to be so much fun to have you in the group!"

"I guess," Sam said, looking dubious.

But Tara noticed he didn't pull his arm away, just gazed at Jenny's hand for a moment before standing and shuffling off to the elevators.

CHAPTER 12

IN THE ELEVATOR, SAM REGARDED the bag with dismay. He'd expected to give it to the shawl people, but somehow they'd roped him into learning how to knit. It had been a totally frustrating experience. He had new respect for Dorothy. She'd kept at it, hour after hour, making beautiful things out of yarn.

As he stepped out of the elevator, Eileen, the weekend charge nurse, waved him over.

"What did you bring Dot today? She loves your presents."

"I didn't bring her anything today," Sam said. "This is some yarn and knitting needles."

"Not for Dot, though?" Eileen's eyebrows disappeared under her soft brown bangs.

"Well, they are Dorothy's, but I don't think she's interested anymore. I brought them for those knitting ladies in the lobby."

"That's so thoughtful of you." Eileen gave him a beaming smile. "My prayer shawl is very special to me." Eileen reached behind her and lifted a deep green shawl from her chair.

Sam reached out and touched the shawl. It was soft and still warm from the nurse sitting against it.

"The group in the lobby made this for you?" Sam asked, mostly to delay the embarrassment of having to peek at Dorothy around the edge of the door to the dayroom instead of striding right in to sit with her.

Eileen grinned. "No. It was the craziest thing. I was at the café in the bookstore at the mall, and there was this group of women knitting. This shawl was on the table. I mistook it for a scarf and wanted to buy it. It would have been a great gift for my sister. But they said it wasn't a scarf and wasn't for sale. It was a prayer shawl and could only be given as a gift for someone who needed it. I felt like crying. I suddenly wanted that shawl so much." Eileen gathered the shawl in her arms and hugged it.

"So, how did you get it? Don't tell me you stole it," Sam said with a wink.

"That's the great thing. I didn't have to steal it or even buy it," Eileen said. "One of the ladies gave it to me and said I looked like I needed it. And she was right. I really did. I was facing my first Thanksgiving without my father. It had only been a few months since he'd passed away, and everything was hard. Before I knew it, I was sitting at their table telling them all about my dad." Eileen's eyes were soft with memory.

"That's quite a gift," Sam said, remembering the weeks and weeks it used to take Dorothy to make an afghan. "Did you ever see them again?"

"If you've talked to the group downstairs, you've probably met Rose," Eileen said.

Sam nodded. Rose, who didn't seem able to take no for an answer.

"She was one of the ladies at the mall, if you can believe it. Anyway, when they gave me the shawl, one of them seemed concerned their pastor hadn't prayed over it. There was a tag attached to the shawl with the church's address, so I went to the early service on Sunday and asked him to pray over it. I've been going there ever since. I have to hurry to get here for work after the early service, but it's worth it."

"That's nice," Sam said to be polite. He'd always wanted to sleep in on Sundays, but Dorothy had insisted they go to church. He hadn't missed it when she'd started to forget about going. He'd had enough going on trying to keep track of her both day and night, without getting up early, trying to get her dressed (appropriately), and getting there on time. It had been hard enough to manage timing for medical appointments. And then there had been that terrible night when he'd been sure she was sound asleep, so he jumped at the chance to shower . . . He closed his eyes as if to shut out the memory.

"Sam? Sam?" Eileen said.

Sam started and blinked. "Oh, sorry."

"Where did you go? You were lost in your thoughts, and they didn't seem like happy ones."

"Enough about me," Sam said. "How's Dorothy today? I don't know if they told you, but they'd rather I didn't visit with her, at least for a while. They say it upsets her too much. She's taken it into her head to be afraid of me."

"I'm so sorry, Sam. She's doing fine, enjoying the roses you brought her. She invites people into her room to show them off," Eileen said. "It's sweet of you to bring her flowers every week."

Sam didn't trust himself to speak for a moment. Eileen didn't deserve the tirade he felt rising in his throat. That was what got to him about Dorothy's situation. There was no one to take it out on—not the staff, not Dorothy herself. It wasn't their fault she didn't know him from Adam, didn't know the flowers came from the love of her life. And the disease itself didn't care. It was heartless.

But he was grind-your-teeth, clench-your-jaw, pound-a-fist-on-the-table angry.

Finally, he cleared his throat. "I'll just go and take a peek. See for myself." He knew he sounded gruff, but it was the best he could do. He moved away from the reception desk and positioned himself to the side of the entrance to the dayroom. There she was, at one of the tables, chatting away with three other residents of the memory care unit. She was talking with her hands, waving them in lively, expressive arcs. Her tablemates burst into laughter. Sam turned away, no longer in on the joke.

Rose watched as Tara doggedly practiced her newly acquired and hard-won skill. She certainly had the patience and perseverance to be a knitter. Tara glanced up and caught Rose looking at her.

"I can make a prayer shawl now, can't I?"

"Yes, if you want," Rose said with a smile. "Is there someone in particular you want to make one for?"

"I want to do it like the Woolgatherers—just make it, not knowing who will get it. I kind of like that idea. It's like that random act of kindness thing people do, like paying for somebody in line behind you at Starbucks."

"Hey, I like that," Laura said. "Random acts of knitting." A chuckle ran around the circle, stopping at Edna, of course.

"And crocheting," Laura hastened to add.

Edna completed the stitch she was making before she responded.

"It's a bit more work than paying for somebody's coffee."

Tara's cheeks flushed.

"Both of them are special because you're doing something for someone you don't know." Jenny rushed to Tara's defense. "And when I'm making a shawl, all the wondering about who's going to get it makes me feel bigger inside, somehow." Now it was Jenny's turn to blush.

"I couldn't have said it better myself." Mr. Peabody favored Jenny with a beaming smile.

"What pattern can I do now that I can purl?" Tara wanted to know.

"You could do the Trinity pattern," Susan said. "That's what I'm doing." She held out her work for Tara to examine. "You knit three, then purl three, ending with a knit three. Then on the next row, you do the same thing, but you're knitting the purl stitches and purling the knit stitches."

Tara frowned. "It looks a lot like garter stitch. I already know how to do that."

"Stand back farther," Rose said. "It looks different from further away."

Tara did as Rose suggested. She tilted her head and considered. "Oh, I get it now. It makes columns, but . . ."

"Here," Rose reached into her capacious knitting bag and pulled out a pattern book. "Look through this. Each pattern is labeled with a difficulty level. Even though you know how to purl now, you'll still want to choose one in the easy category."

Tara pored over the pages of patterns, running her finger down the directions to find the difficulty level. Finally, she pointed to the last pattern in the book. "This one. 'Cape Cod Shawl.' We went there one summer when I was little for vacation. I still have the shells I collected on the beach with Grandma Becca." She pointed to the picture of the shawl, indicating the shells sewn at intervals at each end of the shawl.

Taking the book from her, Rose examined the pattern. "Yes, you'll be able to do this one."

At that moment, Nan and Samantha emerged from the elevator. Tara met them halfway across the lobby, waving the pattern book. "Mom, can we stop at the craft store on the way home? I'm gonna make my first prayer shawl, and I need yarn and needles. I still have Christmas money," she finished in a wheedling tone.

Nan shot a look of gratitude Rose's way. "Yes, we can," she told her daughter.

"Great! Let's go." Tara grabbed her coat and backpack. "Rose, can I . . . ?" She hugged the pattern book.

"Yes, you can borrow it," Rose said with a smile.

As Nan and her daughters stepped out into the blustery March morning, Rose heard a sniff beside her.

Apparently, Susan heard it, too. "Laura, you're not coming down with a cold, are you?"

"No," Laura said, pulling a tissue from her pocket for the tears about to brim over. "She could spend her Christmas money on any of the myriad of things teenagers want. But she's buying yarn to make a shawl to give away."

CHAPTER 13

On Monday, as Nan stopped to talk to the Woolgatherers on her way to Memory Care, Edna noticed the line between Nan's eyebrows. She'd felt the same worry line form on her own face many times over Stanley.

"I need some advice," Nan told the group. They all looked at her expectantly. "I'm wondering if I should keep making Tara come to visit Mom every week. She was really hurt on Saturday when Mom mistook her for me. It doesn't seem to affect Samantha. She's always been more easygoing than her big sister. But Tara takes things to heart. Maybe I'm expecting too much from her."

"Don't matter," Edna said. Her heart gave a lurch as she thought of Stanley. "She ought to be visiting her grandma every chance she gets. When her grandma is gone, she'll be gone—and there won't be no going back."

"Regrets *are* hard to deal with," Laura said. "No matter how much you wish you'd done things differently, you can't turn back time and do it over."

"But she's so young to be dealing with Alzheimer's," Jenny said. "You should just let her remember her grandmother the way she was before. Then it will be all good memories and no sad ones."

"Except for the sad fact that she didn't spend time with her grandma once she got sick." Edna's mind swept back to grim-faced doctors and hopelessly bad news. Back to being there for people she loved, no matter what.

Susan nodded in agreement. "She might feel sad about it when she gets older."

"So, I should keep making her go? Tell her she'll thank me later?" The line between Nan's eyebrows deepened.

Rose, who had been quiet until now, weighed in. "I have an idea. She's knitting her first prayer shawl, right?"

"It's already four inches long."

"Suppose we invite her to join the Woolgatherers? She can spend a little time with Grandma Becca, like she did last Saturday, and then come back here to knit with us."

Edna frowned. Tara would still be missing time with her grandma— time she'd never be able to get back. *What I'd give for more time with . . .*

"That would be wonderful," Nan was saying. "Tara would get to do what she wants to do, which is knit with all of you, but she'll still be visiting Grandma Becca. Are you sure you wouldn't mind?"

"Won't Samantha be jealous Tara's getting to cut her visit short?" Susan asked.

Nan chuckled. "She'll think she's getting the better end of the deal, getting Grandma Becca all to herself."

Edna gave an approving nod. The child couldn't knit worth beans, but she knew what was important.

"There's Sam," Jenny said, looking past Nan. "Yoo-hoo, Sam."

Sam waved and kept right on walking.

"Stop by on your way out," Jenny called after him.

"No shame, that one," Edna muttered.

"I'm just being friendly, Edna O'Brian." Jenny tossed her head. "He could use some friends."

Nan hurried after Sam, who held the elevator for her.

"Those sure were some pretty flowers," Laura said after the elevator doors closed. "Tulips always look so cheerful this time of year."

"I still prefer roses," Jenny said. "I love the ones you sent me, Alistair." Jenny turned her blue eyes on Mr. Peabody, who gave a seated bow.

"My pleasure, dear. It was kind of you to make sure Dorothy got hers last week."

Edna, however, was gazing across the lobby at the elevator.

"Sam didn't bring his knitting," she said.

"Not a problem," Laura said. She reached into her knitting bag and produced a set of size 8 bamboo needles and a skein of yarn. "He can use these."

In the elevator, Sam found himself traveling to the seventh floor with the woman with knitting needles sticking out of her bag.

"You knitters seem to be everywhere," he said.

"It's something I do with my mother," the woman said. "Lately, she doesn't remember me, but she does remember how to knit. We knit together when I visit."

"My wife used to knit and crochet," Sam offered. "I don't know if she still remembers how or not."

"Might be worth a try," she said. "I'm Nan Sheffield, by the way. I think we have some mutual friends—the Woolgatherers?"

"Sam Talbot," Sam said. "Your friends the Woolgatherers think I should be knitting, too."

"What a great idea," Nan said. "You could try knitting with your wife."

"With me, knitting is trying in more ways than one," Sam said. "They've tried to teach me, but I'm not doing very well. This dog's too old to learn new tricks."

The elevator doors slid open. "I'd keep at the knitting if I were you," Nan said as she stepped out. "The Woolgatherers are a nice bunch. And it really might be something you could do with your wife. You never know." With a wave and a smile, she headed toward the dayroom.

"Problem is, I do know," Sam muttered to himself. He walked straight to the nurses' station and handed over the bunch of tulips to Patsy.

"Oh, these are lovely! I'll put them in the vase in Dot's room right away. She's going to love them." Patsy bustled off.

Sam craned his neck across the reception desk to look through the open doors of the dayroom. Yes, there was Dorothy, chatting away with her tablemates, living in the moment. *Life is so much simpler for them*, he thought. No past, no missing the way things used to be. No future, no worrying about what might happen. That fell to other people, to their caregivers. For Dorothy, there was only now. A now without him in it. With a sigh, he turned to leave.

"See you Thursday, Sam," Patsy called.

He didn't look back but simply flapped a hand in her direction as if waving her away. He just wanted to be left alone.

Sam meant to walk straight past the group of yarn ladies, hoping they wouldn't notice him hurrying through the lobby. Unfortunately, Jenny had eagle eyes.

"There he is," she said as soon as he stepped out of the elevator. "Sam, come on over here."

Every head in the lobby turned, first to look at Jenny, smiling and waving, and then at the object of her attentions. There was nothing to do but walk over to the prayer shawl group.

"You didn't bring your knitting," Jenny said. She stuck out her lower lip just the tiniest bit. Sam felt a hitch in his breath.

"I, uh . . ."

"Not a problem." Laura produced a set of needles and a skein of yarn. "You can use these. Come sit." She patted the empty space on the couch between her and Jenny.

Sam hesitated. It was discouraging enough having to keep a low profile with Dorothy without adding the frustration of trying to get the hang of knitting. But what if he did get the hang of it and could take his knitting to Memory Care? Might Dorothy see him as the Knitting Man? Would she let him sit with her? Would she maybe even remember how to knit and knit with him, like Nan's mother? A wave of longing swept over him. He knew it was a long shot, but maybe, just maybe . . .

"Okay," Sam said.

Laura was patient as ever, and it was a pleasure to sit next to Jenny, who kept up a lively banter. The knitting itself, however, was every bit as frustrating as it had been the first time he'd tried. He kept dropping the needles and having to retrieve them from under his chair. When he did manage to hold on to them, the yarn seemed to have a mind of its own. His fingers felt fat and clumsy, as if he had ten thumbs instead of only two.

"There you go," Laura encouraged as he managed to grip the needles, get the tip of the right-hand needle into the loop on the left-hand needle, and wrap the yarn around the right-hand needle. "Now, just—"

"Argh." The yarn slipped out of place for what seemed like the fiftieth time. Discouragement descended on him like a dark cloud. Who was he kidding? He couldn't learn to knit, and he was a fool to think Dorothy would take up knitting again anyway.

"You almost had it," Jenny said.

"No, *I've* had it." Sam thrust the yarn and needles at Laura. "I can't do this. It was very nice of you to try to teach me, but I'm just not cut out for it."

"He's right. Some people aren't cut out for knitting." Edna pointed her hook at Sam.

"Exactly," Sam said as he started to stand. "Well, ladies, I'd better be—"

"But just about anybody can learn to crochet," Edna said before he could finish. "You sit tight while I make you a swatch, and then we'll see what's what."

Sam looked across the circle at Edna, with her fat pink crochet hook and wild gray hair. He wasn't sure he wanted to learn anything from this woman.

"What a great idea," Laura said. "I don't crochet, but Edna is really good at it."

Edna didn't even look up to acknowledge the compliment. She had already pulled yarn and a hook out of her bag and busily set to work creating a small square of crochet.

"Stay and crochet," Jenny said.

Sam looked into her blue eyes and felt a flicker of hope. He decided he could at least give it a try.

"All right, come on over here," Edna said a few minutes later. Once he was settled in the chair next to her, she gave him the square of crochet and the hook. The hook was smaller than the big pink one she was wielding.

"This here's a size H hook, good for beginners. You right-handed?"

Sam nodded.

"Okay," she said. "Hold the hook in your right hand. You can hold it like a pencil, like this." She demonstrated. "Or you can hold it like a knife, like this. Whichever you want." She held the hook as if she were about to cut into a steak.

Sam tried both and settled on the knife hold. The "steak grip" felt more manly.

"Then you hold this swatch in your left hand," Edna instructed. "Like this." She pinched the swatch between her thumb and third finger. "And you put the yarn over your pointer finger."

Over the next few minutes, Edna guided Sam through a row of what she called "single crochet." It was awkward at first, every bit as awkward as the attempts at knitting had been. But eventually, he caught the rhythm of sticking the hook into the stitch, maneuvering the yarn over the hook, pulling through, getting the yarn over the hook again, and pulling it through the rest of the loops. At the end of the row, Edna examined his work.

"It'll do," she said. "For now." She talked him through making a single loop she called a "chain one," and showed him how to turn his work and start across the row again. Each stitch was a little easier than the last. Soon he was absorbed in forming the stitches, barely aware of the conversation that flowed around him. Stitch after stitch, turn after turn, row after row, he worked on, until someone touched his arm. He looked up to find Jenny beside him.

"Sam, it's time for us to go."

"Lunchtime," Alistair said.

Sam blinked, returning to awareness of the lobby, the people around him, and the state of his own stomach, ready to start growling any minute. Across the circle of chairs, Laura and a few of the other ladies sat with their heads together in earnest conversation.

"Why don't you join us for lunch?" Laura said to Sam when they broke out of their huddle.

"I couldn't," Sam said. "I don't live here."

"You'll be our guest," Laura said.

"I'll pick up the check," Alistair said, puffing out his chest a bit.

"Don't listen to him," Laura said. "Our meal plans include the occasional guest."

Sam considered the alternatives—either the leftover pizza in the fridge or stopping for a burger and fries on the way home.

"Of course he'll have lunch with us," Jenny said with a warm smile, which seemed to settle it.

"Here, let me have those." Edna took the yarn and hook away from him. "I'll keep hold of them for now." She stuffed Sam's work into her crochet bag. "You can have them back after lunch. Now, come on. I'm hungry."

CHAPTER 14

St. Patrick's Day at Fair Meadows Retirement Community dawned blustery but bright. Mr. Peabody arrived at breakfast wearing a green T-shirt that invited all and sundry to "Kiss me! I'm Irish!" A large button pinned to his shirt proclaimed the same message, adorned with flashing lights to emphasize the point. Rose watched with amusement as a number of ladies favored him with kisses on the cheek as he went through the line at the breakfast buffet.

"Hmph." Edna sniffed as he arrived at their table. "Everybody wants to be Irish on St. Patrick's Day, but Peabody is an English name."

"I really am Irish," Mr. Peabody said. "On my mother's side. She was a Kennedy. No relation to the famous ones, but she was plenty proud of the name all the same."

"Well, even if you are"—Edna looked askance at the flashing button—"don't expect me to kiss you."

"I wouldn't dream of it, ma'am." Mr. Peabody gave her a little bow from where he was seated across the table.

Rose stifled a giggle at his antics.

"Now, O'Brian is a *real* Irish name," Edna went on as though Mr. Peabody hadn't spoken. "It's a lucky name, and my Stanley had all the luck that goes with it, the luck of the Irish. He won. He won a lot."

"You mean like at poker?" Mr. Peabody asked.

Edna sent him a look so sharp it made him flinch.

"My Stanley was *not* a gambler," she said with a fierce lift of her chin.

"Then what did he win?" Laura asked. "Now I'm curious."

"Everything where there was luck involved. Raffles, bingo, and"—
she paused, with a proud and triumphant smile—"the lottery."

I don't think I've ever seen her smile before, Rose thought. *At least,
not like that. Why, she looks like a completely different person. Happy,
for once.*

"You mean like the scratch-offs at convenience stores?" Susan asked,
a hint of disdain in her voice.

"Hmph," Edna said with answering disdain. "Small potatoes. He
won the lottery with a capital L. The Big One." She leaned back in her
chair and crossed her arms over her chest. She didn't even have to say,
"So there."

"Wow!" Jenny said. "He really won the lottery? What did the two
of you do with the money?"

"Jenny," Rose said in a warning tone.

"Did you travel? Buy a big house? A Rolls-Royce?" Jenny pursued,
ignoring Rose.

"Nah." Edna waved Jenny's questions away. "Stanley knew enough
not to trust the luck. He paid the taxes and put the rest away for a
rainy day. 'Got to take care of you, Edna,' he said."

"It's just sitting in a bank account somewhere?" Jenny asked,
incredulous.

"Some of it," Edna said. "But most of it's here." She made a sweep-
ing motion with her arm. "Never could have afforded this place if
we'd squandered the winnings on cars and cruises. It's a good thing
we didn't, because right after he won the Powerball, Stanley's luck left
him."

"You mean he stopped winning?" Laura asked.

"The Old-Timer's Disease took his luck right away." The light faded
from Edna's face, and Rose's heart sank.

"It started with the bingo. Stanley used to be able to keep eight
cards going all at once." Edna swept her hand across the table, and
Rose could almost see the cards laid out. "Then he could only manage
seven, then six, until he couldn't even keep his mind on one."

A murmur of sympathy rippled around the table.

"Stanley really loved his luck. I tried to help him keep it, but it just ran out. That's the thing about luck. You can't trust it. Sometimes it just runs out. It runs out right when you need it most."

"He still had you." Rose ventured to lay a reassuring hand on Edna's skinny arm. "I'd say that was pretty lucky."

"What's the point, if the other person don't even know you?" Edna burst out. "Easy for him, hard for me." She threw her napkin on the table, grabbed up her cane, and stomped out of the dining room.

"Oh, dear," Laura murmured.

"Shoulda known better," Edna muttered to herself as she gave the third-floor elevator button a savage jab.

"Hold the elevator, please."

Nan hustled across the lobby, her knitting bag bumping wildly against her hip as she hurried toward the elevator. Edna did not put out her arm to keep the doors from closing. With a scowl, she punched the button to close them instead.

"That's the last thing I need this morning," she told the empty air around her once the doors were safely shut. "Knitting Nan, on her way to knit with her knit-wit mother. Shoulda known better," she told herself again. "Shoulda stayed in your apartment on St. Paddy's Day, especially with that Peabody fool running around trying to be Irish."

The elevator settled to a stop at the third floor and the doors slid open to reveal a chattering group of women clad in various shades of green, one in a particularly loud fluorescent lime.

"Happy St. Patrick's Day!" they chorused.

Without returning their greeting, Edna shouldered past them and stumped down the hall to her apartment. Once inside, she leaned against the door and let the tears fall. It had been a near thing. She'd almost lost control. She pushed herself away from the door and headed for her bedroom, where she made a beeline for the old brown cardigan that had once been Stanley's. She thrust her arms through the sleeves and pushed the worn leather buttons through the buttonholes. Then she made her way to the sitting room. Edna sank onto the couch she and Stanley had splurged on, one of their few indulgences after the Big One. It was the most comfortable piece of furniture they'd ever owned, with butter-soft leather in a deep, luxurious brown. She sat in the place that had always been his. It still smelled faintly of English Leather aftershave. She'd often teased him about being an Irishman wearing English Leather, but she wouldn't have wanted him to wear anything else. The scent was quintessentially Stanley.

She breathed it in now as she reached for the picture on the end table. There he was, her lucky man, holding the giant Powerball check with all those zeroes. There hadn't been quite so many zeroes after they'd paid taxes on it, which Stanley had patiently explained to the relatives, friends, and friends of friends who'd suddenly remembered "Stanley old pal" after the win. Edna mentally kicked herself for blabbing about the Big One to the Woolgatherers. They all seemed well-off, but how long would it be before one of them came to her with her hand out? Edna still budgeted according to what Stanley had earned as a mechanic, even though he'd urged her to spend more after he saw how much she enjoyed the couch.

"I want you to have everything you need, Edna. And the things you want, too."

She couldn't bring herself to do it, though. Who knew how long the money would have to last? Especially once that Old-Timer's had showed up. It wasn't the kind of disease that killed a person outright or even had a timeline. Why, she knew someone whose father had had it for twenty years and was still going strong (and driving his daughter crazy in the process). The doctor had given Stanley four to eight years and said a lot depended on the care he received. Edna had chosen to spend the money making sure her Stanley had everything *he* needed, for however long he would need it.

She stared into the happy, triumphant eyes in the photograph. It was an 8 x 10, but it didn't seem big enough to contain his joy. His grin filled the whole picture. She smiled back at him and stroked the glass. Then her chin began to quiver all over again.

Oh, Stanley, I miss you so much!

She wrapped her arms around the frame and laid her cheek along the top edge. With a long, shuddering sigh, she let the tears flow, soaking the sleeves of the old brown sweater.

Rose gazed after Edna's swiftly retreating back with dismay. She'd meant to comfort Edna, but the attempt had clearly backfired.

"I wonder how long she's been widowed," Laura mused aloud.

"Is she widowed, though? She's still wearing her wedding band," Jenny said. Jenny tended to notice that kind of thing.

Rose held up her left hand, where a wide gold band and a diamond ring glinted in the sunlight.

"It's been ten years, but I still wear mine," she said.

"If you took them off, you might get some dates," Jenny said.

Rose smiled and shook her head. "My Ray was the best. No one else will do. He'd be a hard act for anyone else to follow, at least in my eyes."

"Isn't it lonely sometimes, though?" Jenny asked. "And boring?"

"I have so many good memories with him," Rose told her. "More than enough to go on with."

"I have plenty of good memories, too," Jenny said. "But I'm always open to making new ones." She flashed a smile at a man passing their table on his way to the buffet. He winked as he passed.

"Don't encourage her," Susan muttered.

"Girls just wanna have fun." Jenny grinned and tossed her head.

"Hey, your Cyndi Lauper imitation is pretty good," Mr. Peabody said.

"Who's Cyndi Lauper?" Susan asked, her eyebrows pulled together over her nose.

"A singer in the 80s," Mr. Peabody told her. "She had a song called 'Girls Just Want to Have Fun.' Here, I'll pull up the music video for you." He pulled out his phone.

"Never mind." Susan waved the phone away. "I stopped listening to new music when my kids were teenagers. It was loud enough back then."

"Don't be such an old fogy," Jenny told her.

Susan glared at Jenny. "I may be old, but I am not an old fogy."

"Oh, lighten up, Susan," Jenny said. "Have some fun."

"But life isn't all about having fun," Susan told her.

"It is about living, though," Jenny said. "Not just about trying to stay alive."

Susan gasped and opened her mouth to retort, but Jenny spoke first.

"Now, if you'll excuse us, Alistair and I are on our way to dance lessons. We're learning to salsa this week."

Once Jenny and Mr. Peabody were out of earshot, Laura said, "I wonder how you salsa with a walker?"

"If anybody can figure it out, it's Mr. Peabody." Rose chuckled.

Rose missed Edna at lunch, dinner, and breakfast the next morning. The more she pondered the outburst at breakfast the day before, the more she regretted any way she might have added to Edna's grief. It didn't usually work that way. Rose was used to being able to comfort grieving people. Long after others had tired of hearing about Fran's sudden widowhood, Rose had created space for her to talk about it, over and over. With a few kind and well-placed questions, Rose had encouraged Eileen to talk about her dad with the Heavenly Hugs, bringing him to life for a little while as she shared special memories. With Edna, however, she had failed so colossally that she'd actually inflicted pain. Facing Edna to apologize made Rose's stomach clench. She might make a mess of things all over again. Nevertheless, Rose squared her shoulders and rode the elevator to Edna's after breakfast.

"Oh, it's you." Edna's frowning face peered around the edge of the door.

"I came to see if you're all right," Rose said. "I haven't seen you at meals."

Edna opened the door a little wider but not much.

"There. You seen me." She started to close the door.

Oh, no you don't, Edna O'Brian, Rose thought. Not giving herself time to think about it, she stuck out her cane to keep the door from closing.

Edna glared with such force that Rose almost took a step back. She stood her ground, however, fighting the urge to turn tail and avoid this confrontation. She swallowed hard. "I also came to apologize. What I said clearly upset you. I didn't take the time to think of how uncomforting my words would be."

Edna continued to stare.

"I'm sorry, Edna. I really am." Rose's voice caught in her throat.

"Not your fault," Edna said after an uncomfortable moment. "Not nobody's fault." She opened the door all the way and stepped aside. "You might as well come in."

Not the most gracious of welcomes, but I'll take it. Rose took in the tidy, sparsely furnished sitting room. It was dominated by a chocolate brown leather couch flanked by end tables that had seen better days. She could tell one end of the couch was Edna's spot by the mug on a crocheted coaster on the end table and the crocheted throw Edna must have pushed aside to answer the door. She took a seat at the other end of the couch.

"I just put some coffee on." Edna pulled her brown cardigan around her as if she felt a chill. "Want some?"

Rose hoped this meant she was forgiven. "Yes, please."

While Edna busied herself in the kitchen, Rose examined the framed photographs on the end tables. The man with a huge grin holding an oversized check had to be Stanley. Next to it was a picture of a young girl in a cheerleading uniform, one hand holding a pom-pom on her hip while the other held a pom-pom high over her head. Her grin matched Stanley's. Rose peered more closely at this picture. In the bottom right corner, a curl of coppery hair nestled under the glass.

"That there's Stanley, when he won the Big One." Edna set a tray on the coffee table.

"He looks so happy," Rose said.

"It was a great day," Edna said.

"And this one?" Rose asked about the other picture. "Is this your granddaughter?"

Edna pressed her lips together and shook her head. "My daughter."

"She's beautiful. Does she live nearby? I've never heard you speak of her."

"I don't," Edna said. "She passed."

"Oh, Edna, I'm so sorry." Rose gulped. *I've stuck my foot in it again.*

Edna waved Rose's sympathy away. "It was a long time ago."

How long ago? Rose longed to ask. *Is this the heaviness you carry with you, along with losing Stanley?*

"Her smile is the same as Stanley's," Rose said.

Edna nodded. "Peas in a pod, those two. Always smiling, always looking on the sunny side of life. Penny was a daddy's girl for sure. 'Bout went crazy when the boys started buzzing around. Told her she couldn't date until she was forty and was only half joking. She managed to talk him down to sixteen, but . . ."

Rose took a sip of coffee and waited.

Edna sighed. "She barely got to fifteen. And there weren't no boys buzzing around once she lost her hair." She picked up the photograph and traced the curl of bright hair in the corner with her finger.

"Tell me about her," Rose said. "What was she like?"

"Happy. Had a temper but got over it quick. Loved people, hated making her bed. Smart in school. Straight A's before she got sick."

"So, her hair wasn't the only bright thing about her," Rose said.

"Everything about her was bright." Edna sounded wistful.

"What kinds of things did you do together?" Rose asked.

"She worked on the car with Stanley. He was a mechanic, a real good one. I taught her to crochet." Edna held out the throw. "She made this for me the Christmas she was twelve. She worked on it in secret, never once asked for help. Ain't it something for a girl her age?"

Rose reached out and examined the even stitches, the complicated pattern. "It would be something at any age," she said with admiration.

Edna hugged the throw to her chest.

"She was the light of our lives, that girl. We were so lucky to have her, even for a little while. That's what Stanley always said." Edna's face, open and soft with memory, seemed to snap shut and harden. "The rest of them Woolgatherers don't need to know all this. Didn't even mean to tell you."

"I'll keep it between you and me." Rose sensed Edna had had enough of company and confidences. She thanked Edna for the coffee and took her leave. Rose's steps were slow and thoughtful on the way to the elevator. The enormity of Edna's losses filled her heart and spilled over into prayer.

CHAPTER 15

ON SATURDAY MORNING, TARA SENT a jaunty wave across the lobby as she followed her mother and little sister to the elevator.

"Be back soon," she called.

Rose waved back, delighted with Tara's new Saturday cheerfulness.

"I'm eager to see her progress on her first shawl," Rose said. "I forgot to remind her to remember to move her yarn to the back again when she changes from purling to knitting. She'll get yarn overs and extra stitches if she doesn't."

"She seemed pretty chipper," Mr. Peabody said. "I'll bet she figured it out herself. She's a smart cookie, that one."

The group settled into their work, which consisted not only of making prayer shawls, but also greeting the Saturday Memory Care visitors. Anxious faces eased at the sight of them, and sad ones were momentarily lit with smiles in response to the Woolgatherers' waves.

Half an hour later, Tara stepped out of the elevator and came over to the group.

"Mom said you want me to knit with you. You want me to be a Woolgatherer?" she said, a tentative hope in her voice.

"Only if you want to, dear," Rose said. "We weren't sure if you'd want to hang out with a bunch of old fogies like us."

"Speak for yourself." Jenny flashed a look at Susan. "I'm not an old fogy and never will be."

"No, you're not," Tara said with a laugh. "And I really do want to hang out with you."

Once Tara was seated, Rose gave her a card with their shawl-maker's prayer on it.

"We start each session praying this together."

"I pray it every time I work on my prayer shawl," Laura said.

"Okay," Tara said. "Do I, like, read it out loud now, before I start? Or can I pray it in my mind? I've never done this before."

"Whichever feels more comfortable to you," Rose told her. "God hears you either way."

"I'll whisper it, if that's okay." Tara bowed her head over the card.

The rest of the group returned to their work. Seated next to Tara, Rose could hear the softly repeated words of the prayer. When she finished, Tara unzipped her backpack and pulled out her shawl. She had chosen a variegated yarn in shades of ocean blue, much like the yarn that had captured Susan's attention at The Tangled Thread.

"You're really making progress." Rose ran a finger over row after row of perfect stitches. "You must have twelve inches at least. I forgot to remind you to move the yarn to the back every time you changed from purling to knitting, but I can tell it wasn't a problem."

"It was at first," Tara said. "I kept getting these extra stitches. Not only extra stitches, but holes. Holes! I was freaking out!"

"How did you figure out what the problem was?" Laura asked.

"I thought if I took it back to the mistake, I'd be able to tell what was going wrong. I know how to tink, but I had to learn how to lurp on YouTube."

"Lurp?" Susan asked.

"That's what my little sister calls undoing purl stitches. She says it's *purl* spelled backward. It's not really."

"Close enough." Laura chuckled. "It'll never be on a spelling test."

"Anyway, when I lurped, I saw what had happened. I'd forgotten to move the yarn to the back after purling at least once on nearly every row, so I just ripped it all out and started over."

"And you've gotten this far since then," Laura said. "Impressive."

"How is your grandmother this morning?" Rose asked.

"Still knitting," Tara said. "I hope it lasts, for Mom's sake, but I'm not counting on it."

"Can't count on anything with Old-Timer's Disease," Edna said.

She paused in her crocheting to wave her hook at Sam, who was crossing the lobby to the elevator.

Sam waved and gave her a thumbs-up.

Now, that's a hopeful sign, Rose thought.

"How's his knitting coming along?" Tara asked.

"It's not," Laura said. "He got frustrated and gave up."

"But I taught him to crochet." Edna pointed the bright pink hook at her bony chest. "He caught on right away."

At the nurses' station, Eileen greeted Sam with a friendly smile. "What do you have there?" She gestured at the paper sack Sam carried. "A present for your wife?"

"Uh, no. Nothing for Dorothy today. Those women in the lobby have roped me into learning how to crochet, of all things."

"Weren't they teaching you to knit?"

"I couldn't get knitting at all, but before I knew it, that woman named Edna had me crocheting." He pulled out his practice piece to show Eileen.

"Not bad," Eileen said. "You seem to be getting the hang of it. Are you enjoying it?"

Sam felt his face redden. "I know it's not really a guy thing, but I am enjoying it. I'll just look in on Dorothy and then head downstairs."

Sam positioned himself next to the doorway of the dayroom. He saw Nan and her daughter sitting and knitting at a table with a smiling, white-haired woman. As he watched, Dorothy drifted over to their table and stood watching. A man with a full head of graying hair and a thick mustache followed close behind her. A little too close, in Sam's opinion. His heart pounded, and he opened his mouth to tell the guy to back off. Then he clamped his lips shut, realizing the scene it would cause. All he could do was stand there, keeping vigil over Dorothy until she drifted away from the knitters and turned toward the door of the dayroom. The man came after her, and she spoke to him. He caught the word "nap" and was relieved when the man didn't follow. Then Sam crossed swiftly to the elevator and kept his back turned, hoping she wouldn't realize the Fat Man was only a few feet away. He let out a sigh of relief as she passed him without incident.

"Whew, that was a close one," he said to Eileen. "The guy in the dayroom, the one with the mustache . . ."

"Mr. Montoya. Rafe." Eileen supplied the man's name. "What about him?"

"Is he bothering Dorothy? Every time I've come to visit lately, he's been hanging around her."

"He does seem to enjoy her company," Eileen said. "But it doesn't seem to bother her."

"If he was bothering her, the staff would do something about it, wouldn't they?"

"Of course," Eileen said. "We would find a way to distract or redirect him if he was upsetting her."

Somehow, Sam did not feel reassured by this. As he turned back toward the elevator, he found himself wishing Rafe's interest did bother Dorothy.

In the lobby, the Woolgatherers hailed Sam like a long-lost brother. Once he was seated, he pulled out his hook and practice piece. Edna took it and examined it closely.

"Not bad, not bad," she muttered. "Now it's time to learn half double crochet."

This turned out to be a bit trickier than single crochet. He had to remember to yarn over before he stuck the hook in the stitch and then to maneuver the hook through three loops instead of two at the end. Even so, he found it absorbing to form the stitches and satisfying to watch the piece grow row after row.

"You're really getting the hang of that," Tara said. "Do you like it?"

"I didn't think I would," Sam said. "But I do."

"So, you'll be back?" Rose asked.

Sam nodded absently as he worked another stitch.

"Yes, he will," Edna said in a tone that brooked no argument.

Sam smiled to himself. Edna sure got bossy over crochet, but he was enjoying himself too much to mind. And Dorothy had sure seemed interested in the knitting that was going on upstairs. Maybe someday he'd sit down in the dayroom with his crochet and she'd come over to watch what he was doing and . . .

"Ta-da! It's done." Across the circle, Jenny stood and draped the shawl around her, throwing one end dramatically over her shoulder amid oohs, aahs, and applause.

"It's gorgeous," Laura said.

"Just like you, Jenny," Alistair added.

Sam groaned inwardly. That Peabody never seemed to pass up a chance to flirt.

Rose pulled a tag out of her tote and attached it to the end of the shawl. Tara leaned over and read out loud, "This shawl was made for you with love and prayer by the Woolgatherers." She turned it over and read the other side. "You are not alone."

"I finished one last night, too." Edna pulled a long, fluffy shawl out of her bag.

"I'll take them to church tomorrow to get prayed over," Rose said.

"But didn't you already pray over them?" Sam said, confused. "That shawl-maker's prayer, I mean."

"You'd think that was enough, wouldn't you?" Edna said. "But no, they take them to Rose's church, too."

"*I* really enjoyed going to church with you the last time, Rose," Laura said, with a quelling glance at Edna. "It's probably too late to arrange for Gus to take us again."

"Ask for what you want or be content with what you get." Jenny pulled out her phone and tapped a few keys.

"She's got Gus's phone number?" Susan said incredulously to Rose.

"Of course I do." Jenny winked. "Oh, Gus, there you are. This is Jenny. Could you find it in your heart to give some of us a ride to church tomorrow morning?" She tilted her head and gazed at her scarlet fingernails as she listened to the answer. "Oh, thank you, Gus. You are so sweet. See you tomorrow morning."

Jenny tucked her phone into her knitting bag, giving it a little pat of satisfaction. "Gus said he'd be delighted to take us, and he'll take care of the paperwork. It will be lovely to see that nice Clive Stanhope again."

Alistair sat a little straighter in his chair. "Clive Stanhope?"

Sam suppressed a snort. The man was so obvious.

"Oh, yes." Jenny nodded. "I met him at the bishop's luncheon."

Alistair turned to Rose. "What time do we leave for church again?"

"You're more than welcome to come, too," Rose said to Sam.

"Maybe not this time." Learning to crochet was one thing, but going to church was quite another.

The knowing smile with which Rose received this answer gave Sam the uneasy feeling that someday, somehow, he would be going to church.

CHAPTER 16

THE FOLLOWING MORNING, A CONTINGENT of Woolgatherers assembled in the lobby to await the arrival of Gus and the Fair Meadows van. Mr. Peabody was the last to arrive, a snappy bow tie showing between the lapels of his black wool overcoat. He had his "Meat and Potatoes" shawl draped over his arm.

"Good morning, ladies." He lifted one hand from his walker to tip his fedora. He passed the shawl to Rose. "I stayed up late to finish it last night. Didn't want to arrive empty-handed."

"You look quite dashing, Alistair," Jenny said, admiration in her voice.

"Why, thank you, ma'am." He gave a little bow. "And all of you ladies look lovely this morning." A titter of pleasure ran through the group.

Rose wondered what the widows of Hope of Glory would make of this charming man. If she knew the widows, they would make much of him, and Mr. Peabody would enjoy the coffee hour at Hope of Glory very much indeed.

The van pulled in under the porte cochere.

"All aboard!" Gus called out as he came around to open the sliding van door. "This van is bound for glory—Hope of Glory, that is."

"The invitation to come in with us is still open," Rose said as Gus helped her alight from the van a little while later.

"I really do appreciate it," Gus said. "But I have to study." He turned and ran ahead to make sure Mr. Peabody made it up the church steps.

"Such a nice young man," Laura said to Rose as Gus guided Mr. Peabody to the top of the steps with both his body and dignity intact. "He's going to be a wonderful doctor."

"Indeed he is," Jenny said. "He's just perfect for my great-niece Lacy. I plan on introducing them the next time she comes to visit me. She really needs a boyfriend who treats her well. Her last few have been, well, less than satisfactory. She really needs to let me pick for her."

"Will she mind your matchmaking?" Laura asked with a chuckle.

"She doesn't know yet." Jenny gave a conspiratorial wink. "But once she meets Gus, she'll be glad for it, I think. Besides, everyone needs love."

"More shawls already, ladies?" In the foyer, Howard relieved Rose of the bag of shawls.

"And gentleman," Rose said, and introduced Mr. Peabody.

"I made that one," Mr. Peabody told Howard, indicating the shawl at the top of the bag.

"Really?" Howard took a closer look at the shawl. "Fran's been hinting about me learning to knit. I might be able to do something like this."

"One of the perks is spending time with lovely ladies," Mr. Peabody told him.

Howard gave Mr. Peabody a conspiratorial wink. "Indeed." He ushered them into the nave.

As she settled into a pew with her knitting friends, Rose reflected on Jenny's words about everyone needing love. For Jenny, that seemed to mean attention, and lots of it. She thrived on it. At that very moment, the flamboyant redhead was fielding admiring glances and flashing her dimples.

Rose watched as Howard spread the prayer shawls they'd brought along the altar rail. There were three of them: Jenny's vibrant emerald-green creation, Mr. Peabody's "Meat and Potatoes" shawl, and the one Edna had contributed. What a pity Edna wasn't here to enjoy this. *There* was someone, in Rose's opinion, who needed love. Not a romance, but the love of friends, of people who cared for and valued her. Since her visit to Edna's apartment, Rose had been gaining a new and deeper understanding of the crotchety crocheter. At first she had marveled at Edna's patience as she taught Sam to crochet, but now she knew what had made Edna such a good teacher was being a mother to Penny.

Beside her, Jenny craned her neck to look around. *Probably scoping out eligible bachelors*, Rose thought with an inward chuckle.

When Jenny spoke, however, it was not to comment on any of the parishioners.

"This church is beautiful, Rose. The colors in those windows. So rich, especially with the sun shining through them."

"The ones in the Prayer Chapel are even more beautiful. I can show you after church if you'd like," Rose said.

"Yes, I'd—" Jenny began, but fell silent when a burst of organ music signaled the start of the service.

At the end of the announcements, Father Pete drew the congregation's attention to the shawls the Woolgatherers had brought.

"Rose and her friends from Fair Meadows have brought some shawls today for us to pray over. These will be given to those who have the challenging job of caring for people with dementia." Father Pete walked along behind the altar rail, laying his hand on each one. Then he stepped to the center, knelt, and spread his arms to encompass the shawls as well as the congregation. "Let's pray."

Rose bowed her head along with her fellow parishioners.

"Thank you for these beautiful shawls and the caring hearts that made them," Father Pete prayed. "May these shawls shelter and comfort the caregivers who receive them, giving them courage and kindness to care well for those who depend on them."

Later, as the final organ notes of the recessional hymn died away at the end of the service, Jenny turned to Rose.

"Can we go to the Prayer Chapel now?"

"Follow me," Rose said.

The rest of the Woolgatherers turned toward the parish hall and the spread of treats, so only Rose and Jenny stepped into the tranquility of the chapel moments later. Sunlight streamed through the stained-glass windows, pooling in vibrant colors on the floor. Jenny stopped in the middle of the center aisle and turned slowly, taking it all in.

"You left *this* to knit at the mall?" she asked Rose, as if she couldn't believe it.

"Yes," Rose said. "We had to find another place to knit."

"Now I understand why some of you didn't want to leave here. I thought it was just some musty old room in a musty old church. I didn't know it was like this. I can't believe the Heavenly Hugs decided to keep knitting at the mall."

"It's become much more about the people than the place," Rose said.

Jenny wrapped her arms around herself. "But this place. It makes me feel so . . . so . . ."

Rose waited for Jenny to find the words.

"So *loved*," she finally said. "It would be wonderful to simply sit here and knit while gazing at those gorgeous windows."

"Hey, there you are."

Rose turned. Clive Stanhope peered around the edge of the chapel door.

Jenny started and turned away from the windows to favor Clive with a warm smile.

"C'mon. I saved you some streusel cake." He held out a paper plate.

"Uh-oh," Rose said. "You'd better take that cake back to the parish hall pronto, before Margaret catches you strewing crumbs from one end of the nave to the other."

"Huh?" Clive glanced at the crumbly cake.

"This is just so sweet." Jenny took the plate. "Let's get a cup of coffee to go with it, shall we?"

Rose watched Jenny glide smoothly down the aisle in her three-inch heels, her hand tucked in the crook of Clive's elbow, chatting away and not dropping a single crumb.

Rose didn't follow right away. Instead, she sat down in one of the pews and gazed at the windows. As she mulled over Jenny's emotional response to the chapel, she felt a delighted grin spread across her face.

"Whatever you're up to," she prayed, "I'm in!"

When Rose arrived in the parish hall, the first thing she noticed was the table where the Woolgatherers sat enjoying coffee, refreshments, and the attention of a number of parishioners. Jenny held court at one end of the table while at the other end several ladies plied Mr. Peabody with baked goods.

Over by the coffee urn, Rose saw Father Pete surveying the scene with satisfaction. She made her way over to him.

"Way to go, Rose. Your friends are quite a hit!"

"I hope church will be a hit with them," Rose said. "I'd love more folks from Fair Meadows to come here on Sundays."

"That would be wonderful," Father Pete said. "Your friend Jenny seems quite taken with the Prayer Chapel. She's asked if she can knit there sometimes during the week. I told her she's welcome to do so any time the church is open."

After chatting with her pastor for a few more minutes, Rose joined her fellow members of the Heavenly Hugs, who were seated at a table with coffee. Fran bubbled over with excitement about her upcoming move.

"We start moving things over to my new place this week."

"Moving is a lot of work," Margaret said.

"Oh, I have lots of help," Fran told her. "Eddy and Howie, of course, plus Jane, her husband David, and her girls—they'll all help with the boxes. I've hired movers to bring the big things on Saturday. I can hardly wait!"

All too soon, Gus strode into the parish hall in search of his charges.

"Sorry to break up the party," he said to the group. "I have to return the van by one."

They gathered and donned their coats (there was a bit of jockeying for who would help Jenny into hers) and said their goodbyes to the members of the Heavenly Hugs.

"I'll be by soon to knit in the Prayer Chapel. I'm sure my daughter can drop me off when she's running errands," Jenny told Father Pete when he came over to see them off.

"You're going to knit in the chapel?" Margaret's eyebrows drew together.

Jenny nodded. "It's such a beautiful and peaceful place."

"It *is* beautiful." Margaret gave Jenny an appraising glance. "But I wouldn't count on it always being peaceful."

CHAPTER 17

ON THURSDAY MORNING, SAM GRABBED his old briefcase as he got ready to go to Fair Meadows. There were any number of tote bags to choose from in Dorothy's craft room, but they all had flowers or cute sayings. He knew he'd feel silly and self-conscious carrying any of them. The briefcase, so vital to his working life, had sat on the floor of the closet since his retirement. The handle felt good as he picked it up. Sam carried it to the kitchen, where he set it on the counter and flicked open the catches with his thumbs. That felt good, too.

It was empty inside, cleared of all the papers, pens, and pencils he used to carry from work to home and back again. Sam retrieved his crochet from the living room. The skein of yarn fit inside, and the pockets that had once held writing implements turned out to be a good place to put the hook.

Sam caught a glimpse of himself in the hall mirror on his way out the door.

"Nope, nope, nope," he muttered as he took in the sweatpants, sweatshirt, sneakers—and briefcase.

He set the briefcase by the front door, where he used to place it every night before going to bed. Then he headed for his closet. He changed into slacks and a button-down shirt. He dusted off his wing tips and unearthed a pair of black socks from the drawer. He dithered over wearing a tie. It would cover some of where the shirt gapped across his middle, but one of the great things about being retired was not having to wear one anymore. In front of the mirror, he held first one tie and then another up to his neck and finally decided to leave the shirt open at the collar. He reached for his comb to give his hair a once-over and noted he could use a trim. Maybe he'd stop at the barber shop on the way home. How long had it been since he'd talked basketball while Leo snipped away? He couldn't remember.

In the front hall once again, Sam stood in front of the hall mirror holding the briefcase. *Yes, that's better.* He threw his shoulders back. *Much better.*

Sam felt almost jaunty as he swung his briefcase out of the trunk of his car in the parking lot at Fair Meadows. The brown leather case was considerably lighter than when it was filled with papers from work, but it still felt good to be carrying it. He felt like he was going somewhere important.

"Good morning, Sam." A chorus of greeting rose from the Wool-gatherers as he strode through the lobby doors.

"I'll be back in a little while. Just have to check on Dorothy."

Moments later, Sam stepped out of the elevator and crossed the reception area to the nurses' station. "Good morning, Patsy."

"Hello, Mr. Talbot. You're looking spiffy this morning."

"Had to do the briefcase justice," Sam said with a grin. He set the case on the counter for Patsy to admire.

"My, you're ready to do business." Patsy smiled at him.

"Actually, it's got my crochet supplies in it." He dropped his voice to a mock whisper. "I couldn't find anything in Dorothy's craft room I'd want to carry around."

"I can understand that," Patsy said.

"So, how's my best girl this morning? Does she have everything she needs?" Sam asked.

"Yes, but there's something we need to talk about, Mr. Talbot."

"I'll just peek in on her, then we can talk." Sam turned toward the doorway to the dayroom.

"Really, Mr. Talbot, we should talk before you do that," Patsy said. Sam waved her off and peered around the edge of the doorway.

There was Nan, sitting on the couch and getting out her knitting. Beside her, a plump, white-haired woman sat with her hands on top of the knitting project in her lap. He watched as Nan put her own knitting down and tried to hand the needles to the woman, but the woman made no move to take them and knit.

"It's okay, Mom," Sam heard Nan say. "We can just sit together, and I'll knit. Is that all right with you?"

The woman stared blankly at Nan and shrugged again. Nan's bottom lip trembled as she took up her own knitting.

"Mr. Talbot." He heard Patsy at his elbow. "I really need to tell—"

Sam didn't hear the rest. He'd been searching the room for Dorothy, and he'd finally spotted her at a table in the farthest corner of the room. She wasn't by herself. That man, the one who'd been hanging around her, the one with the thick hair and huge mustache, was sitting next to her. The man said something that made her laugh. Sam could hear her delight from where he stood by the door. Then the man reached for Dorothy's hand and raised it to his lips.

Sam tensed, waiting for her to snatch her hand away, maybe even deliver a well-deserved slap.

"Mr. Talbot, come away." Patsy laid her hand on his arm. "We need to talk."

"No, *we* need to talk!" Sam shook off Patsy's hand and stepped into the doorway and pointed at the man who was still holding his wife's hand.

Conversation died away as everyone in the room turned to look at Sam.

Dorothy shrieked, "Oh, no! Oh, Rafe, it's the Fat Man."

"Don't be afraid, Dot. I'm here." The man put his arm around her.

"Her name is Dorothy," Sam said as he strode into the room. "And I'm not the Fat Man. I'm her husband!"

Dorothy cowered and buried her face in Rafe's shoulder. "No, no! Get away."

Rafe stood and put himself between Sam and the sobbing Dorothy.

He raised his chin and his fists. Sam clenched his fists as well. That thrust-out chin practically begged for an uppercut.

"Mr. Talbot, please." Patsy had followed him into the dayroom and now gripped Sam's arm. He tried to shake her off but found the nurse to be surprisingly strong.

"Let go. Let me at him!"

Patsy, however, hung on. "Don't make me have to call an aide," she growled.

"But—my *wife*. My wife—she's married. To *me*." Through the haze of shock and anger, however, Sam could see the terror in Dorothy's eyes. Not because of this Rafe person, but because of him. With one last blistering glare at Rafe, he turned and let Patsy steer him out of the room.

Patsy quickly arranged for another nurse to cover the nurses' station. Then she led Sam to the break room, grabbing his briefcase on the way. While Sam paced in fury, she fixed him a cup of tea.

"Chamomile, with sugar," she said. "Good for nerves and shock."

"What the—what in the world is going on here?" Sam waved the tea away. "Eileen told me the staff would let me know if that guy was bothering her. How could you let something like this happen? She happens to be married."

"I'm so sorry, Mr. Talbot," Patsy said. "I tried to catch you at home this morning, but you'd already left. Please, have some tea."

"You shouldn't have let this happen." Sam gripped the mug handle. "You're supposed to be taking care of her."

"And we are," Patsy said.

Sam snorted.

Patsy gave him such a look of patient kindness that Sam had to fight the urge to pitch the mug across the room.

"Sam, you know your wife is married. I know your wife is married. But she doesn't. In her mind, she's perfectly free to accept the attentions of a man she likes."

"But—but—you were supposed to do something about it if he was bothering her," Sam said.

"He's not bothering her," Patsy said. "She seems to be enjoying spending time with him."

"Well, he's sure bothering me," Sam said through gritted teeth. "Don't I get any say in the matter?"

"I'm sorry, Mr. Talbot." Patsy's brown eyes were warm with sympathy. "This happens sometimes. Tomorrow things may be totally different, if it's any comfort to you."

"It's not. It should never have happened in the first place. This is all your fault, and I expect you to put a stop to it. You keep that guy away from my wife."

Patsy looked Sam squarely in the eye.

"I am not the enemy here, Mr. Talbot. And neither is Rafe. It's the disease."

Sam clenched his fist and fought the urge to smash his mug against the wall, tea and all, since he couldn't deck either the nurse or this nebulous, all-consuming entity called Alzheimer's.

"So, I just have to stand here and take it?" he said. "Just let it do whatever it wants?"

"Mr. Talbot, it's easy to feel alone in the fight, but you're not. There are support groups for family members that really help."

"Bunch of strangers," Sam muttered.

"Who will quickly become friends, because you're all in the same boat on the same stormy sea," Patsy said.

"I don't want to sit around and talk about this. It won't help. Nothing can help. Dorothy's gone, and she's not coming back. And neither am I." Sam slammed his mug on the table, heedless of the sloshing tea, grabbed his briefcase, and stalked out of the break room. When he arrived at the elevator, he kept his back to the dayroom as he jabbed the down button. He clenched his jaw as he waited, focusing all his energy on controlling the trembling of his chin. He heard Patsy's brisk steps behind him. Grateful for the small mercy of the elevator's swift arrival, Sam stepped in and pushed the button to close the doors before the nurse could catch up with him.

All he wanted was to get out of this place and never come back. It had been hard enough when she was afraid of him, when he had to check on her from around the edge of a doorway, like some sort of spy or stalker. A man's gotta do what a man's gotta do, he'd told himself. He certainly didn't want to be the cause of that look of abject terror on his wife's face.

And now . . .

The elevator doors slid open at the lobby level, giving Sam a view of the Woolgatherers sitting in their companionable circle. Jenny waved at him.

"There you are, Sam. We've been waiting for you."

Sam gripped the handle of his briefcase, took a deep breath, and stepped into the lobby. He considered pouring out his anger and frustration to the Woolgatherers. There would be listening ears, sympathy, and . . . pity. They would feel sorry for him rather than feel righteous indignation at this Rafe person and the staff who had turned a blind eye to Dorothy getting involved with him. No, at this moment, he didn't want to hear anyone say, "You poor man." They might even try to comfort him with the same things Patsy had said—"These things happen" and "It's just the disease."

No, Sam decided. He would take his anger home with him and pick up a double cheeseburger and large order of fries on the way. He set his jaw and stared straight ahead as he strode past the Woolgatherers, turning a deaf ear to Jenny calling after him. He was unglued enough as it was. Who knew what would happen if he looked at them, or worse yet, tried to talk about what had happened?

CHAPTER 18

ROSE FELT A RISING CONCERN as Sam strode through the lobby and out the door. His jaw was set and his back stiff. He didn't even turn his head when Jenny called to him.

"What was that all about?" Jenny said. "I know he heard me."

"Everybody heard you," Edna said, her own face set in a concerned frown as she pushed her hook into the next stitch. "He looked like thunder."

"He had a briefcase," Susan said. "Maybe paperwork about Dorothy's stay here?"

"Whatever is going on, he could probably use our prayers," Rose said. They could speculate all they wanted, but God would know what Sam needed.

"What exactly should we say? Are there special words or something, like our shawl-maker's prayer?" Jenny asked.

"We don't even know what to ask for." Laura gave a helpless shrug. "We don't know what's happened."

"Simply ask God to help him," Rose said. "We don't need to know what's wrong to do that."

Silence enveloped the group as they resumed their work and prayed for Sam.

A few minutes later, Rose glanced up to find Nan standing at the edge of their circle of chairs.

"Doing business, I see," Nan said.

"Huh?" Jenny said.

"Praying," Nan said. "You're all so intent."

"We have been praying," Rose said. "Sam walked right past us and left instead of joining us to crochet after checking on his wife. He seemed quite distressed, so . . ."

"I'll say," Nan said. "You all know his wife's been afraid of him for the past few weeks, right?"

They all nodded.

"Well, she's not at all afraid of one of her fellow Memory Care patients. A very handsome one."

Edna looked up sharply. "Who? Which one?"

"A man named Rafe," Nan said. "I've seen him hanging around her when I'm with Mom. He seems to be attracted to her."

Edna turned her attention to her crochet.

"Uh-oh," Laura said.

"Yeah, uh-oh is right," Nan said. "When Sam visits, he checks in at the nurses' station and then kind of peeks around the door just to catch a glimpse of his wife, even though he can't sit or talk with her. Today, he saw Rafe kiss Dorothy's hand."

Susan gasped. "Oh, no!"

"Sam came storming into the dayroom loaded for bear. Dorothy screamed about the Fat Man and hid behind Rafe. Rafe put up his fists to protect her. Sam would have punched him if the charge nurse hadn't grabbed his arm. Do not ever mess with Patsy. She's a lot stronger than she looks."

"Then what happened?" Jenny leaned forward as though enthralled by the drama of it all.

"Patsy hauled Sam off to the break room. I could hear him yelling, but you couldn't tell what he was saying. A few minutes later, he left. He didn't look like he'd calmed down much."

"Men have come to blows over me a time or two," Jenny said, preening a bit. "It's very exciting."

"Maybe for you." Susan frowned. "But I'll bet Sam would be happy to live without that kind of excitement."

"Poor man." Laura shook her head. "I wish there was something we could do."

"We have been doing something," Rose said. "We've been praying."

"It all seems pretty hopeless to me," Susan said.

"You can say that again," Edna said, giving her next stitch an emphatic jab.

"I wouldn't despair just yet," Rose said. "You never know what Alzheimer's is going to do next."

"I can attest to that." Nan heaved a discouraged sigh. "My mom and I have been knitting together for weeks, but today it was like she'd never touched a pair of knitting needles in her entire life. She didn't know knitting, and she sure didn't know me."

A murmur of sympathy rippled around the circle.

"I thought I was holding it lightly, just treasuring each day." Nan's voice trembled with emotion. "But I guess I was enjoying it so much I got lulled into taking it for granted, expecting her to be my knitting buddy, even if she couldn't remember I'm her daughter. I don't know when I'm going to learn to take it one day at a time, to simply take her as she is, and cherish that."

"That Old-Timer's Disease is a mean one, that's for sure," Edna said. "It don't care how no one else feels. Just does what it wants." She examined her work. With an impatient huff, she set to work ripping out her stitches.

"Mistake?" Rose asked.

"Three rows back." She tugged at the yarn with angry energy.

"Easy enough to fix," Jenny said.

Jenny flinched at the disgusted glare Edna shot across the circle.

"*Some* things are," she muttered and went back to pulling out her work.

"Sometimes I catch myself wishing dementia was like a knitting mistake," Nan said. "Something I could unravel, fix, and knit back up again, good as new."

Rose reached over and gave Nan's hand a squeeze. "Do you have time to sit and knit with us for a while?"

Nan nodded. She pulled her work out of her tote, then sat holding her shawl in progress in her lap and staring off into space. Finally, she said, "I guess I'll have to prepare Tara and Samantha for Grandma Becca possibly not knitting with them on Saturday."

"They'll be all right about it," Laura said. "I can see Samantha just knitting and chatting away anyway. And if it bothers Tara, she can come and vent to us."

"Thank you." Nan resumed knitting. "That's such a relief. I don't know how anyone manages the Alzheimer's ordeal on their own. Your support means more than you will ever know."

Halfway through his double cheeseburger, Sam had a thought that turned his stomach. He took another bite to try to make it go away, but the train of thought persisted.

Dorothy was an adult. This Rafe person was an adult. Adults who liked each other, in the way Dorothy and Rafe seemed to like each other, often did a whole lot more than laugh at each other's jokes and give and accept kisses on the hand. Did the laissez-fair attitude the memory care unit had about romance between the patients extend to visits to each other's rooms? At night?

To Dorothy in her right mind, all of this would be unthinkable. While he might not have been the most ardent of worshippers, she had been devout. She was faithful and true, not only to God, but to him. Of that, he was sure. She would've been appalled at what had happened that morning. In a strange way, he was glad she didn't know. He was glad she was spared that pain, even though it hurt him to the core. But that he had to even be thinking about this—that his wife could lose herself so completely, that this could happen . . .

Sam set his burger on the coffee table, the greasy goodness turning to ash in his mouth. The Dorothy he had courted and won had not allowed any of what she'd called "hanky-panky" before their wedding night. She'd been adamant about making those lifelong promises first. She didn't have to insist all that strenuously, though. He was of the same mind about it. His heart lurched, and he closed his mind against the memories of their honeymoon.

She was, however, no longer the Dorothy he had courted, for whom he'd waited, with whom he'd enjoyed a loving honeymoon. Who knew what this Alzheimer's Dorothy would do? If she couldn't remember she was married, would she remember her rules about hanky-panky? He'd read somewhere that sometimes people with dementia had lowered inhibitions. What if—?

He took a savage bite of the hamburger and chewed with fierce resentment. What could he do about this? He'd tried talking to Patsy, but she acted like he didn't have any rights at all in the situation. Dorothy was his wife, *his* wife, for crying out loud. She wouldn't even be at Fair Meadows if it weren't for him. He'd worked hard all his adult life to provide for her and the boys. He'd put a nice roof over her head, and when she wasn't safe there anymore because of the disease, he'd found another nice place for her to live where she *would* be safe.

Only she wasn't safe. She was in danger of being seduced by a charming man with an impressive mustache. And nobody cared. Nobody but him. He stared at the blank television screen across the room and reached for the remote. Soon the room was flooded with someone else's problems, problems that would be solved in the space of an hour, give or take a few commercials. Sam munched on his warm, salty fries and relaxed. It was a relief to forget, for a while at least, the woman who had forgotten him.

Sam started at the insistent sound of his cell phone's ringtone.

"Huh? What?" He wiped his hand over his face to try to wake up. He located the phone on the end table beside his recliner and peered at the screen. It was his son Josh, and it was—what time? Eight o'clock? Had he been asleep all afternoon and into the evening? A further squint at the phone informed him it was eight o'clock in the morning. Friday morning.

"Josh." He forced the sleepiness out of his voice. "How are you, son?"

"I'm great. Dad, you'll never guess what happened."

"What is it?"

"I'm top salesman at the company, the top."

"I could have guessed that," Sam said. "You're good at what you do. A chip off the old block, if I do say so myself."

"Bet you can't guess what I get for being number one, though." Sam could picture his son's triumphant grin.

"That's easy, too," he said. "A big, fat bonus."

"Well, that, too. But I also get a Caribbean cruise. There's room for you, and we want you to come along."

"When?" Sam asked, but already knew how he would answer.

"Dad, I know it's short notice, but it's next week. They're giving me the time off at work, we're taking the kids out of school, and we're going where it's warm, warm, warm."

"Next week? That really *is* short notice. Unfortunately, I can't go. Not with things the way they are with your mother." The reply was automatic. This was what he said every time Josh or Jack tried to pry him away from his duty to Dorothy.

"Dad, she's in a really great facility. You're paying them to take care of her. She'll be fine while you're gone. You deserve to enjoy yourself."

All at once, the situation at Fair Meadows came flooding back—Dorothy, Rafe, Patsy.

"No!" His sharp tone surprised even him. "I especially can't go now. There's a, a . . . situation with your mother I need to keep an eye on."

"Oh?" Josh said. "What's going on? Is she sick?"

Sam was tempted to say, "If only," but resisted the urge to give a reply that would shock and distress his son. The situation was distressing enough.

"No, she's healthy, except for the dementia."

"Then what is it, Dad? What is it that the facility can't handle while you're gone?"

Sam felt the anger rising again. "It's not that they can't handle it. It's that they won't."

"Dad, you'd better tell me what's going on." Josh's voice was serious, concerned.

Sam outlined it as briefly as he could, but it was hard to tell Josh his mother had forgotten even her wedding vows.

"I'm sorry." Josh sounded sad rather than shocked. "This whole thing has really been hard on you. But this is all the more reason to get away. Forget about it all for a while. Get a change of scenery. Enjoy your grandkids. C'mon, Dad. Come with us."

"No," Sam said. "I can't just forget about it the way you do and just go have a good time. I can't go while that guy is sniffing around your mother."

"I don't forget about her," Josh shot back. "I miss her. I miss who she was. I miss her face lighting up at the sight of me, the smile in her voice when I'd call her on the phone. But I can't do anything about it, so I'm going to take this trip and enjoy my own wife and kids while I can. I'd like to enjoy my dad, too."

"I can't just sit by and let it happen," Sam repeated.

"Even though you can't do anything about it?" Sam heard the frustration in his son's voice. "I really wish you'd reconsider, Dad. I think it would be good for you."

Sam felt his hackles rise. "Oh, you do, do you? *I* don't have dementia yet. I still know what's best for me—and your mother."

"Be that way, then," Josh snapped. "Far be it from me to try and help. I'm just your son."

"You could help by coming to visit," Sam said. "You could pay attention to your mother."

"You know it's hard for me to get away, between work and the family. Besides, I just invited you to spend time with us—free of charge, no less."

"And that works great for you, because then you don't have to be around your mother," Sam said.

"As I've said a million times before, what's the point? She doesn't know who I am." Josh's voice was sharp with exasperation.

"The point is," Sam said through gritted teeth, "that you still know she's your mother. It wouldn't kill you to get on a plane and be here every now and then."

"Like I just told you, Dad—oh, never mind. Forget I ever asked."

Sam stared at the phone, realizing his son had hung up on him. The argument was old, repeated in some form or another every few months, but Sam was no nearer to getting his point across. Sure, Josh had time for a Caribbean cruise, but no time at all for his mom and dad. Sure, he'd invited Sam to come along, but he should know by now his parents were a package deal. The united front they'd presented in his adolescence should have more than convinced him there was no Mom without Dad and no Dad without Mom.

Sam pushed himself out of the chair. Time to shower and dress and have breakfast and then . . . what? Sam discovered after his shower that on the agenda after breakfast would have to be laundry, unless he was willing to turn his underwear inside out, as he had been wont to do at summer camp as a boy. The laundry tended to sneak up on him. Hadn't he just done it? Obviously not, since he was nearly out of clean clothes.

He carried the hamper into the laundry room, poured some soap into the washer, and stuffed clothes into the tub. Dorothy had been a stickler for sorting, but Sam put everything in together. As he worked, he considered next steps. He wanted to return to Fair Meadows and deal with the Dorothy situation but decided to wait until Saturday. If he went today, he would be facing off with Patsy again. Maybe things would be different if he appealed to Eileen.

CHAPTER 19

"THERE HE GOES," EDNA SAID on Saturday morning. Sam strode across the lobby like a man on a mission.

"He looks determined," Laura said. "Something about the set of his shoulders."

"I'm not letting him get past us on the way out this time," Jenny said.

Of this, Edna had no doubt. That Jenny was a bold one.

"In the meantime," Rose said, "we need to open in prayer."

"I'll do it," Mr. Peabody said. He pulled out his card, adjusted his glasses, and prayed. "Father God, we ask you to remember all those who have loved ones who do not remember them, especially Nan, Tara, Samantha, and Sam. In the embrace of these shawls, may they be strengthened, encouraged, loved, and known."

"Good morning, Eileen," Sam said as he approached the reception desk. He carefully averted his gaze from the doorway to the day-room.

"Good morning, Mr. Talbot." Eileen's smile was warm and welcoming. Sam liked that she always called him "Mr. Talbot" instead of "Sam." He cleared his throat as he began the speech he'd rehearsed all day Friday and on the way over that morning.

"I have some questions about how some, ah, situations are handled here in the memory care unit."

Eileen looked Sam in the eye. "I think I know the situation you're wondering about. I'll answer as best I can."

"Good." Sam was glad he would not have to tell her about his discovery of the relationship between Rafe and his wife. He'd relived it enough times since Thursday. "I need to know how you deal with, ahem—" He felt his face flush with embarrassment. He went on in a rush. "I need to know if residents are allowed to visit each other in their rooms. At night, I mean."

Eileen nodded. "I understand your concern, Mr. Talbot. The night staff keeps a close eye on residents at night due to the possibility of falls. As I'm sure you're aware, falls can have dire consequences for people at this stage of life. We guide residents who try to wander the halls back to their rooms. We recognize some of our residents have trouble sleeping. They can stay up if they want, but in their own rooms, not the hallways. For safety's sake."

"I'm relieved to hear it."

"If it's any comfort to you, Mr. Talbot, things are holding steady at the hand-holding stage."

Sam gave her a weak smile. "I don't find that terribly comforting."

"I know. I'm really sorry. It's not uncommon, you know. And you never know how long it will last. Dementia wreaks havoc on those relationships, too," Eileen said.

Sam considered this. "So, I should just wait it out? It could change like March weather?"

"It's entirely possible," Eileen said.

"In that case . . ." Sam thought for a moment. The longer he stood at the nurses' station, the harder it was to keep from looking toward the dayroom. His ears were even straining to hear her voice. "No, I can't keep coming here to check on things. It's just too hard. But . . . I don't know what to do."

"You could call instead," Eileen said.

"Kind of hard to ask if my wife still has a boyfriend." Sam's stomach lurched at the idea. "Patsy and I had words over it."

"Call on Saturdays, when I'm here," Eileen said. "I know Mr. Montoya isn't your only concern, but I can update you on that, too, when you call."

"Okay." Sam sighed. "I guess that will have to do for now. This isn't who Dorothy really is, you know. She'd be horrified if she knew what she was doing. Look out for her, will you?"

"I will, Mr. Talbot." Eileen gave Sam a reassuring pat on the arm. "It'll be all right. Just you wait."

"I hope so." But his steps were slow and heavy as he made his way to the elevator.

"There he is," Susan hissed as the elevator doors swept open to reveal Sam.

He looks so discouraged. Rose took in his slumped shoulders and the deep lines on either side of his mouth.

Jenny laid her knitting aside on the couch and stood. She patted her hair and smoothed her just-tight-enough leopard-print tunic sweater over her hips.

"What are you going to do?" Rose asked.

"I'm going to get him to talk to us about what happened on Thursday," Jenny said.

"How?" Susan asked.

"Watch me." With that, Jenny walked toward Sam. *No,* Rose thought as she watched. That was not a walk. That was a sashay.

Jenny intercepted Sam in the middle of the lobby. "Sam, you didn't crochet with us on Thursday. You just walked right by." She favored him with the slightest of pouts. The bright-red lipstick did the rest of the work.

"I, uh . . ." Sam had a deer-in-the-headlights look about him again.

Jenny tucked her fingers around his bicep. Rose thought she saw her give it a slight squeeze.

"Now, come on over here and visit with us." Jenny gave Sam's arm a gentle tug. As if in a daze, Sam "came on over."

Jenny sat on the couch, swept her knitting into her lap, and patted the place beside her.

"Sit right here and tell us all about it."

"All about what?" Sam looked wary but still sat next to Jenny.

Rose leaned forward. "We couldn't help but notice, Sam, that you were a bit upset on your way out on Thursday."

"Yeah," Edna said. "You missed your crochet lesson."

"Anyway"—Rose shot a quelling glance at Edna—"we were wondering, is Dorothy all right?"

"Oh, *she's* just fine," Sam said with a tinge of bitterness.

"But you're not?" Rose asked, her voice soft.

Sam hesitated. "No. No, I'm not," he finally said.

"Do you feel like talking about it?" Rose asked.

"Of course he does," Jenny said. "I always feel better about my troubles after I talk things over with a friend."

"There's nothing I can do about it, so there's no point in talking about it," Sam said.

"Exactly," Edna said. "Leave the man alone."

Rose suppressed the urge to glare at her. Edna might want to keep her troubles to herself, but that didn't mean Sam should do the same.

"Trouble shared is trouble halved, as they say," Mr. Peabody said. "You might feel better if you talk it over with your friends, man."

Sam closed his eyes, and Rose wondered if he was taking a moment to pray. After a moment, he opened them and looked around the group.

"It's Dorothy," he said.

"But you said she's okay," Susan said.

"She is," Sam said. "She's pretty happy, as a matter of fact."

"What is it, then?" Susan said.

"She's happy with somebody else, that's what," Sam blurted out. "There's this guy named Rafe. He's a patient like Dorothy. He's been paying attention to her, and she's not discouraging him. Not at all.

And the staff won't do anything about it, never mind that she's married. To me." This last came out through gritted teeth.

"Oh, Sam, I'm so sorry," Jenny said. "I've heard that happens sometimes."

"And you can't really blame her," Susan said. "She probably doesn't remember she's married."

"There's no one to blame, really," Laura said. "It's the nature of the disease."

Sam slammed his fist on the arm of the couch. "I am so tired of this infernal disease. It gets away with doing whatever it wants."

"Ain't that the truth." Edna sounded every bit as angry as Sam.

"I can understand why the staff won't intervene," Laura said in her understanding teacher voice. "It would be really confusing for Dorothy, and she's confused enough already."

"I guess." Sam shrugged.

"It's still hard to watch, though," Rose said.

"Yeah, I can't go there while this is going on," Sam said. "It's been hard enough not getting to spend time with her since she started being scared of me, but I can't even fathom standing by and watching her with that Rafe guy. At least, without wanting to punch his lights out. And I almost did the other day."

Jenny clasped her hands together. "How romantic."

Rose widened her eyes at Jenny in an I-can't-believe-you-just-said-that stare.

"Yeah," Mr. Peabody said. "Brawling tends to be frowned upon around here."

A smile twitched at the corner of Sam's mouth. His chest puffed out a bit. "I could take him, though. I would have if the charge nurse hadn't stopped me. The weekend charge nurse, Eileen, suggested I call on the weekends to check on Dorothy and the Rafe situation."

"So, you won't be coming to Fair Meadows?" Rose asked.

"No point," Sam shrugged.

"But you could still meet with us," Rose said.

Edna fixed Sam with a piercing stare. "Of course you're going to keep meeting with us. You're learning to crochet. Didn't you bring your work today?"

"Um, no," Sam said.

Edna continued to stare at him.

"Well, actually, it's in the car." He shifted in his chair. "I was so mad about Rafe on Thursday that I forgot to bring it into the house when I got home."

"Go get it and get right back here," Edna said. "You have crocheting to do."

"Well, I don't think—"

"That's right," Edna said. "Don't think. Just get your crochet stuff."

"Okay, okay." Sam raised his hands in mock surrender.

Edna leveled her crochet hook at him. "And don't you even think about getting in your car and taking off for home. Now, get going."

Sam hurried through the lobby doors.

"Whatever happened to 'Leave him alone'?" Susan asked Edna.

"This is different," Edna said. "This is crochet we're talking about."

Moments later, Sam returned with his briefcase.

"Snazzy," Mr. Peabody said as Sam flipped open the latches of the case to reveal his neatly stowed hook and yarn.

"Yeah, yeah," Edna said. "Show me your work."

Bracing himself, Sam handed it over for her scrutiny.

"Not bad. Not bad. There's hope for you," she said, turning the swatch this way and that and finally handing it back.

Sam basked in her approval, only to be brought up short by a sharp nudge of Edna's elbow.

"Now look, this here is the double crochet stitch." He leaned over and paid close attention as she demonstrated. Then he picked up his practice piece and followed along while Edna talked him through the stitch. After some initial fumbling, he got the hang of it. As soon as he finished the row, Edna took the piece of crochet from his fingers and examined it closely.

"It'll do," she said, passing the practice piece back to Sam. "Now, chain three, turn, and do three more rows."

"Chain three? First, you had me chain one when I started a new row, then last week it changed to chain two. I'm confused."

"One is for single crochet, and you chain two for half double because it's taller," Edna told him. "Double crochet is even taller, so the turning chain has to be higher, too."

Sam squinted at his work, pointing his finger first at the rows of single crochet, then the rows of half double crochet, and finally, the row of the new stitch.

"Yeah, you're right. Each one gets a little taller." With that he resumed practicing, muttering under his breath, "Yarn over, into the stitch, pull through . . ."

"Do we have shawls that need to be prayed for?" Jenny asked.

Heads shook all around the circle. No one had a finished shawl in the last week, not even Edna.

"I was hoping someone had," Jenny said. "I want to go to church tomorrow."

"Really?" Laura asked.

"It's growing on me," Jenny said with an oh-so-casual shrug.

"Or is it Clive Stanhope?" Susan said with a slight smirk.

"Clive's nice enough." Jenny shrugged. "But I'm starting to really like church."

"We don't have to wait until we have finished shawls to go to church," Rose said. "All of you are welcome any Sunday. Every Sunday, if you want."

"I'd like to go," Laura said.

"Me, too," Susan said.

"Count me in." Alistair raised his hand.

"How about you, Sam?" Rose asked. "Would you like to come to church with us tomorrow?"

Sam looked up from his crocheting, startled. "Me? Uh, no." He saw the disappointment in Rose's face and added, "Maybe some other time."

Edna gave Rose a sharp and emphatic shake of the head and focused on her work.

"We'll need the van," Jenny said as she pulled out her phone. Moments later she informed the group that of course Gus would be happy to come in on what had been a scheduled day off to give them a ride to church.

CHAPTER 20

"Thank you so much for the ride, Gus," Jenny said as he helped her out of the Fair Meadows van. "It being your day off and all."

"My pleasure." The young man smiled. "I planned to study anyway, and I can do that just as well from the coffee shop down the street. Their coffee is better than mine, anyway."

"You'd be more than welcome at church," Rose told him.

"I know. But like I said, I need to study." He gave the Woolgatherers a jaunty wave as he swung into the driver's seat and pulled away from the curb.

"Such a nice boy," Rose said.

"He works too hard," Jenny said. "He needs to get out and have some fun."

"Said the woman who asked him to work on his day off," Rose said.

"Which he was going to spend studying anyway," Jenny said. "We're giving him a much-needed study break. And he'll make some money." She turned and made her way up the steps. The heavy oak door swept open to reveal Clive Stanhope.

"I was hoping you'd be here, Jenny."

Jenny gave him a gracious smile, then hurried through the foyer to the nave, where the service was getting underway. She didn't want to miss anything.

Susan is wrong, she thought as Howard approached the lectern to read the Bible. Clive was nice and all, but he wasn't the reason she wanted to come to church. Which was strange, because usually basking in the attentions of a handsome man like Clive *would* be her main reason for coming. She let her gaze wander around the church as she listened to Father Pete lending depth and meaning to words she'd never really understood before. She'd tried reading the Bible from time to time throughout the years, but "it's Greek to me" had been her usual quip. As he read Psalm 19, she could picture in her mind's eye the great expanse of the night sky filled with stars, then the strong and magnificent sun traveling from one end of the sky to the other. The rest of it, all the verses about the "law of the Lord" and the "fear of the Lord"—that was a bit hazy. And she wasn't too sure about the part that said those things were better than gold. She had a particularly stunning twenty-two-karat gold necklace . . .

After the service, she made a beeline for the side aisle and slipped into the Prayer Chapel. As she stood drinking in the rich colors of the stained-glass windows and the soft glow of polished wood, she wondered again just how the women of the Heavenly Hugs Prayer Shawl Ministry could bear to meet at the mall when they had this gorgeous place. The colors, the light, even the lemony smell of Pledge filled her soul to the very top.

"There you are, hiding in here again." Jenny turned at the sound of Clive's hearty voice. She sighed and then pasted on a smile.

"Not hiding. Enjoying. This place is wonderful."

"I guess." Clive shrugged. "These Tiffany windows are worth a fortune, anyway. C'mon, it's time for coffee."

Jenny followed Clive out of the Prayer Chapel, giving it one more glance over her shoulder as she left. She promised herself she would find a way to return soon to bask in the beauty of the place unhindered and undisturbed.

Ripples of laughter eddied out of the parish hall as Jenny and Clive crossed the foyer. Jenny grinned as she surveyed the scene from the doorway. Alistair, dapper in his bow tie and sweater vest, was regaling the Hope of Glory widows (and a few of the matrons, too) with stories, quips, and compliments. She took a seat at a nearby table while Clive went to get her a cup of coffee.

"I really like your hair." Jenny turned her attention from Alistair and Clive to find Amy standing by the table.

"I like yours, too," Jenny said. "Although I could never pull off that purple."

Amy tilted her head and considered. "Maybe a silvery purple. It looks good on women your, um . . ."

"Age?" Jenny said with a smile.

Amy blushed.

"That does sound like fun. I like to change my hair fairly often. Don't want to get boring. And purple would definitely make people look twice." Jenny grinned. "So, how's that adorable baby of yours?"

"Check it out." Amy pointed across the room to where Bryson stood holding Heaven Leigh. The baby waved her chubby arms and gazed at her father with impossibly blue eyes. Jenny watched as Bryson returned his daughter's adoring gaze.

"She obviously loves her daddy," Jenny said. "How about you? How are things going with you two? I love a good romance, you know."

Amy, suddenly serious, said, "We're taking it slow. At least, I am. Bry wants to get married, like, last week."

"You have a man who loves you and a beautiful baby with him. What's stopping you?" Jenny asked.

Amy's face clouded. "Hasn't Rose told you Bry used to do drugs?" When Jenny nodded, Amy continued. "He's only been clean a few months. I need to know that once the newness of getting back together and being a dad wears off, he's going to face life head-on instead of running off to use when things get hard. When I get married, I mean for it to be for life."

"I've been divorced," Jenny said. "It's not the end of the world. I thought it was at the time, but I found love again." She smiled at Amy and at the memory of Ben, the man who had helped her put her heart back together after the end of her first marriage.

"It was the end of life as I knew it when my parents got divorced," Amy said. "I don't want to do that to Heaven. I want her to be able to count on us to stay together. I don't want her to have to worry about us, the way I did with my parents. I want to be able to count on us staying together, too."

Jenny thought of her daughter Chloe, her only child. She'd been four years old when her father, a handsome ladies' man, had left for greener pastures. He hadn't liked being tied down by a family. Ben, on the other hand, had reveled in being a dad to Chloe.

Clive arrived with her coffee.

"I'll be back in a few minutes," he said. "One of the guys got a new fly rod and I want to hear about it."

Jenny turned to Amy. "I hope it works out for you. I hope you get your happily-ever-after."

Amy gazed across the room at Bryson and Heaven. "Me, too," she said. "For all our sakes. It means a lot to me that the Heavenly Hugs are praying for us."

Jenny's heart warmed to this young mother with startling hair. She surprised herself by saying, "I'll pray, too."

All too soon, Gus appeared in the doorway of the parish hall. "Time to go," he called.

Jenny was uncharacteristically quiet on the way back to Fair Meadows. Praying for caregivers in general was one thing, but telling Amy to her face that she'd pray about her relationship with Bryson was another. She realized she now had a stake in how things turned out for the little family. It mattered whether she prayed for them or not.

"Are you all right, Mrs. Alderman?" Gus said after several blocks. She sat, as usual, in front with him. "You're pretty quiet."

Jenny shook herself out of her reverie and flashed a smile at Gus. "I'm fine," she said. She had a sudden thought and blurted it out. "Gus, is there anything I can pray about for you?"

The way Gus's eyebrows shot up made Jenny wish she hadn't said anything. Who went around just asking to pray for people?

"I'm good, thanks," he said. "Although . . ."

"I knew it," Jenny said. "You really want a girlfriend. Never fear. I have just the girl for you. My niece Lacy. You're going to love her."

"Whoa, whoa, the last thing I need is a girlfriend," Gus said. "I'm studying my brains out. I don't have time for a relationship."

"Of course you need a girlfriend," Jenny said. "You study too much. You need to have some fun once in a while."

"Girlfriends don't want to be 'some fun once in a while,'" Gus said. "And they're absolutely right. No, I'm planning ahead for med school. What I need is to find a roommate, or I won't be able to afford an apartment there."

"If you married Lacy, you'd have a roommate," Jenny said, unwilling to give up on the idea.

Gus took advantage of a stoplight to look askance at Jenny.

"Okay, okay, I'll pray for you to find a roommate for medical school." She raised her hands in surrender.

CHAPTER 21

WHEN SAM WOKE ON MONDAY morning, he stared at the ceiling, trying to orient himself. It was Monday, so he'd need to stop at the florist on the way to Fair Meadows. No, wait. He wouldn't be going to the memory care unit. Couldn't. Mad and hurt as he was, though, he wouldn't let Dorothy wait for her flowers in vain. He decided he'd have them delivered.

He shoved his feet into his slippers, dragged on his bathrobe, and headed to the kitchen. As the coffee maker chugged and wheezed, he called April Showers to arrange for a dozen red carnations to be delivered to Dorothy. The shop owner, April, asked what he'd like on the card.

Sam considered for a moment. Since he'd always delivered them himself, he'd never included a card. The way things stood, he wasn't sure he should include one now. She wouldn't recognize his name. It might confuse or even frighten her.

Finally, he said, "No card."

"No card? Are you sure?" April asked. "Don't you want her to know who they're from?"

Of course I do. Sam's heart ached, but he didn't feel up to explaining the situation. "The important thing is that she gets the flowers, okay? No card."

"All right, if you say so." April sounded dubious.

"Thank you." Sam ended the call.

Over coffee and a Pop-Tart, Sam considered how he would spend the rest of his day. Without his Fair Meadows routine, he had nothing to do until the basketball game was on in the evening. Oh, and it was trash day. When he returned from taking the trash to the curb, Sam passed his briefcase, right where he'd dropped it when he'd come home on Saturday.

He picked it up. It felt good in his hand. It felt so good that once again, he dressed in slacks, button-down shirt, wing tips. A glance in the mirror sent him to the phone to ask if his favorite barber was at the shop that day.

When Sam strode into the lobby at Fair Meadows, a chorus of greetings rose from the circle of chairs and couches occupied by the Woolgatherers.

"Looking sharp there, Sam," Alistair said.

"Yes, indeed," Jenny said.

"It's about time you got here," Edna said. "Today you're learning shell stitch."

"Goodness, Edna, let the man catch his breath before you start barking orders at him," Susan said.

Sam, however, dutifully took his seat next to Edna, balanced his briefcase on his knees, and flipped the catches. Edna reached for his practice piece and gave it a once-over.

"You haven't done a darn thing since Saturday. How do you expect to learn to crochet if you don't practice? Here, do some double crochets, *if* you remember how." She shoved the yarn and hook at him.

"Course I remember," Sam muttered as he closed the briefcase and set it on the floor. He stuck the hook into the next stitch.

"Yarn over first," Edna said, then coached him through the rest of the stitch. "This is why you have to practice. Now, do two more rows of double and then we'll see if you can do shell stitch." It sounded as though she had her doubts.

Sam bent over his work, repeating the steps under his breath. The Woolgatherers' conversations swirled around him.

"I have a couple of things to add to our prayer list," Jenny said.

"We have a prayer list?" Susan sounded confused. "Don't we just pray our shawl-maker's prayer at the beginning of our meeting?"

"We have one now." Jenny pulled a cloth-covered journal out of her knitting bag. "When my daughter gave me this for Christmas, I couldn't for the life of me imagine what I would write in it. But now I'm thinking we can use it to write prayer requests in, like the Heavenly Hugs do." Jenny opened the journal to reveal prayer requests written on the left-hand page. "We'll write the answers on the right-hand side." She passed the journal around. Sam juggled his yarn and hook to hand the book off to Rose.

"Oh, good," Rose said as she read the requests. "Amy and Bryson need all the prayer we can pour on them. Gus needs a roommate for med school? We can certainly pray about that, too. This is a wonderful idea, Jenny."

"We should add Nan and her mom," Laura said. "It can't be easy for Nan not to know from one day to the next what things are going to be like with her mom."

As Jenny copied that concern into the journal, Rose turned to Sam. "Can we put something on the list for you?"

"What?" Sam paused his double crochet practice.

"Is there something we can pray for you?" Rose asked.

Sam shifted uncomfortably in his chair.

"We could pray Dorothy stops being afraid of you," Laura said.

"And tells Rafe to leave her alone," Susan said.

Edna frowned. "That Old-Timer's Disease does what it wants."

"We could simply put Dorothy's and Sam's names on the list," Rose said. "God knows what he wants to do about it. Would that be all right with you, Sam?"

Sam shrugged. "I guess. I don't know too much about this praying business." He passed his double crochet practice to Edna for her inspection.

"It'll do," Edna said after peering, poking, and prodding at Sam's work. "This here's shell stitch. Pay attention." Sam did. It looked hard, but Edna patiently guided him through one shell and then another, all the way across the row.

A little while later, Nan stepped out of the elevator and made her way across the lobby to the prayer shawl group.

"How's your mother?" Rose asked as Nan sat next to her.

"Knitting again, at least for now," Nan said. "This is what I worked on today with her." She pulled out her work in progress, a lacy crescent-shaped shawl in shades of purple.

"It's coming along beautifully." Rose brushed her fingers over the feather-soft shawl. "I love the way the plum shade is at the neck and how it gets lighter and lighter as you go. By the time you get to the pale lavender, it will look like it's floating away."

"It's the hardest pattern I've done so far," Nan said. "When I started, it seemed miraculous that a whole shawl could grow from the few stitches at the beginning of the pattern. It still seems like a miracle. I've been tempted to quit more than once."

"What keeps you from quitting?" Susan asked.

Nan chuckled. "The better question is who keeps me from quitting."

"Who keeps you from quitting, then?" Susan said.

"My mom," Nan said. "Every time I hear myself say, 'This is the hardest thing I've ever done. I can't do this,' I realize it's not true. It's not even close. Caring for my mom through her dementia is the hardest thing I've ever done. Mom puts everything into perspective."

"You're doing well at both." Rose stroked the shawl.

Nan sighed. "I still struggle with having to put her in Memory Care. But it got hard to keep her safe. I had to watch her every second, even at night."

Sam looked up at this. "Especially at night," he said.

"You, too?" Nan asked.

"Me, too," Sam said.

"What happened?" Rose asked, her voice soft.

Sam took a deep breath as if to steel himself. "Understand, she kept me busy all day long. Even before her memory started to go, she always

162

had a honey-do list a mile long. Don't get me wrong, I liked it, especially after I retired. Doing things for her filled my days in the best way. She filled my days."

As the Woolgatherers listened, their hands stilled, and their knitting lay forgotten in their laps. Edna alone kept at her work with her head down.

"I always took my shower at night, when I was sure she was sound asleep. One night she wasn't in bed after my shower. I found the front door wide open. In my robe and slippers, I grabbed my phone and went straight out to find her. I was frantic. It was dark. She could fall and break something, get hit by a car, get picked up by some unscrupulous person. I was about to call the police to activate a Silver Alert when my phone rang. It was one of the neighbors. Dorothy had come visiting—at eleven o'clock at night. Once I got her home, I stayed awake the rest of the night to keep an eye on her."

"I've been there, too," Nan said.

"I installed those latches that go way up on the door the very next day, and it worked for a while," Sam went on. "But one night, I woke to her yelling and pounding on the front door. She was convinced the school had called to tell her our son Josh was sick and needed her to go get him, never mind that Josh is grown with kids of his own and it was the middle of the night. She was beside herself. It took a long time to calm her down. I didn't get any sleep that night, either."

"It's the short nights that get to you," Nan said.

"More like no nights," Sam said. "Nights where you don't get any sleep at all."

"Did you—" Laura started to ask.

"I know what you're going to say." Sam cut the question short. "I did get someone in to be around for the nights, but it didn't help in easing my mind. If I slept at all, it was with one eye and both ears open. Finally, my sons caught wind of the situation. They came and staged what they called an intervention, like I was an addict or something. They said I couldn't go on like this."

"They live too far away to come and help out?" Laura asked.

Sam nodded. "They were right, though. I couldn't keep their mother safe all by myself, and the other options weren't working. They helped me find this place and stayed long enough to get her settled. So, here we are. She doesn't even know who I am anymore. I keep thinking if only I'd kept her at home, she'd still know me."

Rose reached out and squeezed Sam's hand.

"I'm so sorry," she said.

"That's so hard," Laura murmured.

"I'll live," was Sam's gruff reply.

"Enough of this," Edna said. "You got those three rows yet?"

Sam concentrated on his crochet again. Rose thought he seemed relieved not to have to talk anymore.

"So, your mom knitted today?" Rose asked Nan, to divert attention from an obviously uncomfortable Sam.

"Like nothing ever happened."

"I suppose it's something of an adventure, isn't it?" Rose said.

"I've never really thought of it like that," Nan said. "It's not exactly an Indiana Jones movie, but there are twists and turns. It can be scary and sad, but sometimes there are moments so sweet they nearly break my heart."

"How do the girls deal with the unpredictability?" Laura asked.

"Samantha chatters and knits away no matter what's going on with Grandma Becca," Nan said. "I can tell it bothers Tara more. Thank you for inviting her to be a Woolgatherer. Hanging out with all of you helps."

"We're happy to have her," Rose said. "She's making great progress on her prayer shawl."

"She's a natural," Nan said. "Once she learned to purl, she really took off."

"What about Samantha's knitting?" Laura asked.

Nan laughed. "It's wonky as ever, but she doesn't care. She's having fun."

"Not bad, not bad." Edna's voice carried across the circle. She squinted at Sam's crochet, then showed it to the rest of the group. She turned to Sam. "On Thursday, bring four skeins of the same color wor-sted weight yarn and a size K hook. You're gonna start a prayer shawl."

"What? I don't know how to do any of that. What's 'worsted weight?' What's a K hook? And I really don't know about this praying thing." The words came out in a slightly panicked rush.

Edna dug around in her crochet bag and produced a crochet hook. It was thicker than the one Sam had been practicing with, but not nearly as big as the pink one Edna used. She showed him the letter *K* embossed on the handle.

"Just go through your wife's hooks until you find one like this," she said.

"And this is how to figure out yarn weight." Mr. Peabody showed Sam how to read the label on one of his skeins of yarn.

"Here, I wrote it down for you." Laura handed Sam a piece of paper, ever the organized teacher.

"We'll show you how to do the praying thing," Rose said.

"Okay, I guess." Sam put his yarn, hook, and the paper into his briefcase. He stood to take his leave of the group.

"Until Thursday, then." Jenny gave him a smile that deepened her dimples considerably.

Sam sucked in his stomach and stood a little straighter. "Thursday it is."

As Sam turned and made his way out of the lobby, Rose thought she detected just the slightest spring in his step.

Once he returned home, Sam kept crocheting. He didn't drop the briefcase by the door. He carried it into the living room and set it by the recliner. For the next couple of nights, after his microwave dinner, he reached for the remote and clicked around until he found the bas-ketball game. Then he pulled his crochet out of the briefcase and set to work to the squeak of basketball shoes on the court and the blare of buzzers. He made rows and rows of double crochet. Then he made more rows of the half double crochet and single crochet. He was determined not to get caught flat-footed and have to be reminded how to do it at the next Woolgatherers meeting.

Before he settled in front of the television on Wednesday night, he went to Dorothy's craft room to find the hook and yarn Edna had commanded him to bring. The hook was the easy part. In the bag by the rocking chair, Sam found a zippered case. When he opened it, there stood crochet hooks in neat rows, each in its own snug pocket, arranged in alphabetical order. He located the one with the K on it, then decided to take the whole case to show Edna.

Then he turned to the problem of yarn. He reviewed the requirements on the page of notes Laura had given him. Worsted weight, four skeins. Then mentally he added his own requirement. It had to be brown or gray or blue, not pastel or pink in any form. He might be learning to crochet, but he still had his dignity.

When he began his search for the yarn, he discovered Dorothy had been just as organized with the skeins as she'd been with the hooks. All the worsted weight yarn was in one section of what she used to call her "stash." A warm golden brown caught his eye. He was in luck, as there were five skeins of it. She'd probably been planning to make yet another of her afghans. He piled the lot into his arms, balanced the hook case on top, and headed downstairs.

Only three skeins would fit in the briefcase along with his practice yarn, so he set the other two on the place on the couch where Dorothy used to sit and crochet while he watched whatever sport was in season. He took out the size K hook and hefted it. He liked the weight and thickness. He swapped out the smaller hook and did a row of double crochet. This was more like it. The stitches were taller and fatter. He'd be able to whip out a shawl in no time. Once he made a shawl, those Woolgatherers would leave him alone, and he could go back to . . . what, exactly? Sam shrugged off the question and focused on getting stitch after stitch right with the new hook. He'd show Edna. She'd have no complaints tomorrow.

Sam arrived as the Woolgatherers were starting their work, in time for Rose to give him a card with the shawl-maker's prayer on it. He felt self-conscious but bowed his head with the rest of the group while Jenny read the prayer out loud. With a small jolt, he realized he was one of the people the prayer mentioned. Did it matter that God remembered him when Dorothy didn't?

"This here's the pattern I found for you." Edna's raspy voice broke into his thoughts. She held out an open book to him. "You can borrow the book, but I better get it back."

First, he examined the photo of the finished shawl. Okay, he could picture it in the yarn he'd picked out for the project. Then he turned his attention to the directions. In his years as an engineer, he'd read many a schematic. How hard could it be?

Plenty hard, he discovered. The only part he could easily figure out was the supply list. "Ch 75" was next. A glance at the glossary of terms at the beginning of the pattern told him "ch" meant "chain." Seventy-five was a lot, but, okay, he could do it. The rest of the pattern instructions, however, was a jumble of letters with some numbers thrown in, none of which resembled an algebra equation in the slightest. He could have figured out an algebra problem standing on his head with one hand tied behind his back. But this? This jumble of letters and numbers made him want to give up before he even started.

"Show me what you're going to make." Jenny crossed the circle and sat next to him. "Ooh, I like it. What yarn are you going to use?"

Surrounded by Jenny's enthusiasm and the scent of her perfume, Sam chained his seventy-five stitches and was soon single crocheting across to begin to form the border of the shawl.

"Count your stitches," Edna said when he came to the end of the row. As he did, he was relieved to discover he had the required number.

"You're going to do fine," Jenny said as she returned to her chair. Every now and then Sam would notice her smiling encouragement at him. Talk swirled around him as he worked. He only half listened as Rose filled the others in on those people named Bryson and Amy again. She had a great deal to say on the subject, ending with, "So, we need to pray."

Silence descended on the group and Sam realized suddenly that it was because the Woolgatherers were actually praying. Not out loud, thank goodness. As he gazed across the circle, he saw Jenny's lips form the two names. He quickly bowed his head over his work again. Whoever Bryson and Amy were, he wished them all the best, but he wouldn't know the first thing about praying for them.

Before he knew it, the dining room doors opened, and residents began streaming in for lunch.

"Want to join us again? My treat," Alistair said with a wink.

When Sam hesitated, Jenny jumped in, urging him to stay and have lunch with the rest of the Woolgatherers.

"It's squash soup today," Rose said.

"Squash?" Sam grimaced.

"So healthy." Susan beamed.

"It tastes much better than it sounds," Rose said.

With a laugh, Sam accepted the invitation and was soon seated next to Alistair and across from Jenny. He enjoyed the chatter and banter Jenny deftly kept going around the table. He was still chuckling as he walked to his car after lunch. He couldn't remember the last time he'd laughed so much. On his way home, he found himself looking forward to Saturday. He'd been dreading it since he knew he'd be calling Eileen to check on Dorothy. He wanted to know his wife was all right, but he also knew he'd have to hear about Rafe whether he liked it or not. But now, Saturday would also be full of laughter, with some crochet thrown in. The crochet was growing on him, he realized. So was the laughter.

CHAPTER 22

Jenny waved goodbye to her daughter while standing on the curb in front of Hope of Glory Community Church, knitting bag on her shoulder. Chloe had agreed to swing by Fair Meadows on her way to run errands on Friday, drop her mother off at the church, then come by for her when her errands were done. Jenny felt the sun warm on her face, which boded well, not only for the arrival of spring, but for just the right light in the chapel as well.

She stopped in the office before she went to the Prayer Chapel.

"Father Pete said I could come and knit in the chapel," she told Lucille, the church administrator.

"Yes, he mentioned you might come by," Lucille said. "The church stays open until five."

Jenny made her way across the foyer. When she stepped into the nave, she was startled to see that the cross behind the altar was draped in black. And it seemed like something was missing. As she continued to gaze at the front of the church, she realized that the altar was bare, stripped of its cloth and candles. She gave a little shiver as she continued along the side aisle of the nave.

When she pushed open the door of the chapel, she caught her breath. In contrast to the dark emptiness of the nave, it was as if a wave of greeting had wafted out to her, enveloping her in a warm welcome. Was it the light? The colors? The stillness? She stepped deeper into the embrace and barely noticed when the door softly closed behind her.

Jenny walked slowly to the front pew on the left, taking in the beauty of the chapel as she went. The polished pews gave off a soft glow due to the spring sunlight that filtered through the stained-glass windows. A collection of hyacinths was clustered on the table at the front, its scent filling the space. The splotches of color on the floor reminded her of the springtime puddles of her childhood, bright with the reflections of blue sky and clouds. She settled in front of the window with an angel. The woman kneeling in front of the angel must be Mary, she concluded. She vaguely remembered the story about the angel telling Mary she was going to have Jesus.

Jenny reached into her bag and pulled out her knitting and the Woolgatherers' prayer journal. She'd taped their Woolgatherers prayer to the inside of the front cover. She read it out loud, then propped the journal against the arm of the pew before setting to work on her latest prayer shawl. This one was also in bright, vibrant colors, shades of yellow, red, and orange that chased each other across the rows. She watched her fingers form the stitches, over and over, and considered the people on the prayer list.

Amy and Bryson—now that was a cause she could get behind, Jenny thought happily. Ah, romance . . .

"Don't let Bryson mess it up," Jenny prayed. "Help him stay off drugs. Help Amy stay strong about it. Help them be the best people they can be for their beautiful baby."

Jenny's imagination drifted to picture Amy and Bryson getting married at Hope of Glory. She wondered what kind of dress Amy would choose and smiled at the idea of Bryson in a tux, spiked green mohawk and all. She hoped Heaven wouldn't be old enough to be a flower girl before this happened.

There were, however, more names on the list. Jenny mentally shook herself and focused on the next item—Gus. Now there was a young man who needed more than a roommate. From what she could tell so far, this medical school thing was a hard slog, and he hadn't even started yet. He needed someone to cheer him on.

"Gus says he needs someone to share an apartment with," Jenny confided to the air around her. "But it would be better for him to have someone to share life with. Maybe you've got someone in mind? I really do recommend Lacy. She'd be perfect for him."

However, nothing came to mind as Jenny tried to picture Gus and Lacy holding hands and gazing into each other's eyes. In her mind's eye, Gus kept turning his head to study a textbook. She sighed. This might take more prayer than she'd thought.

Next on the list were Nan and her mother. The light dimmed in the chapel as if a cloud had passed in front of the sun outside. Jenny found this one hard to swallow. Nan and her daughters were nice people. What had they done to deserve such sadness? What to pray? It's not like Nan's mom would be healed of dementia. The disease was heartless, raising hopes and then dashing them as more and more memory disappeared. And it was relentless. There was no way to stop it, to keep it from taking everything away.

And yet, Jenny had seen Nan's face when Rose gave her that first caregiver's prayer shawl. The tears, the whispered words, "You don't know what this means to me. Most days she doesn't hug me back." She had to believe that somehow a prayer shawl could make things better for those who loved and cared for people with this heartbreaking disease.

Then there was Sam. The man was such a romantic, it was a shame Dorothy couldn't enjoy it. Flowers every Monday, the little gifts, the faithful visits. What in the world could she pray for that lovelorn, lonely man? Rose said he needed friends. That was why they'd invited him to join the Woolgatherers instead of simply making him a shawl.

"I can't get Dorothy back for him," Jenny said into the dim light. "But I can be a friend."

The door behind her creaked. She turned to find Father Pete framed in the doorway.

"I'm sorry," he said. "I didn't mean to disturb you."

"No, Father. It's all right. I'm just about done." She packed her knitting and the journal away as the pastor came toward her.

"I'm glad the chapel is getting some use," he said.

"It's a beautiful place to pray," Jenny said.

Father Pete nodded. "I pray here often, in front of this same window. I call it the Impossible Window."

"The Impossible Window? Why? I'd call it the Angel Window."

"Look." Father Pete pointed to its base.

As Jenny once again turned her attention to the window, the room brightened again, highlighting a rectangle of golden-yellow glass at the bottom. There was writing on it. She leaned forward to read it.

For with God nothing shall be impossible.
Luke 1:37

"Do you really believe that?" she asked Father Pete.

"I do. I've prayed for some pretty hopeless situations in front of this window."

"And God fixed them?"

"He intervened." Father Pete lifted an eyebrow and gave her a wry smile. "Not always, or even usually, in the way I thought he would. God is full of surprises."

"I guess he is." Jenny's eyes widened as she realized the surprise that had already happened to her. "I never pictured myself coming to a place like this just to pray."

"You're most welcome here," Father Pete said. "I'm glad you've been coming to church with Rose lately. You're enjoying it, I hope?"

Jenny nodded. "More than I expected. I mean, I went when I was a child. My parents made me. I stopped going once I got to college, though. I was usually out late having fun on Saturday nights, so I slept in on Sundays."

"No more partying on the weekends, I take it?" The pastor grinned.

"Oh, I still know how to have fun," Jenny said with a wink. "But this church thing, this praying thing, is growing on me."

"Good. Will we see you on Sunday? It's Easter, you know." Father Pete's face glowed with anticipation.

"Is it?" Jenny blurted and then felt her face get hot as realization dawned. The baskets of ceramic eggs in the dining room at Fair Meadows, spring decorations in the lobby . . . and, oh, my, that black cloth on the cross behind the altar . . . it was Good Friday. "They keep moving the date around." She gave a little laugh to cover her embarrassment.

"They do," Father Pete said with an understanding nod. "But I do hope you'll come. We'll be celebrating the very best of God's surprises."

Jenny's phone chimed. She dug it out of her purse and checked the screen.

"My daughter. She's here to give me a ride home."

Father Pete walked Jenny out to the curb where Chloe waited.

As he opened the car door for her, he leaned over and said, "I'm here most days, should you have questions or need to talk."

"I'll keep it in mind," Jenny said, just to be polite. All she really wanted was to knit in the beautiful Prayer Chapel, not discuss whatever it was pastors discussed with people.

On Saturday morning, Jenny woke resolved to embark on Operation Friendship. She talked to her fellow prayer shawl makers about it over breakfast.

"I feel so bad about the situation with Sam and Dorothy," she began. "He's a really sweet man, and he loves her so much."

"It is sad," Laura said. "I wish there was something we could do."

"There is something we can do." Jenny leaned forward, eager to share her idea.

"Can't do nothing about that Old-Timer's Disease," Edna said.

"I know," Jenny said, slightly irritated.

"Then what?" Edna's raised eyebrows practically dared Jenny to say something positive.

Jenny let go of her irritation and decided to rise to the challenge. She'd show that old pessimist.

"It's like Dorothy is Sam's whole world, and without her, he's lonely and lost. He doesn't have to be lonely, though. He needs friends." She paused for effect. "He needs us."

"He needs to stop having a pity party, that's what," Edna said.

"So, we invite him to *our* party instead," Jenny said.

Rose smiled at Jenny across the table. "This is exactly what I had in mind when I suggested we invite him to become a Woolgatherer. You can count me in."

"I'll ask if he watches basketball," Mr. Peabody said. "They're showing the Final Four on the big screen. We'll have snacks and everything."

"That's a great idea, Alistair." Jenny beamed at him.

"And Edna's teaching him to crochet," Laura said.

"I wish he'd come to church with us," Susan said.

"We'll keep inviting him," Rose said. "And praying for him."

CHAPTER 23

JENNY GLANCED OFTEN AT THE lobby doors while waiting for Sam to arrive, eager to get Operation Friendship underway. Finally, she saw his car pull into the parking lot.

"There he is." Jenny nudged Mr. Peabody with her elbow as Sam stepped into the lobby. "Everybody, act friendly."

"We don't need to act friendly," Laura said. "We *are* friendly. Calm down, Jenny."

Mr. Peabody stood when Sam arrived at the seating area and pumped Sam's hand in welcome. "Glad you're here, Sam."

Sam shook hands with Mr. Peabody amid a chorus of hellos and then sat next to Edna.

"What do you think?" He showed her his project.

Edna scrutinized the work and finally handed it back.

"Not bad, not bad. You know how to follow directions," she said.

Sam's smile transformed his face. He looked like a wonderfully different man when he smiled. Jenny resolved to do what she could to inspire that look more often.

Rose called the meeting to order, Laura read the prayer, and the Woolgatherers began to work on their prayer shawls. They greeted the regulars, people who came to spend time with loved ones in Memory Care on Saturdays, and gave a shawl to a particularly distressed son on his way to visit his dad. They caught a glimpse of him hugging it to his chest as the elevator doors closed.

Nan and her daughters waved as they went past, Samantha nearly bouncing in eagerness on the way to the elevator.

"Wait till I show you." Tara patted her backpack.

Meanwhile, the Woolgatherers plied Sam with questions. Did he follow college basketball? (Mr. Peabody). Did he have grandchildren? (Susan). What did he like to read? (Laura). Had he seen any good movies lately? (Jenny).

Every now and then, Sam would raise a forefinger to indicate he needed to count his stitches, which earned an approving nod from Edna.

"Quit pestering the man and let him work." She glared at the rest of the Woolgatherers.

"It's all right. I'm still on track." Sam displayed the shawl, now at least a foot long.

"Here comes Tara," Jenny said.

"It's a wonder you get any knitting done," Laura said with a laugh. "You're always watching what's going on in the lobby."

"I can knit without looking," Jenny said and promptly dropped a stitch. "Most of the time," she said with a sheepish grin.

"Ta-da!" Tara pulled her work out of her backpack with a flourish. Her finished shawl unfurled in all its glory. She swirled it over her shoulders and did a slow model's turn.

"What do you think?" she asked, although the group was already showering her with praise.

"Lovely."

"Nice work."

"I can't believe you finished it already!"

"Those shells on the border are a great finishing touch."

"Now it just needs to go to church to get prayed over," Jenny said.

"About that," Tara said. "I know you take the shawls to Rose's church, but I was wondering if it would be okay if I took it to my church and asked my pastor to pray over it."

"Does your church have a prayer shawl ministry, then?" Rose asked.

"Well, no." Tara shifted from one foot to the other. "But I'm starting to think it ought to. I mean, going bowling with the youth group is fun and all, and the summer mission trip is important, but . . ." Tara groped for words. "But there's got to be something between having fun and taking a trip to help people who live far away."

"You mean like a youth group prayer shawl ministry?" Jenny asked.

"Yeah," Tara said. "I brought my knitting to youth group last week, and some of the kids thought it was cool." She made a face. "Some of them think it's weird I hang out with a bunch of—" Tara reddened.

"Old people?" Rose supplied.

"Yeah," Tara said. "Sorry."

"They don't know what they're missing." Mr. Peabody grinned.

"That's what *I* said." Tara grinned, too.

"Starting a prayer shawl group with the kids at your church is a wonderful idea." Rose's face shone. "By all means, take your shawl to your church for prayer. They don't have to get prayed over at Hope of Glory."

"Are there any other knitters in your youth group?" Laura asked.

Tara shook her head. "There are a couple of girls who know how to crochet, though."

"So, you'll have to teach them to knit," Laura said.

"I learned on YouTube. I'll bet they can, too."

"That could very well work. People seem to be able to learn so many things right from the internet these days," Laura said. "But if you run into any snags, I'd be happy to help."

"Really? You'd come and teach us?"

"I'd need a ride. I'm a member of the my-kids-won't-let-me-drive club," Laura said.

"I'll bet my mom would give you a ride," Tara said. "That would be really great."

"Hey, don't leave me out," Jenny said. "I'd love to show them just how cool knitting can be."

"Sure, Jenny," Tara said with a laugh. "You can come, too."

"Now we have that settled," Rose said. "What are you going to knit next?"

"Another shawl." Tara pulled two pattern books out of her backpack and gave one to Rose. "Here's your book. I found another prayer shawl book last week. I just started this one." She turned to the pattern she'd chosen for her next shawl. She'd marked the place with her Woolgatherers prayer card. While Rose read the pattern, Tara pulled her new project out of her backpack.

"Ooh, pretty." Jenny admired the variegated shades of purple, green, and blue.

Rose glanced up from the pattern book. "This has a crocheted edge. Do you know how to crochet?"

"No," Tara said. "But I can learn on YouTube."

"Maybe," Edna said.

"I'm sure Edna would be happy to help you if you run into trouble," Rose said.

With a sidelong, apprehensive glance at Edna, Tara said, "I'll probably be okay."

Edna shrugged and returned to expertly flicking yarn over her hook.

Tara murmured the Woolgatherers prayer, then set to work on her shawl.

Mr. Peabody waited until Sam finished counting his latest row, then said, "Do you want to watch the Final Four here tonight? They're showing it on the big screen, and there will be snacks."

"Healthy snacks," Susan said.

"Don't let that deter you," Mr. Peabody said. "I went last year, and they were pretty good."

"I guess so," Sam said. "I was just going to watch it at home."

Jenny beamed at him from across the circle.

"You like basketball, too?" Sam asked her.

"Not really," Jenny said. "I'm more of a movie person. We won't be having movie night until next Saturday because of the basketball." She shook her head in mock disgust. "But when we finally get the media room back, we'll be watching *The Mouse That Roared*."

"Is that the one where Peter Sellers plays all the parts?" Laura asked.

Jenny nodded. "It's hilarious. You want to come, Sam? We always have popcorn."

Sam looked a bit shell-shocked at the barrage of invitations. "You're allowed to have guests at these things, too, like at meals?"

"Yes, we are," Jenny told him. "You'll be Alistair's guest for the basketball and mine for the movie."

"Okay. Sure, I'll go to the movies with you," Sam said.

"Good," Jenny said, pleased she had two Saturday nights planned for him. He wouldn't be lonely anymore. Not if she had anything to do with it.

Jenny dressed carefully for church on Easter morning, remembering the flowered, ruffly Easter dresses of her childhood, the frilly socks and shiny patent leather Mary Janes. She chose a pale green sheath dress with matching slingback pumps. Grabbing a shawl to ward off the spring chill, she hurried down to the lobby. Rose had said they should get to church early to make sure they got seats.

Rose wasn't kidding, Jenny thought as she settled into the pew. The church was so full that the ushers were already setting up folding chairs at the back of the nave. She sat back and drank it all in. Sunshine streamed through the windows, filling the room with light. The scent of the Easter lilies that flanked the altar wafted over the congregation. The cross was draped in white and the walls reverberated with triumphant organ music. Jenny's heart swelled at the beauty all around her.

At the last chords of "Christ the Lord is Risen Today," Father Pete stepped into the center aisle, looking like he could barely contain himself.

He thrust his hands in the air and shouted, "Christ is risen!"

"The Lord is risen indeed! Alleluia!" Jenny found herself shouting with the rest of the congregation.

"Welcome to the celebration of the biggest surprise of all," Father Pete continued, his face suffused with joy. "But why was it such a surprise? Jesus told his disciples what was going to happen, but they didn't seem to be able to grasp it. It was just way too good to be true. You may be having a hard time grasping it, too. You may be thinking that the promises of new life and the goodness of God are too good to be true. I tell you they are not. The grand surprises of God are for you, too. Come and celebrate. Come and be surprised!

Jenny felt her heart rise. She'd never pictured Easter as a party, much less a surprise party. She found herself paying even more attention than usual, wondering what would happen next. She was not disappointed. At the end of the service, as she turned to gather up her purse and shawl, she caught sight of Gus among the folding chairs. She waved her arm to catch his attention and hurried to join him at the back.

"You came! You have to meet Father Pete." Jenny steered Gus over to the door of the nave where the pastor stood shaking hands with all and sundry.

"I wasn't planning to come," Gus said a bit sheepishly when he was introduced. "But the coffee shop where I was going to study was closed for Easter." He stopped and cleared his throat as though overcome with emotion. "I can see why the ladies keep coming back here. This place is alive with hope."

Father Pete clapped Gus on the back. "We're not called 'Hope of Glory' for nothing. And I hope we'll be seeing more of you, Gus."

"Maybe," Gus said. "At least until I leave for medical school."

Jenny smiled at this, but Father Pete's face grew serious.

"You have a long and demanding road ahead of you. Please do come and gather strength for the journey."

Gus returned the pastor's gaze. "Yes, sir. I will."

CHAPTER 24

OVER THE NEXT FEW WEEKS, the Woolgatherers kept Sam busy. He and Alistair discussed past March Madness games as they stitched. He yelled and cheered and groaned right along with the Fair Meadows basketball fans during the Final Four games. Everyone except Edna went to the movie. Sam sat next to Jenny, so he could hear her laugh. He laughed, too, more than he had in a long time. And Edna made sure he kept crocheting.

His Saturday morning calls to Eileen kept him informed about Dorothy. She was fine and enjoying the flowers he continued to send on Mondays.

"She waits for them," Eileen said. "She's actually a bit agitated until they arrive. She's not always oriented to the time or the day of the week, but somehow, she knows when her flowers are supposed to come."

"It's about the only thing I can do for her now." A wave of sadness washed over him.

"It means a lot to her," Eileen said.

"And Rafe?" He made himself ask.

"Still in the picture," Eileen said. "But, um, not making any progress."

Sam appreciated Eileen's tact. The image of Rafe kissing Dorothy's hand still rankled. He tried not to dwell on it.

"Gotta go now." Sam always ended his call to Eileen the same way. "It's time for me to leave for Woolgatherers."

"Say hello to Rose for me," Eileen would answer.

"Will do," Sam said, his mind already turning from Dorothy and Memory Care to his crochet project and spending the morning with his new friends.

His crochet had improved so much he didn't have to sit right next to Edna anymore. He took to arriving early enough to make sure he could sit next to Jenny. He liked to listen to her chatter and joke. Next to her, he could forget about everything else, at least for a while.

By the third Saturday in April, Sam was nearing the end of his first shawl. He sat between Susan and Jenny, chatting with both. Susan was in the middle of a story about her second youngest grandchild, who was, apparently, the epitome of cuteness, when she broke off to say, "Uh-oh."

"What?" Sam and Jenny said together.

"Look." Susan pointed one of her knitting needles toward the elevator. Sam watched Tara cross the lobby toward the group. From the way her face was puckered and crumpled, he thought she must be trying hard not to cry.

Rose stood when Tara arrived at the circle of seats and put her arms around the girl. Tara sobbed into Rose's shoulder. Susan quickly produced a packet of tissues and had one at the ready when Tara finally lifted her head.

"It's so awful." Tara wiped her eyes with the tissue, then blew her nose.

"Tell us about it," Rose said. Laura vacated the chair next to Rose.

Tara sat and let out a shaky sigh.

"It's fine spending time with Grandma Becca when she's knitting, even on the days she doesn't know me. It feels halfway normal when we can knit together. But some days, it's like she never saw a knitting needle in her life."

"She just sits and stares?" Sam said, remembering the time he'd seen Nan and her mother together in the dayroom.

"I wish," Tara said fervently.

"What, then?" Rose asked.

"If she just sat there, I could take it, but instead she keeps picking at lint on her clothes, only there's no lint. It's so creepy." Tara shuddered. "She's picking and picking and there's nothing there. It really got to me today, and I thought she might calm down if I held her hand, but she jerked away so hard, I thought she was going to hit me." Tara's chin trembled. "My Grandma Becca. I thought she was going to hit me." Tears slid down her cheeks.

"She needs a twiddle muff," Edna said.

"A-a what?" Tara swiped at her face with the tissue.

"Twiddle muff," Edna said. "Gives 'em something to pick at when they get like that. I made one for Stanley." She pulled a pattern out of her bag and passed it to Tara. "You crochet a rectangle, then sew the long ends together to make a muff. Then you sew on all kinds of things the person can fidget with, like buttons and ribbons. You can sew things on the inside, too."

Tara examined the picture in the pattern.

"Could you make my grandma one?" Tara asked.

"I've got a better idea," Edna said. "How about you make her one?"

"But I don't know how to—" Tara began. At the look Edna gave her, she finished with, "Right. YouTube. But can I borrow the pattern?"

"Don't lose it," was all Edna said.

"I'll make a copy when I get home and bring this back next week," Tara said. She tucked the pattern into her backpack and pulled out her current shawl. The Woolgatherers admired it and complimented her on her progress.

Laura peered at Tara over the top of her glasses. "You're knitting a lot. Are you still getting your homework done?"

"I'm still passing everything," Tara said with a grin.

"Just passing?" Laura said with mock sternness.

"I'm teasing. I'm doing fine. Knitting makes a great study break. I need lots of study breaks," Tara said with a mischievous wink.

"I'm glad I don't have to take tests anymore," Jenny said.

"I'll bet you aced them," Sam said. "You're smart."

"You're so sweet, Sam," Jenny said with a winsome smile. "But mostly I just squeaked by. I was more of a social butterfly in college."

"Is that what they called a party girl back in your day?" Mr. Peabody teased.

Sam glared at Mr. Peabody, but Jenny just laughed and gave him a playful swat on the arm.

"Oh, you! Let's just say I was the life of the party."

"You still are." Mr. Peabody winked.

Sam shook his head. Alistair Peabody was incorrigible, the way he flirted.

"Here comes Gus." Jenny waved at the young man as he strode across the lobby toward them.

After greeting the group, Gus said, "I wanted to let you know I spoke to my boss, and it's all right with her if I give you all a ride to church every Sunday."

"What about your day off?" Rose asked with concern.

"I don't mind," Gus told them. "In fact, I've decided to start coming to church with you."

The group greeted this news with broad smiles and applause.

Gus's cheeks reddened. "See you tomorrow morning." He strode off to the van, where a group of Fair Meadows residents waited for him to chauffeur them on an outing.

"He probably just needs the extra money," Edna said.

"So what?" Susan said. "He's going to be a doctor, after all. We're helping him get enough money for school."

"The best thing," Rose said, "is that he'll be coming to church. I was so happy to see him there on Easter. We'd love for you to come to church with us, too, Sam," Rose said.

"Oh . . . um . . . well." Sam was startled by the invitation.

"Unless you go to church somewhere else, of course," Rose said.

"Oh, no. I don't go anymore. It got too hard to take Dorothy," Sam said.

"But she's in Memory Care now. You can go to church again," Rose said.

"C'mon, come to church tomorrow." Jenny didn't flutter her eyelashes, but she might as well have. Sam felt slightly dazed.

"Maybe," he said when he finally found his voice.

"Good," Jenny said, as though it was settled. "The service starts at eleven."

"What church is it again?" Sam asked, not entirely sure why he was asking. Church had been Dorothy's thing.

"Hope of Glory Community Church," Jenny said. "Third and Lewiston. Be there or be square."

Sam nodded, but mentally consigned himself to being square. Just about the last thing he wanted to do was go to church.

On Saturday evening, Sam yawned. It was only nine o'clock, and he'd planned on watching a few more episodes of *NCIS*, his latest binge. But he would have to rewatch the latest one since he'd dozed off toward the end and only woke when both the remote and his crochet hook clattered to the floor. He rolled up his work and went to bed.

Sam woke to a hallelujah chorus of birds outside his bedroom window. He turned over with a groan and pulled a pillow over his head. Sure, it was spring, but did they have to make such an infernal racket on a Sunday morning?

Sunday morning. Sunday morning? Something about Sunday morning . . . Sam pushed the pillow away and glanced at his bedside clock. Seven fifteen. He hadn't been awake this early since . . . since Dorothy had gone to live at Fair Meadows. Fair Meadows, Sunday, the Woolgatherers—ah, that was it. Gus was driving the Woolgatherers to church this morning. And church was at eleven. He considered the matter. He was now wide-awake. He could go if he wanted to. Oddly, Sam found he wanted to. He'd have to iron a shirt, though. He had a feeling Jenny would be dressed to the nines, and he wouldn't want to look scruffy next to her. And Alistair Peabody would probably be dapper as well. He didn't want to look scruffy next to him, either. Sam rolled out of bed, scratched his chin, and set to work.

By ten thirty, Sam was ready for church. His suit jacket strained across his midsection when he tried to button it, even when he sucked in his stomach. In the end he decided to leave it unbuttoned. He told himself it was to show off his tie.

To his astonishment, Sam managed to arrive a little early for the service at Hope of Glory. He was crossing the parking lot as the Fair Meadows van pulled to the curb in front of the church. He joined Gus in the task of helping everyone out of the van and up the steps.

"I hoped you'd decide to come," Jenny said when she saw him. "I wasn't sure you would."

"I did say 'maybe,'" Sam said.

After extricating his hand from Howard-the-usher's hearty welcome, Sam took a seat between Jenny and Laura. A flash of purple hair caught his eye a few rows ahead. Next to her sat a young man with a blue-eyed baby peering over his shoulder. This must be Amy, Bryson, and Heaven Leigh. So young, the three of them, with so much of life still to come. Sam remembered Dorothy as a new mother, proudly holding Josh in church, dressed in his baby Sunday best. The picture dissolved when Heaven gave him with a toothless grin. Sam grinned, too, and sent up a prayer on their behalf.

Sam followed the service with interest. This Father Pete person was a bundle of energy. He didn't stay behind the pulpit to preach. He strode back and forth across the front of the church and even came down the center aisle a few times. He waved his arms and raised his voice at times to get his point across. But he wasn't berating the congregation. Sam leaned forward. Father Pete was passionate, not only about Hope of Glory but the world outside of the church as well. He urged the congregation to find ways to connect the two.

"Not so this church can grow, but so people can know God and find the hope only He can bring."

Knowing God . . . now that was a scary thought. Sam had never wanted to get too close to that intimidating entity, not even at church, much less anywhere else. But now, here in the nave of Hope of Glory, sitting with his friends in the warm sunlight that streamed through one of the stained-glass windows and being the object of the friendly, interested stare of Heaven Leigh, it didn't seem quite so daunting.

At the close of the service, Jenny steered Sam to the line of people waiting to greet the pastor.

"Pleased to meet you, Sam," Father Pete said when Jenny introduced Sam as one of the Woolgatherers. "So, you live at Fair Meadows, too?"

"No, my wife is in Memory Care there. I got to talking with the Woolgatherers one day, and before I knew it, I was one of them," Sam said with a rueful grin. "I told them I didn't know how to knit, but they wouldn't take no for an answer."

"They're teaching you to knit?" Father Pete asked.

"Nope." Sam chuckled. "I was a hopeless case. But Edna taught me to crochet, and I'm half done with my first shawl."

"Edna?" Father Pete raised his eyebrows. "The one who makes those beautiful crocheted shawls? The one I haven't met yet?"

"We keep inviting her," Jenny said.

"I hope she comes." Amy joined them, Heaven on her shoulder. "She's a baby whisperer." Amy went on to describe the morning she'd spent with the Woolgatherers getting help with the baby hat Heaven now adorably sported.

"I guess we'll keep trying, then." Jenny patted the baby's back. "C'mon, Sam, I want you to meet Clive."

Soon Sam was standing by the coffee urn in the parish hall chatting with Clive Stanhope.

"She's something else, isn't she?" Clive waved his coffee cup toward the table where Jenny was charming one and all.

"She is." Sam nodded.

"How do you know her?" Clive gave him a narrow look. "You live at the retirement place?"

"No," Sam said. "I'm there a lot, though."

"Oh, really?"

Sam sighed inwardly and took the plunge. "My wife lives there. I met Jenny and the other Woolgatherers on one of my many trips back and forth from the memory care unit."

"Oh, man. I'm sorry to hear that," Clive said. To Sam, however, the man sounded more relieved than sorry. "Yes, indeed, Jenny's quite a woman," Clive continued with an air of self-satisfaction. *So that's it*, Sam realized. *Clive doesn't want any competition as far as Jenny is concerned.*

"Good to have you here. You're welcome anytime." After shaking Sam's hand, Clive went off to join the group gathered around Jenny.

"Like moths to a flame." Sam turned to find Alistair at his elbow.

"Are you comparing Clive to a moth?" Sam asked.

"I'm comparing us *all* to moths." Alistair winked and elbowed Sam in the ribs. "She's bright and warm. Who wouldn't want to be close to her? But not too close. That wouldn't be a good idea."

"Why do you say that?" Sam wondered if Alistair was warning him off, too.

"As she has said herself, 'Girls just wanna have fun.' It wouldn't do to take her seriously."

"No worries," Sam told him.

Gus began to move about the room, suggesting to the Woolgatherers that it was time to leave. They departed in a flurry of farewells. Sam started to cross the parish hall to follow suit, only to be waylaid by Father Pete.

The pastor reached out and clapped Sam on the shoulder. "Good to have you here, Sam. How did you like the service?"

"It was fine. A bit different from the church I used to go to with my wife."

Father Pete raised his eyebrows. "How so?"

"The sermons weren't as . . . well, as lively as yours," Sam said.

The pastor's laugh was as lively as the sermon. "Gotta keep the folks awake."

"I've been known to doze off a time or two," Sam said. "My wife used to elbow me in the ribs. No chance of falling asleep in church today."

"There's a lot more where that came from. I hope you'll come again."

Sam looked into Father Pete's friendly gray eyes and heard himself reply, "Maybe I will."

CHAPTER 25

"THERE YOU ARE, TARA," ROSE said the following Saturday as the teen joined the Woolgatherers after her visit with Grandma Becca.

To Rose's surprise, Tara scooted past the empty seat by her and made a beeline for Edna.

"Mrs. O'Brian, I need your help."

Edna paused in her crocheting to focus her attention on Tara.

"I know I said I could learn to crochet on YouTube, but I can't. It keeps coming out like this." Tara pulled her attempt at crochet out of her backpack.

Edna laid her shawl aside and spread Tara's work on her lap. Rose leaned forward with interest.

"I keep getting fewer and fewer stitches, and I can't figure out why." Indeed, the piece resembled a Mayan pyramid rather than the rectangle it was meant to be.

"What did them videos tell you?" Edna said. "Crochet to the end of the row?"

Tara nodded.

"Bet they didn't tell you the last stitch can be hard to find. It's almost like it's hiding. Lemme show you."

Edna pulled out some stitches, then reworked them up to the place where Tara had ended her row and turned her work.

"Look. Right there." Edna poked at Tara's attempt at crochet with the pointy end of her hook. "That *there's* the last stitch."

Tara peered at her work. "*That's* the last stitch? No wonder . . ." She reached for her work.

Edna passed it to her. "You do the last stitch, then I want you to show me what you've been doing at the beginning of the next row."

"Yes, ma'am," Tara worked the last stitch, then turned her work. She pulled the yarn through the loop to make a turning chain.

"That's right, that's right." Edna sounded delighted. "Now, where are you gonna make the first stitch?"

Tara pointed with her hook, but Edna shook her head. "Too far."

"Here?" Tara pointed again.

"Now you've got it," Edna said.

Tara made the stitch, then examined the result. "Now I get what I was doing wrong. I was skipping the turning chain and the first stitch, instead of just the turning chain. Thank you, Mrs. O'Brian."

"You probably don't want to hear this, but you'll have to start over." Her voice was so gentle Rose caught a fleeting glimpse of a younger, happier Edna, teaching Penny to crochet.

"I don't mind," Tara said cheerfully. "I want it to come out right. This is for my grandma." Tara set to work pulling out stitch after stitch and rolling the yarn back around her skein. She talked as she ripped. "I know this pattern is for a muff, but I want to make it so you can lay it out flat, too. Grandma Becca tends to pick at whatever's in her lap. I want to put some loops on one side and big buttons on the other, so she can use it both ways."

"And she can fiddle with the buttons, too," Laura said. "That's so creative and thoughtful, Tara."

Tara blushed at the praise. "I just want to help my grandma."

"It will," Edna said. "My Stanley—"

But whatever Edna had been about to say about her Stanley was lost in the chorus of greetings as Sam arrived.

"Sorry I'm late. It took me a while to get ready."

Jenny smiled at him. "You look nice, Sam. That color suits you."

Sam gave a nervous tug at the tail of his royal blue polo shirt, then sat next to Jenny. He pulled his shawl in progress out of his briefcase and set to work.

"Let's see," Jenny said.

Sam lifted the pile of crochet to reveal at least two feet of shawl.

"You've made a lot of progress," Rose said.

Edna leaned forward and peered at the shawl.

"Not bad," she said. "You're coming along."

"Well, I think he's doing great," Laura said.

"Are you coming to church tomorrow, Sam?" Jenny asked.

"Are you going?" Sam asked.

"Of course! We're regulars now, aren't we?" Jenny swept a glance around the group.

"Not me," Edna said.

"And why not?" Jenny asked.

"I have my reasons."

"What reasons?"

Rose hastened to intervene. "Edna, you're welcome to come to Hope of Glory with us anytime. But it's entirely up to you. No pressure." Rose finished with a warning look at Jenny.

Edna nodded and returned to her crocheting.

"To answer your question, Jenny, I'll be at church tomorrow," Sam said. "I could give you a ride if you'd like."

"No need." Jenny waved one of her knitting needles airily. "I'll ride in the van."

Tara looked up sharply from her work. Rose saw her lips compress in apparent disapproval. Tara gave Jenny a hard stare, but Jenny didn't appear to notice.

Conversation ebbed and flowed around the circle. Laura beamed with pride over her youngest grandchild's latest school progress report, Jenny displayed her work for everyone to admire, and Susan expressed her great relief flu season was almost over.

"Did you get your flu and pneumonia shots this year, Sam?" Susan never missed an opportunity to urge people to take care of their health.

"I don't need to," Sam said. "I've never gotten the flu."

"Oh, you need to, all right," Susan said. "There's a first time for everything, and at our age, flu and pneumonia are nothing to sneeze at. You really should protect yourself."

Sam's eyes widened at her vehemence. "I'll think about it."

"Don't just think about it," Susan said. "Do it."

"It's probably too late to get one now," Laura said. "You just said the season's almost over."

"*Almost*," Susan said. "It's not over yet, and it's never too late." She stared at Sam and raised her eyebrows.

"I've never gotten the flu," Sam said again.

"Don't come crying to me if you get it, then." Susan pointedly returned her attention to her knitting.

"Wouldn't dream of it," Sam muttered.

An uneasy silence descended on the group until a beeping sound emanated from across the circle.

"That's me." Sam turned off the alarm on his phone. "I have an appointment to get my car serviced this morning. Gotta go." He packed his crochet into his briefcase.

"Pretty soon, your shawl's not going to fit in your briefcase," Mr. Peabody said. "What are you going to do then?"

Sam considered. "My gym bag might work."

Susan wrinkled her nose. "Your *gym* bag?"

"Well, yeah, I'm not really using it anymore," Sam said. "It doesn't have slots for my hooks, but there's a zippered inside pocket I could use."

"But—" Susan wrinkled her nose again.

As if finally catching her drift, Sam said, "I'll wash it first, of course." Sam shut his briefcase. "I'm off for an oil change."

Amid the chorus of goodbyes, Susan called after him, "And get a flu shot while you're at it. Take care of your car *and* yourself."

Sam waved the comment away as he went out the lobby doors.

After Sam was out of earshot, Tara turned to Jenny and fixed her with a hard stare.

"He likes you," she said.

"Of course he likes me." Jenny preened a bit. "Everybody likes me."
Edna rolled her eyes.

"Well, they do," Jenny said.

"No, I mean he *like* likes you," Tara said.

"I don't know where you get that idea," Jenny said.

"Oh, please," Tara said. "He offered you a ride to church when you can just as well get there in the van like you've been doing."

"He was just being nice. Being a gentleman."

"I'd give you a ride if I could," Mr. Peabody said.

"See?" Jenny said.

"I see all right." Tara crossed her arms in front of her chest.

"What?" Jenny's voice had an edge to it now. "Tara, Sam was just being nice. He's married."

"Yes, he is," Tara said. "But that doesn't stop you from flirting with him, does it?"

"Oh, *that*," Jenny gave a dismissive wave. "Everybody knows I don't mean anything by it. I'm just flirting for fun."

"When it comes to Sam," Tara said, "I think only one of you is flirting 'for fun.'"

Jenny drew herself up to stare down at Tara. "And you know so much about this kind of thing how?"

Tara rolled her eyes. "Uh, duh. I'm in high school."

Laura drew in a short, sharp breath.

"Tara," Rose said in dismay.

Tara's cheeks reddened. "I'm sorry. It was really rude to say it like that. Please don't tell my mother."

"You're forgiven, and my lips are sealed," Jenny said in a conspiratorial stage whisper.

"She's right, though," Edna's sharp tone made everyone jump. "You be careful. That man's heart is already broke over Dorothy. Don't you go raising no false hopes, toying with his affections."

Jenny's jaw dropped. "I am not 'toying with his affections.' Everybody around here knows I'm just being friendly and charming."

"So you can get what you want," Edna said.

Jenny gave an elegant shrug.

"But if you don't want *him*, don't act like it!" Edna's voice echoed in the lobby.

"Well, I never—" Jenny said. "He's married, for heaven's sake."

"If you ask me, he's feeling less married all the time." Edna leveled her crochet hook at Jenny. "You be careful with him, missy."

CHAPTER 26

WHEN JENNY'S DAUGHTER MENTIONED SHE had errands to run on Tuesday, Jenny had jumped at the chance to knit in the Prayer Chapel again. She had some things on her mind, and the Prayer Chapel seemed like the best place to sort them out.

She settled in front of Father Pete's Impossible Window.

"Impossible is right." Jenny's needles clacked furiously. "Edna O'Brian is impossible. Imagine her telling me to leave Sam alone. He's alone too much. That's why we invited him to be a Woolgatherer. I think she's just jealous."

Jenny bent her head over her knitting as if her last statement settled the matter. The knitting, however, failed to soothe her ruffled feelings. In her agitation, she dropped three stitches. After she recovered them, Jenny let her knitting fall into her lap and gazed at the angel in the window.

"I mean, can you believe what she said to me? That I'm leading Sam on? He's married, for heaven's sake. He knows I don't mean anything by it. I'm just being nice. That woman wouldn't know nice if it walked up and handed her a dozen roses."

Jenny was about to dismiss Edna and her comments completely when an image flashed through her mind, the image of Edna sitting across from her in the Woolgatherers' circle, teaching both Sam and Tara to crochet in her own no-nonsense but effective way. Jenny began to get the uncomfortable feeling she wasn't being fair. She picked up her knitting, then dropped it again with an indignant huff as she once again remembered Edna's accusation and warning.

"I'm just being his friend," she said. "I got that idea the last time I prayed in here, so it must be okay. That poor man needs some friends."

A thought came unbidden to her mind almost as though someone had spoken out loud.

So does Edna.

Jenny gave an indelicate snort.

"Believe me, I've tried."

Have you? Again, a thought so foreign Jenny wondered if it might be . . . could it be? She felt compelled to answer.

"I knit with her three days a week. What more do you want?"

Knit for her.

Jenny resumed knitting and tried to figure out what that meant. Knit for Edna? Knit what for Edna? A hat? A scarf? Argyle socks? Mid-row, it dawned on her.

"A prayer shawl? You want me to make her a prayer shawl? I don't think it would make a bit of difference. And she's not a caregiver anymore."

As if in answer, a shaft of sunlight illuminated the angel's wings, suffusing them with a soft, golden glow. Jenny dropped her knitting in her lap and stared at the window. Her stomach swooped, and she felt a little dizzy.

"Okay," she said, sounding as shaken as she felt. "If you think it'll help, I'll make Edna a prayer shawl."

And pray for her?

"Um, sure." Jenny shrugged and was finally able to settle in to her knitting.

An hour later, a soft chime sounded from Jenny's phone, notifying her of a text from her daughter.

"Be there in fifteen," it read.

"Have time to stop at The Tangled Thread?" Jenny texted back. She needed to shop for yarn for Edna's shawl.

"Sure," came the reply.

Jenny rolled up her knitting and tucked it into her tote. Then she grabbed her coat and left the chapel. Once in the foyer, she set her tote on a bench and put on her wrap. Father Pete, on his way out of the church office, helped her with the second sleeve.

"Enjoying the Prayer Chapel again, Jenny?" Father Pete beamed with pleasure.

"Enjoying isn't exactly the word I'd use," Jenny said. Margaret's words came back to her, something about the chapel being beautiful but not always peaceful.

"Oh?" The pastor raised an eyebrow.

"Father, can I ask you something?"

"Of course." He extended his hand toward one of the benches.

"I hope this doesn't sound crazy," Jenny said once they were seated, "but does anything ever, well, *happen* in the Prayer Chapel?"

"Well, prayer happens there," he said.

"Do things happen when people pray in there?"

"God has responded to prayers I've prayed there," Father Pete said.

"That's not what I mean." Jenny searched for words to make herself understood without sounding crazy. "Do things happen to people when they pray in there?"

A broad smile spread across Father Pete's face, as though the sun had come out on a cloudy day.

"I think I understand what you're asking. Did you sense God there today?"

Jenny gulped and nodded. "I think he talked to me. Not out loud," she hastened to add. "Here." She pointed to her head. "And here." She pointed to her heart.

"What did he say?" Father Pete asked.

"I was talking to him about this woman in the Woolgatherers who said something really unkind and unfair to me recently. And then I got the crazy idea I should make her a prayer shawl."

"Not so crazy," Father Pete said. "It sounds just like him, as a matter of fact. He told us to love our enemies and pray for those who persecute us."

Jenny raised her eyebrows at this. "An enemy?" Her stomach clenched.

"This woman just tends to be a Debbie Downer. I wouldn't call her an enemy."

Father Pete simply gazed at her with his clear gray eyes. Jenny shifted uncomfortably on the bench.

"I did hear something about praying for her in there," she said after a moment.

"If you ask me—" Father Pete began.

"Believe me, I'm asking you," Jenny said.

"Praying for her would be a good thing. For both of you."

Another chime sounded from Jenny's phone.

"My daughter's here to pick me up," she said after a quick glance at the screen. "She's taking me to the yarn shop to choose yarn for this shawl God wants me to make." Saying it out loud made her stomach swoop again.

Father Pete held the door for her.

"Listen carefully while you choose," he said as she passed through. "Rose tells me it's an important part of the process."

After watching Jenny navigate the steps in her heels to the waiting car, Father Pete closed the door and turned toward the Prayer Chapel. He had phone calls to make and a sermon to get started on, but right now it was time to pray for Jenny and the unknown problematic woman for whom she was making a shawl. He slipped inside and settled himself on his knees in front of the Impossible Window. He should be used to it by now, he thought as he gazed at the words of promise at the base of the window, but it still amazed and delighted him to see prayer shawl ministry in action, comforting the recipients and challenging the makers. He had a feeling it was only a matter of time before he would meet Jenny's "Debbie Downer." He did not find the prospect daunting in the least. He was, after all, pastor to Margaret Benson, the transformed Dragon Lady of Hope of Glory Community Church.

"Do you mind if I don't come in with you?" Chloe asked as she pulled to the curb in front of The Tangled Thread. She cast a longing look at the café next to the yarn shop. "I could use a cup of coffee after running all those errands."

"I don't mind at all," Jenny said. "You go on, and I'll join you in a few. This shouldn't take long."

Choosing yarn for Edna's shawl, however, proved more difficult than Jenny had anticipated. As she dithered over various skeins, Ariadne came alongside her.

"Can I help you?"

"I don't know." Jenny frowned. "It's for a prayer shawl. I usually get whatever yarn catches my eye and run with it. But this is for a specific person, and I don't know what she'll like."

"Hmm . . ." Ariadne tapped her chin with her forefinger. "What colors does she like to wear?"

Jenny wrinkled her nose. "A lot of the time she wears this awful raggedy brown cardigan. The color doesn't do a thing for her. It washes her out."

"So, not brown, then. At least we can eliminate all these." She waved at the many and varied shades of brown yarn hung on pegs on the walls.

Jenny drifted along the rows of yarn hanks, reaching out to savor the softness of this one, the vibrant color of that one. Her fingers closed around a softer-than-soft skein of merino, in much the same way Susan had clasped the ocean-colored yarn she'd loved on the day of the Woolgatherers' yarn outing back in February. Jenny pulled the yarn off the peg to examine it more closely. It was green, mostly. Color swirled through the skein, from the pale green of spring leaves to the green of a lawn in midsummer. The green faded to white, which then gave way to a lavender that gradually deepened to the color of the lilacs that had graced the yard of Jenny's childhood. She tried to imagine a shawl in this yarn wrapped around Edna's shoulders. The swath of purple would probably look ridiculous on her. To her surprise, the image that formed in her mind's eye was not ludicrous but lovely. In Jenny's imagination, the colors, all of them, softened Edna's features.

"What pattern are you going to use?" Ariadne had once again appeared at Jenny's elbow.

"I don't know yet," Jenny said. "So far, I only know I need to make it out of this yarn."

Ariadne grinned. "Sounds like an adventure. But how will you know how much yarn to get?"

Jenny checked the yardage on the yarn label. "Three should be enough," she said. "All the other shawls I've made have never needed more than that."

"Three it is, then." Ariadne pulled two more hanks from the peg. "Do you need it wound?"

"Yes," Jenny said. "I have the feeling I need to get started on this soon." Moments later, Ariadne tucked three tidy cakes of yarn into a Tangled Thread bag.

"Happy knitting. I hope you'll show me when you're done. Whatever you make with this will be really lovely. The person you're knitting for must be so special."

"That's one way of putting it," Jenny said under her breath. With a smile and a wave, she headed out of the shop to enjoy some coffee and conversation with her daughter.

CHAPTER 27

AFTER BREAKFAST THE NEXT MORNING, Jenny walked Rose back to her apartment. She had spent the previous evening poring over shawl patterns online. It turned out to be more difficult to find the right pattern than she'd expected. At last, she'd narrowed it to the three she thought would bring out the best in the yarn. Unable to choose beyond that point, she had decided to consult the Woolgatherers' pattern guru, Rose.

"Do you have time to help me with a knitting question?"

"I thought the shawl you've been working on was going pretty smoothly," Rose said. "Have you hit a snag?"

"No, it's fine. I'm trying to choose a pattern for a new project." Jenny explained her experience in the Prayer Chapel. "I hope you don't think I'm crazy. Nothing like that has ever happened to me before."

"You're definitely not crazy." Rose quirked an eyebrow. "I've had it happen to me, although not necessarily in the Prayer Chapel. I call it the Nudge. It's the urge to make a shawl for a particular person, whether I know why they need it or not."

"We all know why she needs it," Jenny said. "She's always looking on the negative side of things."

"I wouldn't be so sure you know why she needs it."

Jenny stiffened at Rose's mild rebuke. "Why? Is there something you know that I don't?"

"No matter how much we know about someone, God always knows a whole lot more."

Rose's answer only piqued Jenny's curiosity, but she knew better than to push Rose. Whatever Rose knew, she'd guard Edna's privacy like the gold in Fort Knox. "Anyway"—Jenny shrugged—"I need some help choosing a pattern. Here's the yarn I got. I think I got nudged over this, too. I never would have chosen this for Edna myself." She reached into her bag and pulled out the green and purple cake of yarn.

"How beautiful!" Rose gave the cake a little squeeze. "And so soft."

"I know." Jenny smoothed a finger across the spring-colored yarn. "And when I pictured it as a shawl draped around Edna, it softened her somehow. It's hard to explain."

"So, now we have to find out what shawl this yarn wants to be," Rose said.

"Is that what I'm trying to do? I thought I was just having a hard time deciding. Here, let me show you."

Jenny took her tablet out of her trendy tote and pulled up the patterns one by one.

Rose examined the three pictures and patterns.

"This one will stretch you a bit." Rose pointed at one. "But I know you can do it. I can help you if you run into trouble."

"Is this 'the one,' then?"

"There's really only one way to find out." Rose handed Jenny the tablet. "Choose one and start knitting. It will either be right, or it won't."

"Can't you just tell me?" Jenny said. "If it's not right, I'll have to rip it out and start over. It'll take too long."

"How long is too long?" Rose asked. "When does it have to be finished?"

Jenny stared at her, scrambling for an answer that wasn't "as soon as possible so God will leave me alone about Edna." Finally, she said, "I really don't know. I'm just feeling my way along here."

Rose favored her with a delighted smile. "Now you're getting it! That's what happens with the Nudge. There's a lot you don't know, but you find out if you just keep going."

An uncharacteristic tightness formed between Jenny's eyebrows. Rose leaned forward.

"It's an adventure, a treasure hunt. Just start, and along the way you'll discover the right pattern. The shawl will be finished at just the right time, no matter how long it takes."

"Really?" Jenny leaned back in relief. "It's that simple and easy?"

"It's that simple, yes," Rose said. "But it may not be easy. Whatever you do, you have to pray."

Jenny gulped and pressed her hand to her stomach. "That gives me butterflies."

"You won't be alone," Rose told her. "God will be with you."

"That's what's giving me butterflies," Jenny said.

"Being close to God makes you nervous?" Rose asked.

"He's not like I thought he'd be," Jenny said. "I mean, I went into the chapel looking for sympathy, and now I'm making a shawl for the person who was mean to me. Instead of sympathizing with me, he gave me a job to do. I was sure he'd be on my side."

"He still is," Rose said. "Trust me."

"Really?" Jenny had her doubts.

"Better yet, trust him."

Jenny pressed both hands to her stomach. The butterflies were rioting.

That afternoon Jenny met Edna in the hallway. In light of the Nudge, Jenny decided to chat with her instead of giving the nod and wave she would usually have tossed off in passing so she could keep her distance.

"Where are you off to?" Jenny asked.

"Not book club." Edna eyed the paperback Jenny carried.

"You should come sometime." Jenny showed her the cover of the club's latest read, adorned with a woman in a gorgeous emerald-green ball gown. "This is a really good one."

"Don't much like to read." Edna frowned and pushed past as if Jenny had offered her a copy of *War and Peace*.

Jenny cast her eyes heavenward and muttered, "You saw me. I tried."

Jenny usually enjoyed the lively discussion of the latest book chosen by the Fair Meadows Romance Readers. She adored a good love story, complete with a happily-ever-after ending. This afternoon, however, she was impatient for the meeting to be over so she could get started on Edna's shawl. *Of course,* she sighed inwardly, *this* would *be the day the discussion would veer wildly off topic—more wildly than usual, anyway.*

"Why is it," Betty Callahan said, "all the books we read are about young people falling in love? Older people fall in love, too."

"Nobody wants to read about old love," Donna Robinson said. "When I read these books, I feel like I'm young again. I can relive falling in love with Walter."

A collective sigh rose from the group gathered around the fireplace. This escape into memory was one of the joys of reading romance.

"But old love is much more interesting," Betty said.

"Old people falling in love?" Donna frowned. "They meet-cute by crashing their walkers together?"

"No, no, no," Betty said impatiently. "Old people staying in love. All that meet-cute stuff and finally admitting how they feel to each other is just the beginning. The real story is what happens after, when they go through the challenges of life together."

Donna frowned. "But we all know *that's* not happily-ever-after. Bad things happen in real life. Who wants to read about that?"

"I think some of those twentysomethings reading these books want to know love can last, even in the face of challenges. And they need to know love can deepen when they work through hard times together."

"It doesn't always happen that way, though." Donna flung the book into her lap with an impatient huff.

"But it can, and people want to believe it can," Betty said. "Some-times when I'm watching TV with my granddaughters, one of those commercials comes on with an old couple holding hands while they walk together in the park. The way those girls sigh, you'd think it was the 'they're-finally-kissing' scene in a Hallmark movie."

"You may be right," Jenny said, trying to wrestle the discussion back on track. "If you could find a book like that, maybe we could put it on our list to read later. Now, let's get back to this month's book. Talk about a 'they're-finally-kissing' scene!"

After book club, Jenny walked along the winding, flower-lined path to her cottage, enjoying the sunshine and warm spring breeze. The weather was so pleasant that she took her knitting bag and tablet out to the back porch to get started on Edna's shawl. She examined the three patterns again. She decided to start with the one that seemed like it would be the easiest. There was a chance that it would be "the one." And the easier the pattern, the sooner she'd be finished. The less time she spent dwelling on Edna's gloomy outlook, the better.

With the question of the pattern settled (at least for now), Jenny turned to the matter of beginning her knitting session with prayer. Usually, she simply prayed their Woolgatherers prayer since all their shawls were for caregivers. Jenny had the impression Edna had been a caregiver. Hadn't she talked about her Stanley and "that Old-Timer's Disease"? But the way Edna talked about him (on the rare occasions when she did), it sounded like it was all in the past. Jenny decided to pray the Woolgatherers prayer anyway, because it would be good for Edna to be "strengthened, encouraged, loved, and known," in the embrace of the shawl about to take shape under her fingers.

"And maybe make her nicer . . . and happier," Jenny added at the end of the prayer.

Jenny quickly forgot prayer as she became absorbed in following the pattern she'd chosen to try first. She enjoyed watching the green deepen as she worked the bottom border in seed stitch. It was a little more demanding than the simple garter-stitch borders she was used to, but as she held her work out to view her progress, she realized it was worth the effort.

The green began to change to purple as Jenny finished the border.

She worked the first eight stitches in seed stitch for the border and slipped a stitch marker over the end of her right-hand needle as a reminder the border was different from the middle of the shawl.

As she worked on the body of the shawl and the pattern began to appear, Jenny realized she'd found the right one, the shawl this yarn "wanted to be," as Rose put it. She was relieved the pattern was easy. She'd be able to finish quickly. And she wouldn't have to concentrate hard to do it.

For a while, Jenny simply took pleasure in watching the colors change, fade, and then intensify as she worked. Her mind drifted to the book club discussion about "old love" vs. "new love." There was something so thrilling about falling in love. And yet, when she thought about it, it was that very thrill that had spelled trouble for her when she was young.

She usually tried not to think about the man who had swept her off her feet so many years ago. She had met Mark Linfield shortly after graduating from college, at the law firm where she had landed her first "real" job as a paralegal. He'd been a client, a rich one, as were all the clients at Bertrand, Collier, and Dalton. She wasn't supposed to date clients. Mark Linfield, however, had been not only handsome, but also charming and persistent. Before she knew it, she was the star of an extravagant wedding. She joined Mark in his beautiful home and drove the bright-red Jaguar he gave her. Soon there was a baby on the way. Shortly after Chloe's birth, however, the fairy tale began to fall apart. Mark stayed later and later at the office and seemed to have no interest in his daughter.

Then came the fateful evening when Jenny arranged for a babysitter and took a romantic picnic dinner to Mark's office. It was hard to say who was more surprised—Mark, Jenny, or the cute clerk from accounting who was caught in a compromising position. Jenny shook her head at the memory of the next few years. Like a fool, she'd given Mark a second chance, and a few more chances after that, but she'd finally packed up and made a life for herself and Chloe with the help of her well-invested divorce settlement.

She found love again, to be sure. Ben had loved her *and* loved being a father to Chloe. It should have been a fairy-tale happily-ever-after. If Ben hadn't died, it would have been.

Jenny closed her eyes against the memory. She never liked to think past the fairy-tale parts of her marriages. That's why she loved reading all those books about the beginnings of love. She could live in the rosy possibility of happily-ever-after and not remember what happened when the realities of life set in.

This idea of old love—did people really stay in love for years and years? She liked to think she and Ben would have, but she'd never know. Jenny thought of Sam, checking on Dorothy faithfully, bringing flowers every week, looking at her with "his heart in his eyes," as Nan had put it. Sam's devotion was touching but oh, so sad. Jenny sighed and turned her work.

She turned her thoughts to Edna again, since she was supposed to be praying for her while she made the shawl. Edna had a love story, too. Her lucky Stanley, who had been taken from her by "that Old-Timer's Disease." Edna didn't deserve such heartbreak. Nobody did. That breakfast on St. Patrick's Day flashed through Jenny's mind. She remembered the glow of pride on Edna's face when she spoke of Stanley that morning and how she'd caught a glimpse of the hole that his loss had left in Edna's heart.

Jenny found herself whispering, "Comfort her," as the shawl took shape beneath her fingers.

CHAPTER 28

On Saturday morning Sam woke feeling a bit feverish. He put it down to the decision he'd come to the night before. The more he thought it over, the more convinced he was it was time to stop eating his heart out over Dorothy. She'd moved on. It was time he did, too. There was a lot of life to live yet. Jenny had shown him that.

After a quick breakfast of coffee and a Pop-Tart, Sam pulled out the ironing board and pressed one of his dress shirts, the one he'd always worn when he'd had to give an important presentation at work. He pressed his slacks for good measure. He polished his shoes to a glossy glow. Pressed, combed, and shined, he grabbed his briefcase and headed out the door, ready for the mission he'd set himself.

"Don't you look nice," Jenny said when Sam arrived at the circle of prayer shawl makers.

Sam's face heated, but he managed to mumble, "Thank you." He took his seat next to Edna, across from Jenny. The morning sun shone through her hair like a fiery halo.

An elbow to the ribs brought him back to earth.

"Show me your work." Edna held her hand out.

Sam balanced his briefcase on his knees and pulled out the shawl he was working on.

"Mm-hmm. Mm-hmm." Edna nodded as she ran her fingers over it, tugging here, smoothing there.

"You're getting better," she finally said.

Edna had no patience for fools or shoddy work. "Getting better" was high praise indeed. Sam felt his chest swell with pride but soon interrupted himself with a cough.

Susan, however, paid more attention to the cough than Edna's approval of Sam's work.

"Are you feeling all right, Sam?"

"I'm fine," Sam said.

"Are you sure? You're a bit flushed." Susan put out her hand to feel his forehead, but he leaned away.

"I said I'm fine," Sam said, only to cough again.

"That doesn't sound good at all."

"I'm not sick," Sam said through gritted teeth. Today, of all days, he could not be sick.

He had a hard time concentrating on his work what with Jenny sitting right across from him, given what he planned to do after this. He kept having to rip his work out.

"Are you sure you're all right?" Edna asked as Sam pulled his work out yet again.

"Just distracted," he mumbled—and coughed again. "Tickle in my throat," he said when both Edna and Susan looked askance.

A little while later, Tara stepped out of the elevator.

"How is Grandma Becca?" Rose asked.

"It's one of the good days. Look, Mrs. O'Brian!" Tara pulled a crocheted rectangle out of her backpack with a flourish. It was sunny yellow, edged with a row of orange single crochet. There were three loops worked into the edge of one of the long sides. "She can roll it up and make it into a muff if she wants to. I'll put these big buttons on the other long side," Tara explained. Tara pulled three large yellow buttons out of her backpack.

"What other kinds of things are you going to attach to it?" Laura's eyes were bright with interest.

Tara grinned. "I found some really cool stuff." She reached into her backpack again and produced a baggie. Inside, beside buttons of various shapes and sizes, were beads, ribbons, a fuzzy pom-pom, and some plastic charms. "I want to put a crocheted flower on it, too. Can you show me how to do that, Mrs. O'Brian?"

"Yes, I can show you how to make a flower," Edna said, her face softening. "I used to make those with—" Edna clamped her mouth shut.

"With who?" Tara asked.

"Don't matter who," Edna said. "I'll show *you* how to do it."

Tara settled herself in the chair on the other side of Edna. Soon they were absorbed in the creation of a flower using nothing but yarn and a crochet hook.

After what seemed like an eternity to Sam, it was time for lunch. The Woolgatherers stood and stretched. Tara, with a pink and purple crocheted flower tucked into her backpack, headed for home with her mother and sister. As Jenny started toward the dining room, Sam fell in step beside her.

"Jenny, do you have a minute before lunch?" Suddenly, his palms felt sweaty.

"Of course, Sam." Jenny's smile brightened not only her face, but the whole lobby.

Sam stepped over to the side, out of the flow of traffic into the dining room. He fought the urge to stare at his shoes and shuffle his feet. It had been such a long time since he'd done anything like this. He gazed into her eyes, which were alight with expectation.

"I was wondering . . ."

Jenny raised her eyebrows.

"I was wondering if you'd like to go out to dinner with me on Friday night. I mean, if you don't have plans or anything." He felt his throat constrict.

Jenny simply stared at him as if she couldn't quite take in what he'd said.

Finally, she said, "Sam, it's kind of you to invite me, but I couldn't."

Sam opened his mouth to protest, but a hacking cough came out instead. He turned his head and held up a finger for her to wait.

"You already have plans? Some other time? Sometime soon?" he blurted out when he recovered, to get it said before he started coughing again.

Jenny regarded him with concern, then shook her head. "No, Sam, it's not that. I couldn't whether I had plans or not. You're married. I don't go out with married men."

"Not even just as friends?" Sam fought to keep the pleading note out of his voice. His face felt hot, as if he'd been caught in a lie. "It would be just as friends."

"No. It's not a good idea."

"What if I weren't?" Sam asked.

"If you weren't what?" Jenny tilted her head, eyebrows drawn together.

"Married," Sam said, letting himself think it. Letting himself say it out loud. "What if I weren't married?" His stomach lurched. He hoped he wasn't going to hurl.

"But you *are* married," Jenny said.

"But if I weren't?" Sam persisted. *I might as well not be.* The memory of Rafe and Dorothy together hardened his resolve even as his stomach churned. "Would you go out with me then?"

"Really, Sam, I don't think, I mean . . ." Jenny stammered.

Sam stared at her as Jenny tried to regain her composure, his heart somewhere in the vicinity of his shoes.

"I get it." Bile rose in the back of his throat. He swallowed hard to shove the bitterness of rejection down. "I'm the Fat Man to you, too. Not good enough for you or Dorothy. Forget I ever asked. Forget I ever *was*."

Sam turned and strode toward the lobby doors.

"Sam, that's not what I meant at all!" Jenny cried. "Sam, wait! Let me explain!"

But Sam continued across the lobby, through the doors, and across the parking lot. He threw his briefcase into the trunk of his car and shut it with a slam. Sam took one last look at Fair Meadows Retirement Community in his rearview mirror as he pulled out of the parking lot. He was never coming back. There was no point. Dorothy had forgotten him, had forgotten she was even married, and screamed at the sight of him. And he could never face Jenny again, so he wouldn't be going back to the Woolgatherers, either. From here on out it would be microwave popcorn and Netflix binges with the occasional foray to pick up a pizza. He stopped at his favorite fast-food restaurant on the way home, ordering fries *and* onion rings to go with his double cheeseburger. Since it was abundantly clear he was nothing but the Fat Man, he might as well enjoy it.

Jenny stood stock-still, frozen in confusion, as Sam stormed off. What had just happened? She'd simply been being friendly, hadn't she? Everybody knew she didn't mean anything by it when she flirted. Men just enjoyed it for what it was. She hadn't meant to lead him on. She caught her breath as Tara's words came back to her: *When it comes to Sam, I think only one of you is flirting for fun.*

Jenny felt heat creep up her neck. She didn't much feel like facing her friends over lunch. She hurried into the dining room and made her excuses to the Woolgatherers.

"I remembered something I have to do. I better do it before I forget again." She gave an elegant flutter of her fingers out of habit, then clenched her hand to her side as she left the dining room, appalled at how easy it was for her to cover up the truth with charm and smiles.

As she made her way to her cottage, Jenny barely noticed the spring beauty along the path. She realized there really was something she had to do. She could feel the pull of Edna's shawl as she hurried along. Once inside, she lost no time in brewing herself a cup of chamomile tea and settling on the couch with her knitting.

"I didn't mean to. I didn't mean to. I didn't mean to," Jenny whispered as she worked the first three stitches.

"I'm so sorry. I'm so sorry. I'm so sorry," she whispered with the next three stitches. She reached for a tissue as her eyes filled.

"What should I do? What should I do? What should I do?" Tears dripped onto her knitting.

Talk it over with Rose. The thought seemed to come from nowhere. Nowhere in Jenny's brain, anyway.

"Absolutely not. What would she think of me? I'd sooner talk it over with Edna—which I would never do. I can't talk to anybody about this." Jenny set her jaw.

Have it your way, then. It was the same tone she'd heard in the Prayer Chapel. Gentle, but not nearly as reassuring this time.

Jenny knitted into the afternoon, filled with regret and asking over and over what to do. It felt like the butterflies had folded their wings and settled like lead in her midsection. The Nudge, as she'd come to call those thoughts that seemed to come from outside herself, remained silent. Eventually, she began to pray for Edna. Jenny found herself replaying scenes of Edna among the Woolgatherers. There she was alongside Sam, teaching him to crochet. She wasn't lavish with praise, but Sam had kept at it all the same. And while the other Woolgatherers had twittered around comforting Tara over her grandmother, Edna had suggested something Tara could actually do to help Grandma Becca as well as herself. Edna hadn't even said "I told you so" when Tara had admitted she couldn't figure out how to crochet from YouTube videos. Fresh in Jenny's mind were two heads, one frizzled and gray, the other sleek and dark, bent over creating a crocheted flower that very morning.

Most of all, Jenny remembered Edna's warning about Sam. Her words had stung, and Jenny had thought Edna was being so mean when she said them. Now, she realized Edna had spoken the truth out of concern for Sam, not malice toward Jenny. No, Jenny was the one who'd been unkind (without meaning to, she was quick to add). She'd meant to be kind, but Sam took it all wrong, and she came off as unkind. Jenny wished she'd listened to Edna. Oh, how she wished she'd listened. But it was too late now.

When he arrived home, Sam popped the trunk and retrieved his brief-case. He carried it into the house and set it by his recliner before he realized what he was doing.

"Don't need this anymore," he grunted. He started to pick it up again, but all at once it seemed like too much trouble to climb the stairs to Dorothy's craft room. He left it where he'd dropped it and settled into the chair with his lunch and the remote. Three episodes later, he woke with the greasy hamburger wrapping still on his stom-ach. He paused the show, heaved himself to his feet, and staggered to the kitchen trash to throw the stained paper away. He tripped over the briefcase on the way and fought the urge to kick it across the room. When Sam returned to the living room, he glared at the briefcase. He supposed he should take it upstairs.

Before he could succumb to the lure of the recliner again, Sam grabbed the briefcase and trudged upstairs to Dorothy's craft room. He set the case on her sewing table and flipped open the catches. He grasped the half-finished shawl, intending to toss it into the closet and slam the door. His hands, however, lingered on the pile of crochet and squeezed. He gathered the shawl into his arms and hugged it to his chest. Sam stood with his chin resting on the soft creation. He shivered from a sudden chill. He decided to take the shawl down-stairs, where working on it might keep him warm. He settled into the recliner with the length of the shawl covering his lap and knees. The shivering stopped. He crocheted a few rows, but the hook felt so heavy. He closed his eyes, barely aware of the hook slipping from his fingers. Too spent to retrieve it, he fell into heavy slumber.

CHAPTER 29

On Monday morning, Jenny kept an eye on the lobby doors. Sam had said to forget about him, but she found that her regret and dismay wouldn't let her.

"I wonder where Sam is." Rose glanced at her watch. "He's usually here by now."

"I hope he's all right." Susan sounded worried. "He might be sick. He had a cough on Saturday."

"Or he could simply be taking a break," Laura said. "He's had a rough time lately."

"He would have said something to us so we wouldn't worry," Susan said.

"He's a grown man," Laura said. "He doesn't answer to us. He has a life, you know."

"That's the thing," Susan said. "I don't think he does have a life. I don't think he does anything except check on Dorothy and crochet with us."

"He's enjoyed the events here we've invited him to," Mr. Peabody said. "At least, it seems like he's been enjoying himself. And he came to church, too."

"He did indeed," Rose said. "Lately, it does seem like he has more of a life. That's what makes it strange he's not here this morning."

Jenny busied herself with putting her knitting away and didn't join in on the speculation as to Sam's whereabouts. She was secretly relieved she didn't have to face him. Secretly relieved and just as secretly ashamed of feeling that way. She made an extra effort to be entertaining over lunch so no one would suspect.

By Saturday, the Woolgatherers had still not seen Sam at Fair Meadows.

"I was sure Sam would be here today," Rose said. "It's cookie day." A plateful of Laura's pecan sandies was fast disappearing as memory care visitors stopped by for cookies and comfort.

"He had a cough last week. I hope he's not sick." Susan's face was pinched with concern.

"He said it was just a tickle." Mr. Peabody waved a dismissive hand.

"He was flushed, too. And he wouldn't let me feel his forehead." Susan's fingers fretted on the edge of her shawl.

"Maybe he decided to go visit one of his sons." Laura shrugged.

"Wouldn't he have talked about it?" Susan said.

"Could he have come on one of the days we're not in the lobby?" A hint of concern was edging into Laura's eyes now.

"I don't think so," Mr. Peabody said. "He's had a hard time over Rafe. He hasn't been going to Memory Care. He's just been calling to check on Dorothy."

"We should call him," Rose said. "It's better to find out if he's all right than to sit here and speculate. Does anybody have his phone number?"

"I do," Mr. Peabody said.

At this, Rose noticed Jenny catch her breath and turn her head away, looking decidedly uncomfortable. She wondered . . .

"Jenny," Rose said. "You wouldn't know anything about this, would you?"

"Maybe," Jenny answered in an uncharacteristically small voice.

The group waited for her to go on, but her gaze remained on the knitting in her lap.

"And?" Laura finally said, in a tone that demanded an answer.

Jenny mumbled something.

"Speak up," Laura said.

Jenny heaved a sigh and dragged her gaze up. "Sam may have asked me out to dinner."

"*May* have?" Laura said. "Either he did or he didn't. Which is it?"

By this time, all knitting and crocheting had ceased. The attention of every Woolgatherer was riveted on Jenny.

"He did," Jenny said.

"And then what?" Laura said.

"I turned him down, of course. I told him I don't date married men."

"And that was the end of it?" Rose hoped against hope this was the case.

The guilty flush creeping up Jenny's neck told the group that was not the end of it.

"He asked what I would say if he weren't married. It took me by surprise, and I was kind of at a loss for words, and he took it all wrong." This last came out in a rush.

"I don't know why you were so surprised." Tara stood on the edge of the circle, eyes blazing. "I *told* you he liked you. I told you, and you just brushed it off."

Rose took hold of Tara's hand. "Let's let Jenny finish. I have a feeling there's more to this story. What did Sam take all wrong, Jenny?"

"When I didn't answer right away about whether I'd go out with him if he weren't married, he said something like, 'Oh, I get it. I'm the Fat Man to you, too.' Then he said to forget he'd asked. He said to forget about him. I didn't mean to hurt him. Really, I didn't."

"But you did," Tara said. "You can't go around messing with people's feelings like that."

"But I was just being friendly," Jenny said. "Everybody knows I don't mean anything by it," Jenny appealed to the rest of the group.

"Everybody," Tara said, "except Mr. Talbot, a sad, lonely man who's been rejected by his wife's *disease*. He took your flirting to heart. He hoped you meant it. I take it back. You're *not* cool. You're not cool at all." Tara dropped Rose's hand. "I can't knit with you today. I can't even look at you." She turned on her heel and marched to the elevator, back stiff.

"Tara," Rose called after her.

"Let her go," Jenny said miserably. "I should go. The rest of you probably don't want to be around me, either." She stuffed her knitting into her tote.

"Not so fast," Rose said. "I, for one, am still worried about Sam. I'm even more worried now that I know what happened. You sit tight." Rose pointed at Jenny. "And you call Sam." Rose pointed at Mr. Peabody.

"On it," Mr. Peabody pulled his phone from his pocket, scrolled through his contacts, of which there appeared to be a great many, and finally tapped on Sam's contact. Then he pressed Call and put the phone on speaker. The sound of a ringing phone filled the room. It took six rings before a garbled sound emerged. Mr. Peabody lifted the phone to his ear and listened intently, his eyebrows drawing together in a frown. He passed his phone to Rose. "He's not making any sense."

"Sam? It's Rose Harker. Are you all right?"

But all that came through the line was an unintelligible mumble and then a thud that sounded like the receiver hitting the floor.

"Sam? Sam?" But Sam didn't respond.

"You were right, Susan. Something really is wrong." Rose pivoted to face the group again. "We have to get him help."

"We don't know where he lives," Susan wailed. "He could be dying, and we don't even know where he lives."

Rose had already struggled to her feet. "Memory Care will have his address because of Dorothy."

"Will they give it to us, though?" Susan bit her lip. "What with the Privacy Act and all?"

"I know the weekend charge nurse," Rose said. "She can call the police to do a wellness check."

"I'll go with you," Jenny said. "I have to do something."

Together, Rose and Jenny walked to the elevator and rode to the memory care unit.

"Why, Rose," Eileen exclaimed when they stepped out of the elevator. "What brings you to the seventh floor?"

Rose quickly explained their mission. Even as Rose spoke, Eileen began to type on the computer.

"The emergency contact for Dorothy Talbot?"

"Please hurry," Jenny said. "We think it might be an emergency for Sam."

"Here it is." Eileen reached for the phone, placed a call, and quickly and efficiently requested a wellness check for Mr. Sam Talbot while reading out his address.

"Thank you so much, Eileen," Rose said.

"Thank *you* for letting us know. I heard Dorothy was upset when her flowers didn't come on Monday. And when Sam didn't call this morning to check on her, I should have put two and two together. I hope he's okay."

"So do I," Jenny said fervently.

In the elevator, Jenny pulled out her phone. Her stomach was swooping, and it wasn't because of the elevator.

"We need to get there as soon as possible," she said as she tapped her phone.

"The police can take care of it," Rose said. "That's why Eileen called them."

"Who knows how long it will take them to get there? We need to do something now."

"Hello, Gus, it's Jenny," she said into the phone. "The Woolgatherers need the van right away. It's an emergency."

"A knitting emergency?" The young man was laughing.

"No, it's not a knitting emergency." She managed to control her voice. "It's a real one." She briefly explained about their phone call to

Sam as well as Eileen's phone call to the police. "But I'm afraid they won't rush over there, and I have a strong feeling that he needs help fast." She pressed a hand to her stomach to quell the panicked butterflies.

"I don't know. You could call for a car."

"No, a taxi or an Uber will take too long. I don't think we have that much time. I know it's unauthorized, but I'll take full responsibility."

As the elevator doors opened on the lobby floor, Jenny pocketed her phone and hurried over to the Woolgatherers, Rose barely keeping up on her cane.

"Listen, everybody," Jenny said when she reached them. "Gus is taking us to Sam's. Leave your knitting and crocheting here. We've got to go!"

"But shouldn't we let the police handle it?" Laura objected.

"I don't know about Rose, but *I* only asked Eileen to call for a wellness check so I could get the address when she gave it to the dispatcher," Jenny told her. "It could take hours for the police to get there. More than likely they'll have to deal with an accident or some crime before they can get to checking on our friend."

Moments later, Gus pulled the van under the porte cochere. The Woolgatherers surged through the lobby doors with Jenny in the lead. She took her place in the front while Gus helped Rose, Mr. Peabody, Susan, Laura, and Edna into the van.

"Where to?" Gus asked as he settled into the driver's seat.

"212 Wilshire Place," Jenny said.

As she buckled her seat belt, Laura said, "Jenny, are you sure we have to go rushing off like this? Shouldn't we wait for the police to take care of it? It's only a couple of hours."

"No," Jenny said. "I have a feeling Sam doesn't have that much time."

"I think you're right, Jenny," Susan said. "Step on it, Gus."

"Yes, ma'am." Gus gave her a salute and dutifully stepped on it. Only Jenny saw the barest hint of a smile around the corners of his mouth as he glanced into the rearview mirror at Susan, who was not clutching the door handle but leaning forward as if willing the van to go faster.

Jenny was out of the van before Rose could even unbuckle her seat belt. Rose bustled up the walk to 212 Wilshire Place as the other woman pressed the doorbell. Then pressed it again. And a third time for good measure.

"If he's unconscious, he won't be able to answer the door," Laura pointed out, coming up behind her.

"Just giving him a heads-up before we barge in," Jenny said.

"And how do you propose we barge in, since the door is locked?" Laura had already reached around and tried the doorknob.

"Check under the flowerpots." Jenny pointed to the ceramic urns bearing the skeletal remains of an arrangement. "I'll check here." In her three-inch heels, it was easy for her to run her hand along the top of the doorframe. Jenny came up empty, as did Laura.

By this time, Gus had joined them.

"I'll check around back." He disappeared around the corner of the house while Jenny paced the front walk, head down, lips moving.

"Please, God, please," Rose heard Jenny whisper as she passed.

Jenny was on her way back from her third trip down the walk when the front door swung in.

"The key was on the ledge over the back door," Gus said as the Woolgatherers hurried past him into the house.

"Sam! Sam! It's the Woolgatherers!" Jenny called.

A moan came from the hallway to their left.

"Thank God," Jenny said.

Gus made his way to the front of the group. "Let me check on him first," he said. "I was a medic in the army before college."

Gus strode down the hall in the direction of the moans. Moments later, he came out of Sam's bedroom. He had his phone to his ear and spoke rapidly, giving their location.

"I've called an ambulance. His breathing is labored, and he's burning up with fever. He needs to be in the hospital. I'll stay with him in his room. I suggest all of you wait in the living room so you can direct the EMTs when they get here."

Rose was grateful for a chance to sit. She'd been on her feet for a while. In the living room, however, she looked around in dismay. The only clear space to sit was a recliner. It was probably quite comfortable, but she knew she'd have a hard time getting out of it. Without a word, Laura cleared a space on the couch. Rose perched gingerly on the edge and leaned on her cane.

Edna finally said what everyone was thinking. "This place is a pigsty."

Dishes, soda cans, and fast-food wrappers littered the coffee table, while most of the couch was piled with clothes.

"Are these clean or dirty?" Laura wondered. She picked up a T-shirt from the top of the pile with her thumb and forefinger. She gave it a sniff. "They're clean."

"Too lazy to fold them and put them away," Susan said.

"Or maybe he got sick before he could finish his laundry," Rose said, trying to give Sam the benefit of the doubt.

"This place is downright unsanitary," Susan said. "No wonder he got sick."

"I wonder how long it's been since he's vacuumed." Laura kicked at the popcorn that littered the carpet with the toe of her shoe.

"Too long," Susan said as she headed for the kitchen. The rest of the Woolgatherers heard the refrigerator door open and close. Susan returned, shaking her head.

"No wonder. How can you stay healthy eating nothing but junk? All Sam has in there is junk food, hot dogs, leftover pizza . . ."

The sound of the doorbell interrupted this sad litany. Jenny hurried to open the door to the ambulance crew.

"We're so glad you're here," Jenny said, as graciously as if she were welcoming dinner guests. "Right this way." She led them to Sam's bedroom. When she returned, she was pale and wide-eyed.

"He looks awful. He can hardly breathe, but he keeps mumbling, 'Dorothy, Dorothy' over and over."

A frightened silence descended on the group. Soon after, the ambulance crew wheeled Sam, strapped to a gurney and with an oxygen mask covering his face, through the house and out the front door. Gus followed behind but stopped when he reached the living room.

"I wish I could go with him, but I have to get the van—and all of you—back to Fair Meadows. I'm probably in enough trouble already, and I don't want to be late for my next van run."

"I'll go with him," Edna said. "He's got no family around here except Dorothy. It ain't good for him to be alone." She swept her arm to encompass the mess of the living room. Then she hurried off after the EMTs.

Jenny caught up with her at the front door.

"How will you get home? It should be me. I can call my daughter to take me home."

"You've done enough already, missy," Edna said. "Don't you worry about me none. I'll take one of them Uber things when he's out of the woods." With that, she turned and stumped toward the ambulance as fast as her cane would allow.

CHAPTER 30

Gus groaned as he pulled up under the porte cochere. The Fair Meadows bowling team was waiting, none too patiently, at the curb. The last Woolgatherer had barely alighted before they hurried over to the van.

A burly man in a red and black bowling shirt hustled his teammates into the vehicle while Gus stowed their bowling bags.

"Where have you been, young man? We're bowling against the Willows Retirement Community today. They're the best team in the league. We really needed the warm-up time, and now we're going to be late."

Before Gus could reply, Susan turned around and planted herself in front of the captain of the bowling team.

"For your information, Ralph McGuire, he's been saving someone's life. Now, go win your oh-so-important bowling tournament." She turned on her heel, leaving the bowler gaping after her. At a nudge from Gus, he heaved his bowling bag into the van and climbed in. Gus gave a cheerful toot of the horn, and they were off.

When the Woolgatherers entered the lobby, they discovered someone else had been waiting for the return of the van. Rose's heart quailed as she caught sight of Mrs. Hargrave standing in the Woolgatherers' seating area, arms crossed and foot tapping.

"Mrs. Alderman, the Fair Meadows van is *not* your personal car service, nor is Gus your chauffeur."

Jenny, however, was undaunted.

"I know that, Mrs. Hargrave. It was an emergency." As the group gathered around to corroborate her story, Jenny told of finding Sam at his home, ill and in need of immediate medical attention.

"It's a good thing we had Gus with us," Jenny said. "Did you know he was a medic in the army?"

Mrs. Hargrave gave a tight smile. "Yes, I did. His ability to handle medical emergencies is one of the reasons we hired him."

"Oh," Jenny said. She gave the director a dazzling smile. "What a good idea."

Mrs. Hargrave, however, was not swayed by Jenny's charm. "See that you never do this again, Mrs. Alderman. Next time, call a taxi."

"Whew!" Mr. Peabody wiped mock sweat from his brow as Mrs. Hargrave stalked back to her office.

"They do say sometimes it's better to ask forgiveness rather than permission," Laura said with a chuckle. "Most of the time when students quoted that to me, I didn't approve, but it was worth the tongue-lashing this time."

"Yes, it absolutely was." Rose glanced at her watch. "We still have an hour before lunch. I suggest we get busy knitting and praying. Sam needs our prayers more than ever."

The Woolgatherers resumed their work and their prayers, knitting in concentrated silence. Half an hour later, they were startled by the ringing of Rose's phone. Rose glanced at the screen.

"It's Edna," she announced, then accepted the call. "Edna, can I put you on speaker? We're all here, knitting and praying."

"Fine," Edna said. "You'd better keep praying for Sam. He's got double pneumonia."

Susan gasped.

"The docs say it's a good thing he got here when he did, but it's still touch and go. They're gonna take him up to the ICU in a little while."

A murmur of dismay rose from the group.

"I'm gonna stay here for a while. He ain't got nobody but us here. But his boys ought to know. And the Memory Care people, too."

"Good idea," Rose said. "Memory Care will have his sons' contact information. We'll take care of it, Edna."

"Good," Edna said. "Gotta go. They're moving him upstairs now."

"It's a good thing we called Sam this morning," Laura said as Rose returned her phone to her knitting bag.

"And that we got Gus to take us to check on him," Jenny said.

"He should have gotten his pneumonia shot," Susan said.

"I'll go up to Memory Care." Jenny's heels tapped double-time on the way to the elevator.

"Hello again," Eileen greeted Jenny as she stepped out of the elevator.

Jenny quickly filled the nurse in on the events of the morning, ending with the need to inform Sam's sons.

"You're right, Mr. Talbot's sons absolutely need to be informed," Eileen said. "I can call the hospital with their contact information, no problem. As I said before, I should have realized something was wrong when he didn't call this morning."

"Since Sam isn't able to check on Dorothy at the moment, I guess I'd better do it for him."

Eileen smiled. "You're a good friend. She's in the dayroom. Come on, I'll introduce you."

Jenny followed Eileen across the lobby to the doorway of the dayroom. With a pang, she pictured Sam peering around the doorframe to sneak a peek at his wife.

"Mrs. Talbot, you have a visitor," Eileen said as they approached the table where Dorothy sat, pieces of a puzzle spread out before her.

"Her name is Dot." A handsome man with an impressively full mustache strode across the room to stand behind Dorothy.

"And I'm Jenny Alderman."

"Won't you have a seat, Jenny?" Dorothy swept a gracious hand toward one of the seats at the table. "This is my friend Rafe."

Rafe gave Jenny a curt, dismissive nod.

"She's a friend of Dot's family," Eileen said.

A line formed between Dorothy's eyebrows.

"I don't remember you," she said, distress beginning to show on her face.

"I wouldn't expect you to," Jenny said, her voice gentle. "We've never met, but I've heard about you. I was in the neighborhood and decided to stop by to say hello."

The lines of puzzlement smoothed out into a radiant smile.

"Good things, I hope."

"Very good things," Jenny said. "You are much loved. How have you been, Dot?"

"Pretty well, except . . ." Her eyebrows drew together.

"Except what?" Jenny asked.

"My flowers. I don't know where my flowers are."

"I don't know what you're talking about, Dot," Rafe said. "You have flowers in your room."

Dorothy waved his comment away. "Those aren't fresh. I don't know where the fresh ones are. I keep asking about them, and nobody can tell me anything." Her eyes glistened with tears.

"Would you like me to try to find them?" Jenny felt tears forming in her own eyes.

"Oh, could you? That would be wonderful."

"What kind of flowers are they, the ones you're looking for?"

Dorothy regarded her blankly for a moment. Then her face cleared. "Carnations. Red ones."

"I'll be on the lookout for your red carnations." Jenny stood. "I need to be going now, Dot. It's so good to finally meet you. Nice to meet you, too, Rafe." But Rafe had already taken Jenny's seat at the table, wholly focused on Dorothy.

Out in the reception area, Jenny turned to Eileen.

"Thank you. Now we'll be able to tell Sam that Dorothy is fine. I'm not going to mention Rafe," she added. "And I really will do something about the flowers. If anyone knows how important flowers are, it's me."

As Jenny turned to make her exit, a man in a battered ball cap approached the nurses' station.

"Hello, Mr. O'Brian, what can I do for you?"

"Found my lucky hat." He tapped his headgear with his forefinger. "And my lucky dime." He dug a coin out of his shirt pocket.

"Sounds like you're all ready for your scratch-offs on Monday," Eileen said.

"This ain't Monday?" Mr. O'Brian's face clouded in disappointment.

"No, sir," Eileen said. "Only two more days, though."

"Well, all right then. I'll just have to come back. Just hope my luck holds. I'm feeling really lucky today." He pocketed the dime and continued on to the dayroom with a grin and a jaunty wave.

Jenny raised her eyebrows at Eileen.

"Scratch-off tickets?"

"Before he came to live here, Mr. O'Brian bought lottery tickets every Monday. He kept trying to leave the unit to get them. To keep him safe and give him something that has always brought him pleasure, his wife provides scratch-offs for him. He 'buys' them on Mondays at the nurses' station as if it's the corner store where he always used to go for them. I hear he's always so pleased when he wins, even if it's only five dollars. He can hardly wait to tell her about it."

"Her?" Jenny asked.

"His wife," Eileen said. "Sadly, he doesn't recognize her when she comes to visit, but he does remember sharing the joy of winning with her."

An idea began to form in Jenny's mind.

"Mr. O'Brian's first name wouldn't be Stanley, would it?"

"He goes by Stan here," Eileen said. "I call all the residents by their last names, though. Somehow, it helps me remember who they were before they came here, even if they've forgotten."

"I'd better let you get back to work," Jenny said. "Especially letting you call the hospital so they can get ahold of Sam's sons. Thank you for your help, Eileen."

Eileen gave her a cheerful wave as she turned to her computer and reached for the phone. On the elevator ride to the lobby, Jenny mulled over her surprising encounter with Stanley O'Brian.

The Woolgatherers were putting away their knitting projects when Jenny returned from checking on Dorothy. Together they walked to the dining room for lunch. Rose took charge of Edna's crochet bag, left behind in the rush to check on Sam.

"It's been quite a morning." Rose sighed as she settled at a table.

"It sure has," Jenny said. "I discovered something very interesting when I went to check on Dorothy." She lowered her voice and leaned across the table to tell the group about Stanley O'Brian and his scratch-off tickets. She had a feeling Edna wouldn't want everyone in the dining room hearing about this.

"So, Edna's not a widow," Rose said.

"And her husband lives here at Fair Meadows," Laura said. "She never said a word."

"I don't understand why she never told us," Jenny said. "We're all friends here. We would have supported her like we've been supporting Sam."

"I think she almost did on St. Patrick's Day," Rose said. "But clearly, it's hard for her to talk about. Remember how she stormed off?"

There were nods around the table.

"She's a hurting caregiver," Susan said. "The kind of person we make shawls for. I'm ashamed to admit I've been judging her instead, for being so, well, so . . ."

"Negative? Me, too." Jenny's tone was rueful.

"And all this time, she needed our prayers," Laura said.

"No wonder . . ." Jenny said.

"No wonder what?" Laura asked.

"No wonder I got the Nudge to make her a shawl last week. I didn't know at the time that she's a caregiver, but God did." She sucked in her breath and pressed a hand to her stomach.

"Are you okay?" Mr. Peabody asked.

Jenny nodded. "I get this swooping sensation, like butterflies in my stomach, when I think about it. It happened in the chapel when I got the Nudge, too. Excited and scared at the same time."

Laura leaned forward. "What's the Nudge?"

"It's—I don't know how to explain it," Jenny said.

"It's a sense there's something you're supposed to do, something you wouldn't think of yourself," Rose said. "A heavenly suggestion."

"More than a suggestion," Jenny said.

"True," Rose said. "It's more of an 'I want you to do such-and-such' rather than 'How about doing such-and-such?'"

Laura's eyes widened. "*I*? As in—?"

"Yes," Rose said. "As in God."

"Now *my* stomach's swooping," Laura said. "Does God really do that?"

"If I've learned anything making prayer shawls," Rose said, "it's that God really does do that. I've been Nudged so much about yarn, patterns, and people, it's a wonder my ribs aren't sore."

CHAPTER 31

EDNA WASN'T AT DINNER THAT evening, so Rose called her during dessert.

"I'm gonna stay here tonight," Edna said. "Them boys can't get here until tomorrow, and I ain't gonna leave him alone. Somebody's got to look out for him."

"How is he?" Rose asked.

"Holding steady," Edna said. "Still pretty out of it, but he's hooked up to an IV and breathing better with the oxygen mask."

"What's in the IV?" Susan had leaned in so she could hear.

"No idea," Edna said. "I'm not family, so they can't tell me."

"We'll be praying, then," Rose said.

"You'd better be. Like I said, nobody's telling me what's going on, but we're in the ICU, and nobody's smiling when they come in or when they go out."

"Oh, my." Rose put a hand to her throat. "I'll call the Heavenly Hugs to pray, too."

"Good," Edna said. "From what I can tell, he needs all the prayer he can get."

Rose relayed the news about Sam's condition to the rest of the group and then called each of the Heavenly Hugs.

"It's going to be a long night for Edna," Fran said on the phone.

"Yes, it will," Rose said, remembering hospital vigils in her past. "And she doesn't have her crochet bag with her to pass the time since we all left our work in the lobby when we went to check on Sam. I'm keeping it at my place for her."

"Say no more," Fran said. "Meet me in the lobby with it, and I'll take it to her."

"That's really kind of you," Rose said.

"Not a problem," Fran said. "We all know how comforting it can be to work on a shawl when upset."

"Visiting hours are over," the Red Cross volunteer at the information desk informed Fran when she asked where she could find Sam Talbot.

"I know," Fran said. "I brought something for the person who's staying with him." She showed the crochet bag to the volunteer.

"All right, then." The volunteer turned to her computer. "As long as you know you won't be able to go in. He's in room 602."

"Can I get you anything else?" Fran asked Edna when she emerged from Sam's room to retrieve her crochet bag. "Have you eaten?"

Edna shook her head. "Didn't want to leave him. Them doctors and nurses and what-all keep mumbling about his 'white count,' whatever that is."

"I could get you something from the cafeteria. It's probably just sandwiches at this time of night . . ."

"I'll take anything that don't eat me first. My Stanley used to say that every time I asked him what he wanted for supper." A smile creased Edna's face. The smile disappeared as a nurse bustled into room 602. "Gotta go."

"I'm glad someone's looking out for her," the charge nurse said when Fran returned with Edna's meal. "Because she's sure looking out for him. We don't usually let nonfamily members stay in patients' rooms, but she told the doctor in no uncertain terms that Mr. Talbot shouldn't be alone. When the doctor pointed out that there was an entire ICU staff taking care of him, she stamped her foot and said, 'But he don't know any of you. He needs to see somebody he knows when he wakes up, not a bunch of strangers.' The doctor decided to let her stay. She's going to have a long night of it, though."

So Edna wouldn't feel alone in her vigil, Fran jotted a note on the bag of sandwiches: "The Heavenly Hugs are praying."

It was a quiet and somber group Gus drove to Hope of Glory the next morning.

"Thank you for taking us to Sam's yesterday," Rose told him as he helped her out of the van. "I hope you're not in too much trouble."

"I got a stern warning from Mrs. Hargrave, and the bowling team was unhappy with me on the way to the tournament. But they beat the Willows in spite of not having the extra practice time. They called them the 'Weeping Willows' all the way home, so I'm in their good books again."

"Are you coming to the service again?" Rose asked.

"The semester is almost over," Gus said. "I should be studying my brains out, but I keep getting drawn back to Hope of Glory."

"We're really going to miss you when you leave, Gus." Rose leaned on her cane and gazed at him fondly.

"I'm going to miss you, too." His brown eyes were warm with affection. "Pray for me, won't you? About medical school, I mean. It's already the hardest thing I've ever done, the army included."

Over the lump in her throat, Rose said, "You can count on us. And on God, too. You're going to be a fine doctor."

"And I'll pray for the next van driver, what with Mrs. Alderman and all," Gus said with a wink.

Sam opened his eyes and stared at the ceiling. The light was bright— too bright to be the sunlight coming through his bedroom windows. He turned his head at a rustling sound to his right.

"Edna?"

"Good morning, Sam."

"Where?" He tried to say more, but he was so tired. And there was something on his face. He tried to push it out of the way, but Edna laid a hand on his arm. Not roughly, but not gently, either.

"Leave that. You're in the hospital, Sam, sick as a dog."

"How?" was all he could manage next.

"How did you get here?" Edna asked. "You got the Woolgatherers to thank for getting you here in time. You might've been a goner if we hadn't checked on you. Now, that there is an oxygen mask and without it you'll be gasping like a fish out of water, so you keep it on. You got me?"

Sam nodded and Edna let go of his arm. She settled back in the chair and once again took up her crochet. Sam watched the hook, the yarn, and her fingers forming stitches over and over. Comforted by the steady rhythm, he drifted off to sleep.

Edna listened to Sam's breathing as she worked. It was even and no longer labored thanks to the oxygen mask. It took her back to nights she'd kept vigil over Stanley. After several close calls during nighttime wanderings, during which he'd almost been hit by a car not once but twice, she'd taken to dozing in the chair beside his bed. She didn't dare lie down, afraid of sleeping too deeply. But she'd succumbed to exhaustion one night, and police found him wandering along the highway. She'd put him in Memory Care after that, but it had nearly broken her heart.

She let out a heavy sigh as she thought about broken hearts—hers and Sam's. When Penny passed, Edna had thought she would die, too, it hurt so bad. It had taken seven long, despairing years to finally have a baby, and then to lose her . . . But Stanley always told her how fortunate they'd been to have her for any time at all.

"Sure, we had to wait, but we had a baby at last," he'd tell her. "We were lucky to be a mom and dad. Not everybody gets that."

And when he'd talked like that, Edna reflected, she had felt lucky to have had Penny and to have Stanley loving her through it all. The worse that Old-Timer's got, though, the harder it was to look on the sunny side. Stanley always had. She couldn't keep the clouds away alone.

The soft whoosh of the door to Sam's room roused her from her memories.

"Mrs. O'Brian? I'm Josh Talbot, Sam's oldest son." A thinner, dark-haired version of Sam stood in the doorway.

"It's about time." Edna shoved her shawl in progress into her tote. She struggled to her feet, trying to ease the kinks out of her back. "I'll leave you to it."

Josh, however, didn't move out of the doorway. He looked into her eyes.

"I can't thank you enough for looking out for my dad. The doctors were pretty grim about what would have happened if you hadn't found him when you did. And they said that you wouldn't leave him, that you've been here all night."

Edna scowled at him. "He's not a man who ought to be left alone. You seen his house yet?"

"No, I came straight from the airport."

"Better brace yourself. He's been alone too long." With that, she shouldered past him to arrange for an Uber.

CHAPTER 32

AFTER A RESTLESS NIGHT, JENNY made two calls on Monday morning. First, she ordered two dozen red carnations for Dorothy. Jenny had promised to find the flowers for Dorothy, who would be waiting for them today. It was the least she could do for both Dorothy and Sam. Next, she called her daughter.

"Chloe, I need you to take me to the church today."

"Didn't you go yesterday in the van? Why do you need to go again today?"

"I just do. Humor your mother, honey."

Chloe sighed. "When? This afternoon?"

"I'd like to go this morning," Jenny said.

"I suppose I could," Chloe said with little enthusiasm. "Hey, it's Monday. Don't you have your knitting group this morning?"

"Yes," Jenny said. "I'm still going to be knitting. Just somewhere else today."

"I'll be back in an hour, Mom," Chloe said when she dropped Jenny off at Hope of Glory. Jenny didn't know if an hour would be long enough or not. All she did know was she needed to be in the chapel—desperately. She simply nodded, and Chloe drove off with a wave.

She hurried into the church as fast as her heels would allow but hesitated on the threshold of the Prayer Chapel. What would it be like to step into the chapel with a guilty conscience? Would the air be heavy with disapproval?

To her great relief, she had the same sense of love and welcome as she'd had on her first visit there. She sat in front of the Impossible Window for a moment with her knitting bag in her lap, taking in the light that streamed in through the windows. Wrapped in the warmth of the sunlight, Jenny let out a shaky breath, took out her knitting, and began.

"I'm a terrible person, God. I didn't mean to lead Sam on, I really didn't, but what I meant doesn't matter. Sam thought I really cared about him, and I do, but not the way he hoped I did. Especially not about a married man, not after—well, you know. After Mark. I'm never going to do to some other wife what Mark and those other women did to me. And yes, I know Dorothy wouldn't know she'd been cast off in favor of someone else, but it still wouldn't be right."

Jenny blinked, trying to dispel the tears forming. She hadn't cried about Mark's betrayal for a long time. The memory of being cast off herself swept through her. She caught her breath, cleared her throat, and went on.

"But the worst part is how I made him feel when he asked what I would say if he weren't married. It took me by surprise. I really don't know how I would have answered if he weren't married. I didn't expect him to ask me out at all. Oh, God, I made such a mess of it! And now he's deathly ill. Please help him to get well. Please don't let this whole mess get any worse."

Jenny tried to keep knitting, but her hands were shaking. In the silence of the chapel, she prayed she would have a chance to apologize and make things right with Sam. She laid her knitting aside and gazed at the windows, drawn to the depiction of Jesus on the cross, his mother staring up at him in agony. *What a woman. She stayed with him through thick and thin, even the hardest thing of all.*

"That's love," Jenny whispered. "No matter what, she stayed. Even when it broke her heart." She thought of Mark, who had left when responsibilities loomed and when greener pastures beckoned, breaking her heart. Then she thought of Edna and Sam, continuing to watch over Stanley and Dorothy even as their beloved spouses slipped farther and farther away, breaking *their* hearts. "Stanley and Dorothy are not coming back like you did," she said to the figure on the cross. "Edna and Sam have no hope."

They have love. The words filled Jenny's mind. They conjured images not of roses and candlelight and the breathtaking moments of new love, but of years of keeping promises day in and day out, rain or shine, no matter what. Old love. Tested, tried, and true love. Wrinkled, creased, stained, and worn, like a love letter that's been read over and over again. Her heart ached.

"But Dorothy and Stanley don't know they're loved like that," Jenny protested through the tears that ran down her cheeks.

Don't they? The question brought to Jenny's mind Dorothy expecting her flowers, Stanley buying his scratch-offs and delighting in telling "her" about his winnings. Tucked away in the recesses of their minds remained the sense of being cared for by someone, even if they couldn't remember exactly who.

"But they can't love Sam and Edna back," Jenny said. "Where does that leave them?"

The same feeling that had washed over Jenny the first time she'd visited the Prayer Chapel engulfed her again. She wrapped her arms around herself to hold close the love she felt in the beauty of this room, as real and warm as a prayer shawl. A solid and forever kind of love.

"I wish they could feel this." Jenny stopped trembling. She found she could knit again. As she worked on Edna's shawl, she knitted prayers for Edna and for Sam into it.

"Where were you?" Susan threw the question across the lunch table like a javelin, pointed and sharp.

Jenny felt her face flush. "I was, um, praying."

"So were we," Susan said.

"Sometimes prayer needs to be private." Rose came to Jenny's rescue. "I imagine you had some business to do," she said, low enough for only Jenny to hear. When Jenny nodded, Rose said, "Good," and gave her hand a reassuring pat.

"Well, you missed some excitement," Susan said. "We met Sam's sons, Josh and Jack. They came to Fair Meadows to visit their mother—it's about time, if you ask me—and to thank us for helping their father. Although, I do think rescuing is a more accurate word for what we did."

"Josh did say, 'Who knows what might have happened if you hadn't checked on him,'" Laura said.

"He's asked us to keep helping," Mr. Peabody said.

"How?" Jenny asked.

"I warned Josh to brace himself for the house," Edna said. "But obviously not well enough, because he was still reeling this morning."

"It was kind of a mess." Jenny made a face.

"Kind of a mess?" Susan said. "It looked like a teenage boy's bedroom." She wrinkled her nose. "And it smelled like one, too."

"Jack said the house needed a woman's touch," said Laura, quoting Sam's younger son.

"Like Merry Maids?" Jenny asked.

"More like us," Laura said.

"Hmm," Jenny said, thinking of her manicure.

"We told them boys they were going to have to pitch in, too," Edna said.

"We're going over tomorrow morning." Susan rubbed her hands together. "I've been itching to clean that house since the moment I stepped inside."

On Tuesday morning, a minivan taxi, hired by the Talbot brothers, pulled up under the porte cochere at Fair Meadows Retirement Community. The Woolgatherers, clad in jeans and sweatshirts (even Jenny), climbed aboard. Jenny was inclined to scoff at Rose's whispered "you look lovely." But then her friend squeezed her arm, grinning conspiratorially, and added, "And determined." But even though she was dressed for the occasion, Jenny still had no idea how to tackle the disaster that was 212 Wilshire Place.

Fortunately, the Woolgatherers had their own white-haired natural drill sergeant. As they rode along, Laura produced a clipboard and laid out their plan of action.

"The top priorities are the trash, the dishes, and the laundry. Once those are cleared away, we can start dusting, vacuuming, and scrubbing." She assigned each Woolgatherer a room. In the kitchen, Mr. Peabody would sit at the sink and wash dishes while Jenny dried and put them away. And lest anyone think Jenny was getting off easy, Laura also gave her the job of cleaning the refrigerator. Jenny wrinkled her nose but didn't protest. "The boys" would be doing the heavy lifting and anything that involved getting on the floor, as most of the Woolgatherers felt a bit iffy about being able to get up again.

Josh and Jack met the group at the house and ushered them in. The Woolgatherers stood for a moment of shocked silence in the entryway.

"It's even worse than I remembered," Susan said.

"We can do this." Laura strode into the living room. She opened the windows to let fresh air into a room gone stale with junk food and loneliness. Then she retrieved the television remote from the floor by the recliner and quickly found a music channel. Soon the house was filled with pop songs from the sixties and seventies. As they worked, they sang along and swapped stories about their lives at the time those tunes were hits. Laura turned out to be less drill sergeant and more cruise director, putting fun into what they were doing. Jenny worked with a will and a smile on her face.

Between the two of them, Jenny and Mr. Peabody made short work of the dishes. While Alistair scrubbed the now-empty sink, Jenny turned to the fridge. The smell hit her first and the dismay second.

"There's nothing but leftover fast food in here," she said. "No fruit, no vegetables. No, wait, there's a shriveled-up apple in the back of the crisper. And an orange with mold all over it. No wonder he got . . ." She was about to say "big," but caught herself. "Sick."

Susan came in from the living room to peer into the fridge. She tsked. "It's like he stopped taking care of himself once Dorothy got sick."

"He was too busy taking care of *her*," Edna said from the kitchen doorway. "I sure wouldn't have invited you into my house when I was taking care of Stanley. Stanley came first. The housework could wait."

"Speaking of Stanley," Jenny said. "I had the pleasure of seeing him the other day."

"You what?" Edna reached for the doorframe as if to steady herself.

"When I went to Memory Care to check on Dorothy on Saturday, Stanley came to the reception desk to buy his scratch-offs."

"He must've got his days mixed up. Scratch-offs are on Monday, like Dorothy's flowers. He gets confused sometimes."

"I was confused, too," Jenny said with gentle reproof. "You've talked about Stanley, but you never told us he's in Memory Care. We thought you were a widow."

"I am and I ain't." Edna fiddled with the thin gold band on her left hand. "I'm betwixt and between. I'm married, but Stanley don't know I'm his wife."

"A hard place to be." Jenny had a sudden urge to hug this sad and secretive woman, but held off, not sure how such a gesture would be received.

"Don't want none of your pity." Edna lifted her chin. "Only reason I live at a fancy place like Fair Meadows is to keep an eye on Stanley so he don't have to be alone. Don't need nobody feeling sorry for me. Let's get back to cleaning up this mess. Sam's the sorry one."

"On that we can agree." Jenny dropped the topic, glad she hadn't given in to her impulse.

"From all the debris I had to clean up around the couch and recliner, I'd say he spent most of his time watching television," Susan said.

"That's not much of a life," Jenny said.

"I tried to get him to come on a cruise with us," Josh said, coming in halfway through the conversation. "But he didn't want to leave

Mom. He was pretty wound up about Rafe. I had to take my little brother instead."

"Hey! I heard that!" Jack called as he passed the kitchen with a full basket of laundry.

"Your dad's been pretty concerned about Rafe," Mr. Peabody said.

Josh shrugged. "I told him there wasn't anything he could do about it, so he should come on the cruise with us. It would have done him good to get away. If I'd known he was living like this, I would have worked harder at getting him to come. Instead, I got mad."

Edna gave Josh a level look. His face reddened.

"It seemed so pointless to visit," he said, staring at the floor. Then he glanced at Edna again. "Mom didn't know who I was. It didn't matter to her if I was there or not. It was awful. She used her 'be-polite-to-strangers' manners with us. No recognition at all. It was down-right creepy, like being in an old episode of *The Twilight Zone*." He shuddered.

"Let's face it, Josh. We forgot about Dad right along with Mom," Jack said, coming back from the laundry room. "And it was worse for Dad. The staff in Memory Care told us it's gotten so she's afraid of him for some reason."

Josh nodded. "You're right. We should have been here more, for the both of them. Yeah, it was awful to see Mom like that, but we should have braved it for Dad's sake. We should have come to spend time with him. Hard to think of your parents needing you."

"It's hard for us to admit we need our kids." Mr. Peabody turned toward them from the sink. "I used to be Super Dad, and now—" He framed the sides of the walker with his hands.

"Hey, Super Dad," Jack said. "How about we go grab some pizza for this crew for lunch?"

"And something healthy, like salad," Susan said.

"Good idea," he said, adding, "We'll get some salad, too."

Not too much later, the arrival of the pizza (and salad) afforded the cleaning crew a welcome break. They sat at the now-cleared kitchen table, munching, chatting, and making plans.

"How was it when you visited your mother?" Laura asked Josh and Jack.

"I was prepared this time for her not to know me. It wasn't quite as hard," Jack said. "She's as beautiful as ever. They're taking good care of her."

"That Rafe guy sure does like her," Josh said. "It was really weird to see them together. I can understand now why Dad didn't want to go on the cruise."

"Speaking of your dad," Susan said. "What are the doctors saying?"

"As if double pneumonia weren't enough, he also has the flu," Josh said. "But he's responding well to treatment, and they expect to send him home by the end of the week."

"They're so quick to boot you out of the hospital these days." Susan tsked. "He'll still be weak."

"We're arranging for home health care for a few weeks," Jack told them. "We both have to go home this weekend . . ." Jack raised his eyebrows, hinting and hopeful.

"Of course we'll check on him," Susan said. "It's clear he shouldn't be left to his own devices."

"Is he well enough for visitors besides you boys?" Rose asked.

"He's starting to sit up some. He's mostly watching TV," Jack said.

Edna left the table. She returned from the living room carrying Sam's briefcase.

"He'd be better off doing this instead of watching the idiot box."

"Dad's been retired for years," Josh said. "What's with his briefcase?"

Edna moved the pizza boxes to the kitchen counter, placed the briefcase on the table, and flipped the catches.

"Knitting?" Jack said. "Dad's knitting?"

"Crocheting," Edna said. "I taught your dad to crochet. This here's his first prayer shawl."

The light of understanding dawned on Josh's face. "Oh, now I get it. This is how you know him. He's actually in your prayer shawl group?"

Jack shook his head. "Dad? Crocheting? That's Mom's gig."

"Well, it's his gig now," Edna said.

"I'll take it to him," Jenny said.

"Haven't you done enough damage?" Edna sent a piercing glare across the table.

"Which I need to try to repair with a heartfelt apology." Jenny fiddled with her napkin.

Josh and Jack watched this exchange, eyebrows drawn together. "Are we missing something?" Jack said.

"Maybe Jenny will tell you later," Rose said. "But I think she'd rather not for now."

Jenny mouthed "thank you" at her friend.

Laura stood and began to clear the table. "I, for one, am ready to finish up here. I don't know about the rest of you, but I could really use a nap."

CHAPTER 33

JENNY FELT QUITE ACCOMPLISHED WHEN she finished arranging for her first Uber the next morning. The driver, catching sight of the briefcase she carried along with her flowered knitting bag, asked if she had an important business meeting. The amused smile he wasn't quite successful at hiding irked her.

"Just because I live at Fair Meadows doesn't mean I'm not a force in this world, young man." She fixed him with a direct stare.

"Right. Of course," the driver said, and he lost no time in getting Jenny to her destination, St. Luke's Medical Center.

In a matter of minutes, Jenny stepped out of the elevator on the floor where Sam was recovering. She took a deep breath and gathered her courage. Then she tightened her grip on the briefcase and marched herself to Sam's hospital room.

Sam was sitting up in bed channel surfing when Jenny knocked on the doorframe. When he saw her, his pale face reddened, and he clicked off the television. Jenny showed him the briefcase.

"Edna thinks you should have something better to do."

"Oh. Thanks." Sam looked everywhere but directly at his visitor.

Jenny laid the briefcase on the nightstand, opened it, and handed Sam the shawl and hook. Then she sat in the chair by the bed and pulled out her own shawl in progress.

Taking a deep breath to steady herself, she began. "Sam, I am so, so sorry. I didn't realize—I didn't mean to lead you on—I didn't think, but I should have. Please, please forgive me."

Sam doggedly made stitches. Finally, he raised his eyes to gaze, not at Jenny, but out the window.

"I've had some time to think while I've been in here," he said. "About me, and Dorothy, and Rafe . . . and you." He fell silent.

Jenny waited, anxiously knitting.

Sam turned his head and finally looked at her.

"I was such a fool. Such a fool to ask. Such a fool to even think it."

"I don't think the men who ask me out are fools," Jenny said.

"That's not what I'm talking about. If you had said yes . . ." Sam took a deep breath. "I might as well make a clean breast of it. If you had said you'd go out with me if I weren't married, I was going to leave Dorothy. I had it all worked out. I'd provide for her care, but I wasn't going to care anymore. It all hurt so much. She was happy with Rafe. Why couldn't I be happy, too?"

"Oh, no," Jenny gasped. "You thought you'd be happy with me?"

"I did. You're so full of life. I thought life would be fun again with you."

"Like it used to be with Dorothy?" Jenny's voice was soft.

Sam nodded. "But I thank God you said no. Lying here staring at the ceiling the first few days, I realized it was ridiculous to even consider trying to start a new life with someone else. All I could think about was Dorothy. I did a lot of sleeping, but even then, I dreamed about her. I'm a hopeless case, Jenny. I love my wife, whether she knows me or not. I will always love her, no matter what. You're really great, but you're not my Dorothy." These last words came out as a gasp, as though such a long speech had winded him.

"It's nothing personal with you, either," Jenny said. "I don't want anything serious with anybody. I just want to have fun."

"Alistair tried to tell me that, but I thought—"

"I know what you thought, and it's my fault, not yours."

They were quiet for several moments, knitting and crocheting, mulling things over.

"Doesn't it get lonely, though?" Sam asked. "Wouldn't you like to have a special someone?"

"I did once." Jenny paused as memories of Ben welled up in her heart. "We were so in love, and we had so much fun."

"What happened?" Sam asked.

"He died in an accident," Jenny said. "I never wanted to risk it again. Just keep things light and fun, without falling in love again."

"I'm sorry," Sam said.

"And I'm sorry about Dorothy," Jenny said. "For what it's worth, you have all of us, the Woolgatherers."

Sam smiled. "I do. And so do you. Josh and Jack told me what all of you did at the house. You didn't have to."

"What are friends for, anyway?" Jenny said.

Sam's warm smile filled his whole face. "We are friends, aren't we? I've been thinking about what led to all of this. I've realized all the Woolgatherers were trying to befriend me. Alistair invited me to watch the basketball finals, Laura tried to teach me to knit, Edna got me crocheting, Susan fussed about my health, and Rose kept inviting me to church. It wasn't just you. It was all of you." He paused to catch his breath. "Thank you."

Jenny's fingers relaxed on her knitting needles. She'd been clutching them tightly without realizing it.

"No hard feelings, then?" she asked.

"No hard feelings. Over and done with. Let's forget what an idiot I was."

"You were not an idiot," Jenny said. "I was thoughtless, clueless, and unkind."

"But now we're friends and we'll forget about it," Sam said. "To change the subject, that's a nice shawl you're working on there."

"It's my first Nudge," Jenny said.

Sam raised his eyebrows at her.

"I was in the Prayer Chapel at Hope of Glory," Jenny said. "I like to go there to knit sometimes—and pray, too. I was mad at Edna." She paused, remembering what she'd been mad about.

Sam made a "go on" gesture with his crochet hook.

"Edna said something to me I thought was unkind and unfair. I was complaining to God about her. And that's when the idea came into my mind to make her a shawl. It was not *my* idea, believe me. Rose calls it the Nudge—the feeling God wants you to do something."

"I wonder if it was the Nudge that made Rose call me when I was so sick."

"Could be," Jenny said. She lapsed into grateful silence, sending up a silent prayer of thankfulness for second chances—Sam's second chance at life and hers to become a true friend to him.

They continued knitting and crocheting until Sam's lunch tray arrived. Sam scowled as he lifted the cover. "You never saw so many vegetables in your life. And no dessert, just an orange. I'd even go for green Jell-O at this point."

Jenny laughed. "Just you wait until you get home!"

"What's so funny?" Sam poked at a soggy broccoli spear with his fork.

"You'll see," was all Jenny would say. "Let's just say Susan is busy today."

Susan was indeed busy. She couldn't get the state of Sam's refrigerator out of her mind. And she'd been the one to clear away all those fast-food wrappers in the living room. No way could he go back to eating like that. Not if she had anything to do with it.

So Susan prevailed upon Jack to chauffeur her to the grocery store and purchase the groceries she selected. In Sam's kitchen, Susan tied on one of Dorothy's aprons and got to work cooking healthy meals and stacking meal-sized portions in the freezer. She enlisted the men she insisted on calling "the boys" to wash the pots, pans, and cooking utensils.

"I don't know if our dad will eat turkey burgers," Jack said as Josh handed him a wooden spoon to dry and put away. "Or pizza with cauliflower crust, either."

"He'd better," Susan said. "He was not a healthy man, even before he got pneumonia."

Jack nodded. "I didn't realize he'd put on so much weight. He really wasn't taking care of himself."

"He was used to Mom taking care of him," Josh said. "I don't know if he even knows how to cook."

Susan tapped her finger on the stack of recipe cards she'd compiled for Sam's journey back to health. "He's going to learn."

On Friday, Sam came home from the hospital to find the entryway festooned with a banner that read "Welcome Home Sam."

"The prayer shawl people did that," Jack told him. "I asked them if they'd like to be here to greet you themselves, but they figured you'd need to rest after your exciting car ride home," he finished with a wink.

Sam wasn't about to admit it to his boys that the trip home *had* taxed him. He stepped away from Jack, whose arm he realized he'd been leaning on, ostensibly to tour the work of the Woolgatherers. The house was as neat and tidy as Dorothy used to keep it. The odor of stale popcorn was gone, replaced by the fresh smell of the hyacinths that graced the coffee table.

Josh opened the living room curtains to reveal the yard work he and his brother had done the day before.

"Not bad, not bad," Sam said. "I guess you boys have earned your spending money for the weekend."

"I did more than you." Josh gave Jack a brotherly punch in the arm. "I should get more."

Laughing, Sam pulled out his wallet and counted out some bills.

"Don't you go getting into trouble with this, now." It was the joke that had always accompanied the doling out of chore money.

"It was always enough to have fun, but not enough to get into trouble with," Jack recalled with a grin.

"We were too tired from the yard work to get into any trouble," Josh said with a groan.

Sam rubbed his hands together. "Hey, I could really go for a double cheeseburger. They starved me in the hospital. Which of you wants to make the Burger King run?"

Josh and Jack exchanged uneasy glances. Jack took a step back.

"Chicken," Josh muttered under his breath. Then he squared his shoulders and addressed his father. "Dad, you heard what the doctor said today. All your numbers need to come down, including your weight. No more double cheeseburgers."

Sam stared. "What?"

"You heard the doctor, Dad," Jack said. "You need to eat things like lean meat, lots of leafy greens, vegetables, and fruit."

Sam groaned. "I might as well go back to the hospital. At least they cooked for me there."

"Somebody cooked for you here, too." Jack told him about Susan's marathon cooking session on Wednesday.

"I told her you probably wouldn't eat turkey burgers or whole wheat buns," Jack said. "But she wouldn't listen."

Instead of resisting, however, Sam's chin began to tremble. He cleared his throat and finally managed to speak.

"No one's cooked for me since—" but he couldn't choke out their mother's name.

CHAPTER 34

THE FOLLOWING THURSDAY MORNING, EDNA was delighted to find Amy and Heaven waiting for the Woolgatherers in the Fair Meadows lobby. Heaven was wide-awake and allowed Susan to hold her this time. The baby, however, only had eyes for Edna, leaning forward in Susan's lap to wave her arms and babble.

"I went to the store during my lunch break yesterday," Amy told Rose. "I finally had time to get the yarn for Heaven's sweater, and I can't wait to get started." She pulled a skein of purple yarn out of her knitting bag.

Edna reached over to touch the yarn. "The color of asters in the fall. I love them flowers. You could add yellow buttons, like the middle of asters."

Amy smiled. "I like that idea."

After praying their shawl-maker's prayer, Rose set about coaching Amy through starting the back of the tiny sweater. She'd barely finished the first row when Heaven began to fuss.

"I'll hold her." With Heaven in her lap, Edna breathed in the scent of baby shampoo and happy memories of Penny.

"How is Stanley?" Amy asked shyly. "I hope you don't mind that Rose told us about him."

"Happy as a clam." Somehow, it wasn't hard to talk about him while holding this baby. "He won fifty dollars on his scratch-off this week."

"Maybe his luck's coming back," Amy said.

She knew Amy meant well, but Edna knew better than to hope. "Nah," she said. "It ain't never coming back."

The day came when Sam finally felt strong enough to go to Fair Meadows to meet with the Woolgatherers—and to visit Dorothy. He knew now that as difficult as it was for him that she didn't know him and was even afraid of him, and no matter how hard it was to see her smiling at Rafe, he never wanted to stay away from her again. After a visit to his barber, he polished his wing tips, ironed a shirt, and selected a pair of dress pants. His first inkling of the changes his illness and recovery had brought came when he buttoned his shirt. To his surprise, it didn't strain across his middle. He was even more surprised when he pulled on the pants he'd last worn to Fair Meadows and found they were too big in the waist. He tried a few more pairs and found slacks from his working days that fit. When he put on the matching suit jacket, it buttoned easily. Hmm . . . were the turkey burgers and salads making a difference already?

Sam stopped short when he caught a glimpse of himself in the front hall mirror in his suit, carrying his gym bag full of his crochet. He quickly exchanged the gym bag for the classy leather duffle bag he'd carried on business trips. *Much better*, he thought as he surveyed himself in the mirror again.

Sam felt like he'd been on a long journey since he'd stormed out of the lobby at Fair Meadows, but the Woolgatherers made him feel like he was coming home. He'd barely stepped through the doors when Tara pushed her needlework aside and practically dragged him across the lobby to the Woolgatherers' corner. "How are you feeling? Are you all better now? Do you need to sit?"

"Give the man a chance to answer one question," Edna said.

"I'm feeling much better, I'm not sick anymore, and I'll sit with you after I check on Dorothy," Sam said.

"Won't it be hard?" Susan asked.

"Probably. But it really wasn't good for me to stay away. I need to see my Dorothy, whether she knows me or not."

"We'll pray for you," Rose said.

Sam looked around the circle at his friends. "Will you pray for me now, before I go?"

Collectively, the rest of the Woolgatherers stood and surrounded their friend. They bowed their heads as Rose began to pray.

"Dear God, thank you for Sam. Thank you for helping him get well. Please be with him now as he goes to visit Dorothy. You know how hard this is. Please give him the love and courage he needs for the coming moments."

Everyone joined in on the "Amen."

"You can leave this with us if you want." Tara reached for the duffle bag. Sam relinquished it, squared his shoulders, and marched to the elevator.

The Woolgatherers gazed after him until the elevator doors slid closed, then returned to their seats, their shawls, and their prayers especially.

"I'm so glad you're here, Mr. Talbot." Eileen came out from behind the nurses' station, her face bright with welcome and relief. "We were quite concerned when we heard you were so ill you had to go to the hospital. I heard you had both pneumonia and the flu."

"I was pretty miserable there for a while." Sam gave a rueful chuckle. "Susan will never let me miss my shots from now on. She's had a grand time telling me 'I told you so' every chance she gets."

"I've heard about Mrs. Thomas." Eileen grinned. "She's a one-woman health department."

Sam shifted and craned his neck toward the dayroom. "Speaking of one woman, where's Dorothy?"

"She's running a little late this morning." Eileen glanced toward the hallway that led to Dorothy's room. "Ah, here she comes now."

Sam turned and caught his breath as Dorothy stepped from the hallway into the brightly lit reception area. He knew he should turn around so as not to scare her, but he was rooted to the spot at the sight of his wife. It was too late now, anyway. She'd turned those lovely hazel eyes on him. He braced himself for Dorothy's fear.

He saw her eyebrows draw together as she came across the reception area. She stopped beside him and looked into his face.

"Do I know you?" she asked.

Sam's heart migrated to the vicinity of his throat. How to answer this simple but infinitely complicated question?

Finally, he cleared his throat and said, "Do I remind you of someone?"

She studied him for a moment. "No, but you seem like someone I'd like to get to know. You have such kind eyes." Then she smiled.

Sam smiled back, his heart warm. "I'd like to get to know you, too. Would you like to have coffee sometime?"

"I'd love to. I can't right now, though. My friend is waiting for me." Dorothy continued on toward the dayroom, where Rafe waited for her in the doorway, giving Sam the stink eye.

"That's my cue to leave," Sam said to Eileen with a wink. "I wouldn't want to get into another altercation with Rafe."

"Good idea," Eileen said. "Until next Saturday?"

"I'll be back," Sam said—with a bit of Arnold Schwarzenegger flair.

When he returned to the lobby, Sam barely had time to sit before the rest of the Woolgatherers began peppering him with questions.

"One at a time, please." He held up his hand. "And let me get my crochet out first."

"Did you see Dorothy?" Laura asked.

"The better question is whether Dorothy saw him," Mr. Peabody said.

"You're not going to believe this," Sam began.

"We've been praying, so maybe we will," Jenny said.

"She wasn't in the dayroom when I got there, so I couldn't check on her from around the door. She came through the reception area from her room and saw me."

"Uh-oh." Edna paused in her crocheting.

"I thought so, too," Sam said. "But she didn't start screaming about the Fat Man. She wasn't scared at all. She just looked puzzled and asked if she knew me."

"Of course she didn't start screaming about the Fat Man," Susan said. "You're not the Fat Man anymore. You look more like the husband she knew."

Sam glanced down at the button on his suit coat. He remembered having to leave the jacket open when he'd worn it to church a few weeks before.

"I've been in pajamas and sweatpants since I came home from the hospital," Sam said. "I wasn't really paying attention to how things fit. Now that you mention it, though, my go-to pants were too loose this morning."

"It's all those healthy meals you're eating," Susan said.

"And the unhealthy ones you're not eating," Rose said.

"Not to mention all the housework. The home health care lady said it was part of my therapy, getting up and about and back on my feet. I had my doubts," Sam said with a wink. "It's a lot of work keeping the house like all of you left it. And Dorothy did all those things day in and day out, year after year. I never realized how much she did."

"Don't you ever let it go to wrack and ruin again." Edna pointed her crochet hook at him. "That's no way to live."

"No, ma'am." Sam gave her a mock salute. Then, trying to sound casual, he said, "I asked Dorothy if she'd like to have coffee with me sometime."

"*And?*" Jenny raised her eyebrows.

"And she said she'd like that."

Jenny's eyes lit up, then clouded. "What about Rafe? He's liable to take issue with that."

"Well, I certainly don't want to cause another ruckus. I'll have to figure something out. I was so surprised she wasn't afraid of me that I didn't consider how I'd actually have coffee with her."

"Leave it to me," Jenny said, a scheming look on her face. "I'll help you win her back."

"I'd just like to be her friend for now," Sam said. He surveyed the circle of knitters and crocheters. "There's a lot to be said for having friends."

In the Hope of Glory foyer the next morning, Sam handed Howard Fuller the shawl he'd completed the night before.

"Is there time to put it up front to be prayed over?" he asked. "It's my first one."

"There's time." Howard stepped into the nave with the shawl over his arm.

Sam followed and took a seat in what was fast becoming the "Woolgatherers' pew," since they now almost filled the fifth row on the left every Sunday. Gus slid in next to him.

"That's yours, isn't it?" Rose pointed at the shawl Howard was draping on the altar rail with loving care.

"Finished it last night," Sam said.

A triumphant burst of organ music alerted everyone to the start of the service. Sam stood and joined the congregation in singing the opening hymn, feeling his heart swell with gratitude. He had recovered from serious illness, Dorothy hadn't been afraid of him the day before, and he was making his first contribution to the prayer shawl ministry. How good it was to feel this thankfulness in this place, with these people.

Before he knew it, the time came for Father Pete to pray over the shawl. Before he knelt to pray, Father Pete addressed the congregation.

"I'm sure all of you remember we've been praying for Sam Talbot, who was quite ill and spent some time in the hospital. Thank you all for praying. He has not only recovered, but he's also here with us today. Give us a wave, Sam, so everyone can see where you are."

Sam, red-faced with embarrassment, waved his arm in the air, to the sound of cheers and applause.

"Sam is a member of the Woolgatherers, the prayer shawl group at Fair Meadows Retirement Community. This is his first shawl, which he completed while recovering from his illness." This information inspired another round of applause.

"Now, let's pray." Father Pete knelt as the clapping died down. "Father God, thank you for this shawl. May it wrap both the body and heart of the caring person who receives it in your love and care. May it impart strength and courage to keep on loving in the face of this heartbreaking disease. In Jesus's name, Amen."

After the service, Sam stood behind Gus in the line to shake hands with Father Pete.

"So glad to see you here again, Gus," the pastor greeted warmly. "How did finals go?"

"Fingers crossed, sir," Gus said.

"Better yet, prayers," said Father Pete. "How can we pray for you?"

"Well, the Woolgatherers are already on it, praying I find a roommate for med school. I can't afford to live alone."

"We'll pray, too," the pastor said. "And I hope you'll take Jesus along with you to med school. I can tell you from personal experience that he's a great roommate. He sure got me through seminary."

"Don't tell Mrs. Alderman that," Gus said with a laugh. "Her solution is to set me up with her niece."

As Gus went on to the parish hall, still chuckling, Father Pete turned to Sam. "You're looking well, Sam. I hope I didn't embarrass you too much during service today."

Sam's face flushed all over again. "I didn't know the whole church was praying for me."

"Hope of Glory is becoming quite a prayer community," Father Pete told him. "The Heavenly Hugs blazed the trail, and the rest of the congregation hasn't been far behind. You can imagine how encouraging it is for us to see God's response to our prayers in church this morning."

"Well, I guess if you put it that way, I don't mind," Sam said.

"Is there anything else you'd like us to pray about?" Father Pete asked.

"There is something," Sam said. "But I'd rather keep it between you and me. And God, of course."

"I will keep it in strictest confidence," Father Pete said. "My wife tells me I don't talk in my sleep, although I do snore from time to time."

Sam explained about Dorothy, her illness, her fear of him, Rafe, and the recent, hopeful change in her attitude toward him. "I don't need her to remember who I am. I would simply like to be her friend and spend time in her company," he finished.

"You can count on my prayers, Sam," Father Pete said. "And you can count on God to uphold you, no matter what happens with Dorothy."

Sam chuckled. "Will God hold me up if Rafe tries to deck me?"

Father Pete laughed, too. "More likely he'll help you duck in time!"

CHAPTER 35

"There." The following afternoon, Jenny gave Edna's shawl a little pat as she finished weaving in the last of the ends. Then she folded it carefully, tucked it into a tote, and waited for Chloe to take her to Hope of Glory. She kept her newfound ability to Uber a carefully guarded secret, at least from Chloe. Jenny didn't want to hear, "Can't you just take an Uber?" from her daughter all the time.

"You sure are going to church a lot lately. And not just on Sundays. You're not thinking of becoming a nun, are you?" Chloe's tone was light and teasing.

"And what if I was?" Jenny teased back.

"Never," Chloe said with a chuckle. "You'd have to stop flirting."

Jenny laughed along with her daughter, but inwardly renewed her vow to be more careful about flirting. Careful, yes, but it was too much fun to give up entirely. It could be useful, too. She smiled to herself at the plan that was forming in her mind . . .

Father Pete invited Jenny into his office when she arrived. Lucille brought them mugs of steaming coffee.

"So, you want me to pray over a shawl, and it can't wait until Sunday," he began.

"Yes." Jenny pulled Edna's shawl out of the tote and laid it on the desk. "This is the shawl I made for the woman I was praying about, the one I said was mean and unfair to me."

"Ah," Father Pete said.

"But while I was making the shawl, I discovered she was neither of those things. She was speaking truth, and I should have listened to her."

Father Pete's warm smile encouraged her to go on. "I hope you don't think I'm crazy, but I have a feeling God wants me to give it to her soon." She inhaled and pressed her hand to her stomach. The butterflies were having a wild party in her midsection. "Her name is Edna."

"The Edna who crochets all those shawls?" Father Pete asked. When Jenny nodded, he buried his fingers in the pile of knitted softness and began to pray. "Father God, thank you for Edna, who makes beautiful shawls and speaks truth to her friends, even when it's hard to hear. Thank you for Jenny and her willingness to listen to you. Thank you for opening her heart while she made this shawl. We ask that when Edna wraps herself in this shawl, she will know how deeply you love and delight in her. In Jesus's name. Amen."

"I hope I'll get to meet Edna sometime," Father Pete said as they walked to the outer office, where Chloe was enjoying a cup of Lucille's coffee while she waited for her mother.

"We keep inviting her," Jenny said. "But no luck so far. She's actually a bit hostile about the idea."

"I'm sorry to hear that." Then Father Pete glanced over at Chloe and raised his eyebrows.

Jenny quickly introduced her daughter.

"We'd love to have you at Hope of Glory, too, Chloe," Father Pete told her.

"I'm here so often bringing Mom to do whatever it is she does here, I might as well," Chloe said with a laugh. Jenny laughed, too, but her heart also leapt at the thought of Chloe joining her in the "Woolgatherers' pew."

For the next few days, Jenny stayed on high alert, hoping to sense the Nudge. The shawl, made in the right yarn and pattern, was finished and prayed over. Everything was ready. Jenny felt like a nervous racehorse ready to burst out of the gate as soon as the starting bell rang. But the voice that somehow came from inside of her yet wasn't her remained silent.

"You're awfully quiet lately, Jenny," Rose said as they knitted in the lobby on Thursday morning. "Are you all right?"

Jenny had been listening so hard for the Nudge that it took a moment for Rose's words to register. "What?" she finally said.

"I said 'Are you all right?' You seem preoccupied lately. Is there something on your mind?"

With a sideways glance at Edna, who was focused on helping Sam with his new shawl pattern, Jenny said, "It's that, you know . . . thing God wanted me to do. It's done, but I don't know when . . ."

Rose nodded her understanding. "You can relax about it. You heard him when he told you to do it. You'll hear him when it's time to give it to her."

Jenny lowered her voice. "I'm not so sure. I was clueless about Sam. I might completely miss it when it's time to give it to her."

"You've been praying for her," Rose told Jenny. "You'll know."

Saturday dawned bright and clear, a perfect June day. Jenny hummed "Oh, What a Beautiful Morning" as she dressed for breakfast and Woolgatherers. It was finally sandal weather, and she had found some cute new ones. She enjoyed dithering in her closet over what to wear with her new footwear.

Tea. The thought was sudden and unbidden, sandwiched between Jenny's deciding whether to wear the off-white linen pants or the turquoise broomstick skirt.

"Tea?" she said aloud.

Today. There was an urgency in the word. Jenny's chest tightened and her stomach flip-flopped, the way it had in the Prayer Chapel. Comprehension dawned as clear as the blue sky outside her window. Relief flooded her heart as she realized she had not missed the Nudge, for all her worrying.

"Yes," she said. "I'll invite Edna over for tea this afternoon."

Edna was so taciturn among the Woolgatherers that morning Jenny wondered how she would react to the invitation to tea. The word, however, had been "today," so Jenny mustered her courage and asked Edna to come to her cottage for tea that afternoon.

"I have Milano cookies," Jenny added as a further enticement.

The cookies might have tipped things in Jenny's favor, because Edna rang Jenny's doorbell at precisely four o'clock.

Jenny ushered Edna into the sitting room, where she'd laid out her Royal Doulton tea set and a plate of cookies on an embroidered cloth on the coffee table. She seated Edna on the couch and took her own seat in the adjacent wing chair. As she poured tea for Edna, Jenny said, "I'm glad you could come."

"Mm," was all Edna said.

She's not going to make this easy, Jenny thought as she poured herself a cup of tea. She offered the sugar bowl to Edna.

"Don't mind if I do." Edna plopped three sugar cubes into her tea and accepted a cookie to put on the edge of her saucer.

Jenny took a few sips of tea, then put her cup and saucer on the coffee table.

"Edna, I need to tell you something."

Edna tilted her head slightly. "Oh?"

"Do you remember when you told me to be careful about Sam?"

Edna gave a curt nod.

"I realize now you were right. I should have listened to you, and I'm sorry I didn't."

"It ain't me you need to say sorry to," Edna said. "It's Sam."

"I went to the hospital weeks ago," Jenny said. "I apologized, and he was kind enough to forgive me. But I need to apologize to you, too. I was upset about what you said to me. 'Mean' and 'unfair' are two words that come to mind."

Edna simply gazed at Jenny and stirred her tea.

"I was mad about what you said, so I went to the Prayer Chapel at the church. There's something about that place . . . You're going to think this is crazy, but when I prayed about it, I got this feeling I was supposed to make you a prayer shawl." Jenny took a deep breath. "I did a lot of thinking and praying while I made your shawl, and I realized some things."

Edna narrowed her eyes. "Like what?"

"I realized you weren't being mean, for one thing. You told me the truth. I thought you were unkind because I didn't like what you were telling me about myself. I also realized you weren't doing that for me, but for Sam. You were a much better friend to him than I was. I'm sorry I didn't listen to you. I need a friend who will tell me the truth, especially when I'm wrong." Jenny held out the gift bag she'd stashed next to her chair.

Edna accepted the bag, pushed aside the tissue paper Jenny had tucked into the top, and pulled out the shawl. She stared at it, dumbfounded. With her free hand, she stuffed the tissue paper into the bag and let the bag fall to the floor. Then she gathered the shawl in her arms and buried her face in it. Jenny watched with concern as Edna's shoulders shook with sobs.

Jenny hurried to sit by Edna on the couch. "Oh, Edna, I'm so sorry! I didn't mean to make you cry! I'm so sorry!"

Edna let the shawl fall into her lap, laid her head on Jenny's shoulder, and sobbed some more. Jenny patted her on the back and made noises she hoped were soothing. Finally, Edna gave a great sniff and lifted her head. Jenny passed her a tissue.

"You say God told you to make this?" Edna said when she'd blown her nose and wiped her eyes.

"Yes," Jenny said. "I've been working on it for weeks here in my cottage so it would be a surprise."

"It sure is," Edna said.

"But do you like it?" Jenny wasn't at all sure the answer would be yes, the way Edna had been crying.

Edna simply nodded, as though unable to speak.

"Here, let me put it on you." Jenny stood and gently arranged the shawl around Edna's shoulders. "The same day I got the Nudge, you know, the idea to make it, I went to The Tangled Thread and picked out the yarn. Then I chose three patterns and couldn't decide. Rose told me to just start one and then I'd be able to tell if that was the one the yarn wanted to be. I had visions of having to try all of them, but the first one turned out to be just right."

"It's beautiful," Edna said. "Reminds me of lilacs. My mother had them in our yard when I was a kid."

"Mine, too," Jenny said. "That's why I picked that yarn."

"My Stanley proposed to me by that lilac bush," Edna said. She swallowed hard. "The lilacs smelled so sweet, but nothing was sweeter than hearing Stanley say, 'Will you marry me?'"

"Oh, Edna," was all Jenny could say, sinking back down on the couch beside her.

"It's fifty years today. Since our wedding." Tears streamed freely down Edna's cheeks and soaked into the shawl. "Today is our golden wedding anniversary, and I'm the only one who knows it."

Jenny put her arm around Edna. "Not anymore. Now I know it, too." She looked into Edna's face. "That Old-Timer's Disease didn't steal Stanley's luck. He's been married for fifty years to a woman who sticks by him no matter what. Edna O'Brian, your Stanley is luckier now than the day he won the lottery."

Edna's tears continued to flow, as if they'd been dammed up for a long time and the floodgates had finally opened. She spoke through her tears.

"Stanley forgot me. I thought God did, too." She pulled the shawl more tightly around herself. "But he didn't. And I know it's got to be God, because, no offense, you're the last person I'd expect to do this for me."

"None taken," Jenny said. "Truth be told, I was pretty surprised, too."

In the shelter of her new shawl, Edna reminisced about her wedding, telling Jenny about her dress, the lilacs she carried, and her handsome Stanley waiting for her at the altar.

"He gasped and laid his hand on his heart when I appeared at the back of the church, then grinned from ear to ear my whole way down the aisle."

After Edna left, Jenny got busy on the phone. If Edna was surprised by the shawl, she was really going to be surprised at dinner that evening. Jenny wasn't about to let something as party-worthy as a golden wedding anniversary go uncelebrated. When Edna arrived in the dining room for dinner, she found Sam, Nan, Tara, Samantha, Fran, Howard, Amy, Bryson, Heaven, and Gus were joining the Woolgatherers for dinner. Samantha was full of questions, and Edna found herself regaling the group with story after story about her life with Stanley over the years. Many of the stories highlighted Stanley's optimism and his ability to find the funny side of just about everything. Edna glowed with the happiness of remembering those qualities of her husband and times with him. And then, as though she'd drawn strength from remembering the happy times, Edna talked about Penny and how Stanley's love had sustained her in their loss.

Jenny leaned over to speak to Rose. "What a life she's had. Who knew?" Rose gave her a sideways glance. "Oh, right. God knew."

"And now we're really getting to know her, too," Rose said.

Mrs. Hargrave herself brought a small cake into the dining room and set it in front of Edna. Purple frosting flowers edged the top of the cake, surrounding the words "Happy 50th Anniversary, Stanley and Edna" in elegant gold frosting script.

"Fifty years is something to celebrate," Mrs. Hargrave said amid cheers and applause. "Congratulations."

Over cake and decaf coffee, Tara and Samantha shyly handed Edna cards they had made for her. The one from Tara was adorned with a crocheted flower.

"I sewed a pin on the back so you can take it off the card and wear it if you want," Tara said.

"That was my idea," Samantha put in.

Edna ran her finger over the flower, then gazed around the table at each face gathered there. Her face was radiant even while her chin trembled.

"My Stanley had the luck, but now I do, too."

CHAPTER 36

THE NEXT MORNING, EDNA JOINED the group waiting for Gus to take the Woolgatherers to Hope of Glory. She had the shawl draped around her shoulders, held in place with the pin Tara had made.

"If God's going to go to all this trouble over me," she told Jenny, "the least I can do is go to that there church."

"And the least I can do is let you sit in the front of the van." Jenny laughed and took a seat in the second row next to Mr. Peabody.

Edna sat up straight in her seat and gripped the top of her pocket-book.

"Let's go, young man, and pay attention. We may be going to church, but none of us wants to meet our Maker just yet."

"Yes, ma'am." Gus saluted as he pulled carefully away from the curb.

Edna felt a bit overwhelmed by the warm welcome she received at Hope of Glory.

After the service, at the door to the foyer, Father Pete took her hand in both of his and said, "I'm so glad to meet the maker of those beautiful crocheted shawls."

Edna felt herself blush at his praise.

In the parish hall, the Heavenly Hugs surrounded her, seated her at a table, and plied her with coffee, cookies, and congratulations on her milestone wedding anniversary.

"Rose told us all about it," Jane said.

"I love the shawls you make," Amy said. "After I finish Heaven's sweater, would you teach me to crochet?"

Edna could only nod. Her heart was full to bursting. She leaned over and whispered to Jenny. Jenny nodded.

"Excuse us a moment," Jenny said to the group. "Don't let Gus leave without us."

"As if," Susan said with a laugh.

Edna followed Jenny through the foyer and into the nave. Jenny stopped at the doors to the Prayer Chapel.

"Do you want me to come in with you, or would you rather be alone?"

"Alone, if you don't mind."

"I understand," Jenny said as Edna slipped into the chapel.

Once the door closed behind her, Edna walked to the front of the chapel. The air was cool, and she was glad of her shawl. She pulled it a little more closely around her shoulders as she gazed into the face of the child in the window depicting the nativity, swaddled in a shawl of his own.

"I just wanted to say thank you," Edna said. "Thank you for Penny. Thank you for Stanley. Thank you for the Woolgatherers and this shawl. Thank you for remembering me. Nobody likes to be forgotten. I should know. I forgot you for a while, but I won't anymore."

She stood in front of the window for a little while longer, taking in the peace of the room. Then she turned and headed to the parish hall, where her friends were waiting.

On Monday morning, Fran arrived at the Woolgatherers meeting with four fragrant coffees in a cardboard carrier.

"Your delivery, ma'am." She handed the coffees to Jenny.

"Thanks." At the questioning looks from the rest of the group, Jenny said, "Tara showed me how to order coffee from my phone. All I needed was someone to pick it up."

"Which I'm happy to do," Fran said, "since I'm right across the street."

"Which begs the question of why you ordered four coffees," Laura said, "since there are more than four of us here."

"It's all part of my plan," Jenny said with a conspiratorial wink. "C'mon, Sam. Today you're having coffee with Dorothy."

"What?" Sam gaped at her.

"Oh, and bring your crochet. It might give you something to talk about."

Sam stuffed his crochet in his duffle bag and followed Jenny to the elevator a bit apprehensively.

"What about Rafe?" Sam asked as they stepped into the elevator.

"Leave it to me," Jenny said with an airy wave. "You just enjoy spending time with Dorothy. Now, once we get there, let me go into the dayroom first."

At the nurses' station, Jenny shared a smile with Patsy.

"Operation Coffee with Dorothy is about to begin."

Jenny took two coffees out of the carrier and stood in the doorway of the dayroom until every eye in the room focused on her.

"Oh, there you are, Rafe," she called out. "I was hoping I'd find you here. I brought us some coffee." She sashayed over to a table on the far side of the room.

The expression on Rafe's face was familiar. Sam had the distinct feeling he had looked just as dazed when Jenny had first turned her charm in his direction. The man rose slowly from the table and left Dorothy sitting alone in order to join Jenny.

"Now." Patsy handed Sam the two remaining coffees. Sam took a deep breath and began his trek across the room.

"I hope you don't mind," Sam said as he sat across from Dorothy. "I thought you might like some coffee."

"Oh, hello." Dorothy looked across the table at him. "Yes, thank you, I'd love some."

Sam didn't mind she was using her I-don't-know-you-but-I'm-being-polite manners with him. She wasn't afraid, and what was more, she was smiling.

Three Sundays later, Edna sat in the parish hall at Hope of Glory with Heaven in her lap, adoring the baby's round cheeks and chubby arms. Across the table, she saw Jane nudge Rose with her elbow.

"Will you look at those two?"

Fran and Howard stood in the doorway of the parish hall, hand in hand. They were both smiling. Howard's grin was broad and triumphant, while Fran glowed with quiet happiness.

Edna laughed. "Howard looks just like my Stanley when he won the Big One."

"He does seem awfully pleased with himself," Margaret said. "I wonder what he's been up to."

The couple in question made their way across the parish hall to the table where the Heavenly Hugs and the Woolgatherers were enjoying coffee—and speculation.

"You two sure look happy," Jenny said.

Howard's chest puffed out as he put his arm around Fran.

"Can you believe it? I asked her to marry me, and she said yes." Howard's face shone with wonder and delight.

A cheer erupted from the group. Bryson pumped his fist in the air while Mr. Peabody clapped Howard on the shoulder in congratulation. Heaven waved her arms and gurgled.

"Didn't I tell you he won the lottery?" Edna said.

Fran blushed at this, but Howard laughed. "Indeed I did."

"Fran, didn't I tell you not to rush into things?" Margaret said with a slight frown. At a look from Rose, she added, "But far be it from me to tell you what to do."

"They'll be fine," Rose said as she gazed at the beaming couple.

"I know it hasn't been all that long." Howard nodded in Margaret's direction. "And I'd planned to wait a bit longer, but Edna and Stanley's anniversary inspired me. I want lots and lots of anniversaries with Fran. We might not make it to fifty, but I want to be married to her as long as possible."

"So, tell us how he popped the question." Jenny leaned forward, eager for the story.

"Yeah, did he get down on one knee?" Amy asked, with a sidelong glance at Bryson. Bryson gulped.

Howard shifted from one foot to the other, rubbing the back of his head with the hand that wasn't holding on to Fran's.

"He started to." Fran blushed an even deeper and more becoming pink. "But I told him to kiss me instead."

"I was pretty relieved, believe me," Howard said. "That meant the answer would be yes. And to be honest, I wasn't sure about being able to get up again once I got down there. My knees aren't what they used to be."

Margaret fixed Howard with a powerful stare. "You went ahead and asked, though, didn't you? You didn't simply assume?"

"Of course he did," Fran said.

"So, give us the deets," Bryson said. "I have a feeling I should be taking notes."

"The what?" Fran shook her head in bewilderment.

"Details," Howard answered and pulled a chair over from another table for Fran. She sat, and he stood behind her, his hands resting on her shoulders.

"We went for a walk at the Botanical Gardens," Fran began.

"So pretty and romantic." Jenny gave a satisfied little sigh.

"We meandered our way to the Japanese garden, chatting and enjoying each other's company," Fran continued. "We stopped on the bridge, the one with the weeping willows on either side of the stream."

Edna gave Heaven a little hug as she remembered lingering on the Japanese garden bridge with Stanley a time or two.

"Howard turned to me and said, 'We've had our share of weeping, haven't we? After my Emily passed, I thought I'd never love again.

And then I saw you at the bookstore, reading in the coffee shop. There was something special about you. I couldn't stop watching you.'" Fran reached up and squeezed one of Howard's hands.

"Go on," Jenny said. "This is getting good."

Fran leaned forward. "Do you remember the day we gave the green prayer shawl to Eileen? The day she told us about how hard her first Thanksgiving without her dad was turning out to be?"

Jane and Rose nodded, but Margaret said, "*You* gave it to her. *I* said it hadn't been prayed over yet."

"And it turned out just fine," Rose said with a chuckle. "More than fine, since Eileen started coming to church."

"I suppose," Margaret said. But a smile tugged at the corners of her mouth.

"What does that have to do with Howard proposing? Get back to the story," Jenny said.

"Howard told me he fell in love with me that day, when he saw me give Eileen the shawl and listen to her talk about her father."

"She was so kind and caring," Howard said. "How could I resist?"

Laura sniffed and grabbed her napkin to dab at her eyes.

"I realized where he was going with his story when he started to kneel," Fran said. "At our age, there's no need for that gesture."

Edna saw Amy shoot Bryson a look that seemed to say, "Don't think that lets *you* out of it."

"So, I stayed on my feet and asked her to marry me," Howard said. "And she said yes."

"Ring?" Jenny wanted to know.

"Yes, indeed," Howard said as Fran lifted her left hand from her lap to display a heart-shaped ruby flanked by three small diamonds on each side. "I have Rose to thank for finding out what Fran's favorite gemstone is."

"Excellent," Bryson said.

"Ah, new love," Jenny said with another happy sigh. "I do love a good happily-ever-after." She turned to Amy and wiggled her eyebrows. "Doesn't it make you want to get married?"

"Jenny," Rose said.

"It's all right, Rose," Amy said. "It's wonderful, what Fran and Howard have. They're so blessed to have found each other and to have a second chance at love."

"You've given me a second chance, Amy," Bryson said. "Don't think I don't know it."

Amy held up her hand to Bryson and turned to Edna and Sam. "But I want more than that. I want what the two of you have."

Edna glanced at Sam, startled and confused. Then she focused on Amy. "You want a spouse with Old-Timer's Disease?"

"I want," Amy said, "love like yours. 'For better for worse,' 'in sickness and in health,' 'until death do us part.' That's what I want."

Sam turned his wedding ring around on his finger and shook his head. "I'm not such a good example. I almost broke my promises. You know I was thinking of leaving Dorothy, right?"

Amy waved his words away. "But in the end, you *didn't*. Love won. I want a marriage where love always wins. Even when it's hard. Especially when it's hard."

"It ain't easy," Edna said. "Life is full of hard times. Times when it's hard to hold on. Times when it seems like it'd be easier to give up, if you want the truth."

"The truth is exactly what I want. I want to know how you keep loving even when it's hard. I want a love that will go the distance, all the way to the end, come what may. You and Sam are living proof that people can love like that."

Bryson stared at Amy and swallowed hard.

"You don't want much, do you?" His voice was hoarse, as though he was talking over a lump in his throat.

"There's no point otherwise." Amy locked eyes with him. "All of me for all of you, for all our days. And all for love."

Sam put his arm around Bryson's shoulders. "If I've learned anything lately, son, it's you can't do it alone. We'll all be here for both of you—the Woolgatherers, the Heavenly Hugs—"

"Me," Father Pete, who had quietly joined the group, added. "And especially God."

"Yes, we will." Edna held Heaven close as she spoke to Amy and Bryson. "I thought I was by myself. He did, too," she said with a glance at Sam. "But between the Woolgatherers and God and this here church, we're not. And neither are you. Remember that."

Acknowledgments

WHILE A NOVELIST SPENDS MANY hours alone writing a story, that story does not become a published book without a great deal of help. My heart overflows with gratitude when I think of the people who have helped me in this endeavor:

My agent, Ali Herring of Spencerhill Associates, ever my advocate, cheerleader, wise counselor, and friend. I'm beyond proud to be one of your Ali-ens!

My editor, Janyre Tromp. I'm so glad I got to work with you on this one. You are wise, discerning, and kind, able to bring out the best in me and the story. You made me grow as a writer!

The hardworking folks at Kregel: Catherine DeVries, Katherine Chappell, Lindsay Danielson, Carrie Krause, and the many who work behind the scenes to make books the best they can be before they go out into the world.

Suzi Dorsett, who cheerfully test-crocheted the twiddle muff pattern and found the mistake (so you don't have to!).

Joan Wilson, who calls taking back purl stitches "lurping." Other people may or may not have coined this term, but I heard it from you first, Joan!

All who have shared their journey of caring for a loved one with dementia with me, either in person or through books and articles. I hope so much that you feel seen and loved in the pages of this book.

My husband, Skip Mondragón, the patron of my art, the encourager of my dreams, my number one fan, and my partner in life, through thick and thin.

And lastly, thanks be to God, creator of all things, visible and invisible, including the invisible ideas of stories and the books they become. Thank you for letting me create with you.

Further Resources

Do you feel a tug at your heart to become a prayer shawl maker? Here are some resources to get you started!

Janet Bristow and Victoria Cole-Galo are the founders of the present-day prayer shawl movement. They've authored three books of patterns, prayers, and stories about the effect prayer shawls have on people, makers and recipients alike. They also have a website with patterns, prayers, and an interactive map of prayer shawl ministries across the United States. If no prayer shawl group is near you, both the books and the website (www.shawlministry.com) will tell you how to start one.

Here are the titles and publishing information for their books:

The Prayer Shawl Companion: 38 Knitted Designs to Embrace, Inspire, and Celebrate Life. Newtown, CT: Taunton, 2008.

The Crocheted Prayer Shawl Companion: 37 Patterns to Embrace, Inspire, and Celebrate Life. Newtown, CT: Taunton, 2010.

The New Prayer Shawl Companion: 35 Knitted Patterns to Embrace, Inspire, and Celebrate Life. Newtown, CT: Taunton, 2012.

Any shawl can become a prayer shawl when you make it with love and prayer, and many online sites offer downloadable patterns for shawls. Here are a few online sources for both knitted and crocheted patterns:

www.lionbrand.com/patterns
www.yarnspirations.com/patterns
www.ravelry.com

If you're interested in the spiritual and contemplative aspects of prayer shawl making, I recommend you read *Knitting into the Mystery: A Guide to the Shawl-Knitting Ministry* by Susan S. Jorgensen and Susan S. Izard (Harrisburg, PA: Morehouse, 2003).

Don't know how to knit or crochet? Many people like Rose and the Woolgatherers would love to teach you. Craft and yarn stores often offer classes. YouTube also has great instructional videos.

Some of you may know exactly who you want to make a shawl for while others of you are wondering what to do with your shawl once you finish it. I urge you to pay attention to the people and needs around you as well as nudges from God. Much better than we do, he knows the who, what, where, why, and when for each prayer shawl.

Every shawl is an adventure—where will it take you? Into your own heart, into the places that need to be healed? Into God's heart, to see life and people through his eyes? Into places you wouldn't go if someone there didn't need a shawl? I pray that you'll go boldly, wherever your shawl making takes you, so that just as the Woolgatherers did, you can find the place where courage and kindness meet.

I would love to hear about your adventures. Contact me at www.sharonjmondragon.com.

Edna and Tara's Twiddle Muff

You will need:
- 150–200 yards of worsted weight yarn. You can even use yarn leftover from other projects if you'd like to make it striped.
- Small amount of a contrasting color for the border
- Size H (5 mm, 8) crochet hook
- Three ¾-inch flat buttons

Abbreviations:
ch: chain
hdc: half double crochet
sc: single crochet
dc: double crochet

Special stitch:
Popcorn stitch: 5 dc in 1 stitch, remove hook from loop, insert in 1st dc and then the loop, pull through, ch 1

Instructions:
Ch 45
Row 1: hdc in 3rd ch from the hook. Hdc across, ch 2, turn (43 stitches)
Rows 2–5: hdc across, ch 2, turn (43 stitches)
Row 6: hdc across, ch 1, turn (43 stitches)
Row 7: *sc 3, popcorn stitch in the next stitch* 10 times, sc 3, ch 2, turn (43 stitches)
Rows 8–24: hdc across, ch 2, turn (43 stitches)

Row 25: Repeat row 7 (43 stitches)
Rows 26–31: hdc across, ch 2, turn (43 stitches)
Fasten off.

Border:

With contrasting color, join and work 2 sc in the upper left corner. Sc down the left side, 2 sc in the corner, sc across the bottom edge, 2 sc in the corner, sc up the right side. Now it's time for the button loops. 2 sc in the corner, 2 sc, ch 4, skip two stitches, sc 14, ch 4, skip 2 stitches, sc 14, ch 4, skip 2 stitches, sc 2. Join with a slip stitch to the first sc in the upper left corner.

Now for the fun part! Attach the buttons on the bottom end, opposite the button loops so it can be made into a muff if desired. Then let your imagination run wild as you find things to attach to the space in between the two rows of popcorn stitches—charms, pom-poms, ribbons, fancy buttons. If you'd like a flower like Tara put on Grandma Becca's, simply google "crocheted flower patterns." There are so many different patterns, some simple and others fancy. Have fun with it!

Also by Sharon Mondragón

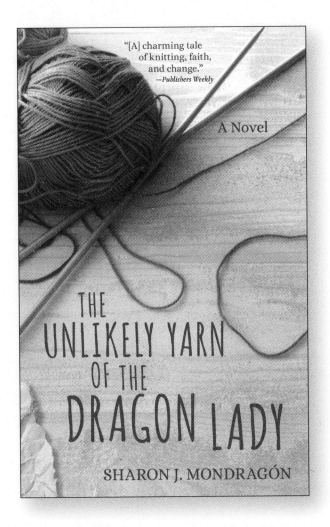

"[A] charming tale of knitting, faith, and change."
—*Publishers Weekly*

A Novel

THE UNLIKELY YARN OF THE DRAGON LADY

SHARON J. MONDRAGÓN

"I love this book. Extraordinary things happen when ordinary knitters reluctantly move a congregation's prayer shawl ministry from a quiet chapel to a busy mall. Their encounters with people they would not normally meet made me chuckle, occasionally weep, and finish the story feeling a gentle nudge from the author to 'go and do likewise.'"
—PATRICIA SPRINKLE, author of *Hold Up the Sky*

KREGEL
PUBLICATIONS